MW01133961

1066 Sons of Pons

IN THE WAKE

OF THE

CONQUEROR

Michael A. Ponzio

Copyright © 2019
Trinacria Publishing Company
BISAC: Fiction / Historical / General
All rights reserved.
ISBN: 1725096447
ISBN-13: 9781725096448

ACKNOWLEDGEMENTS

Cover illustration used with the kind permission of the estate of the late Angus McBride.

Title: "Norman cavalry charge Saxons at the Battle of Hastings 1066" by Angus McBride

Special thanks - Cover created by John Horner Jacobs.

This work of fiction was enhanced by Anne Davis Ponzio.

Thank you Nancy Oberst Soesbee for proofing.

Dedicated to my family.

The Historical Basis of this Novel

1. "Marcus Pontius Laelianus was a Roman senator and officer. He was a military tribune of the Legio VI Victrix. The legion was transferred from Lower-Western Germany to Eburacum, Britain (York) in July 122 AD.

Source: From the Berlin-Brandenburg Academy Corpus Inscriptionum, a comprehensive collection of ancient Latin inscriptions.

2. "The Britons took arms under the conduct of Ambrosius Aurelianus, a modest man, who of all the Roman nation was then alone in the confusion of this troubled period . . . until the year of the siege of Aquae Sulis Hill when took place the slaughter of our cruel foes, which was forty-four years and one month after the landing of the Saxons, and the time of my own birth."

Source: Gildas (c. 500–570) - "On the Ruin of Britain" (De Excidio Britanniae). Gildas the Wise was a 6th-century British monk best known for his history of the Britons after removal of the Roman Legions from Britain and during the subsequent invasion by the Saxons. Ambrosius Aurelianus's leadership of the Britons is considered by many historians to be the origin of the legend of King Arthur.

3. "Pons of County Saintonge. The Lords of Pons in Aquitaine were [among] the most powerful families in France and are frequently mentioned in history. Pontius or Pons, who in 1079 granted a church to the Abbey of Cormery, had four younger sons who went to England, of whom Drogo Fitz-Pons and Walter Fitz-Pons held important baronies in 1086. Their brothers were Richard Fitz-Pons and Osbert Fitz-Pons."

Source: The Battle Abbey Roll (1086 AD) with some account of the Norman Lineages by the Duchess of Cleveland, London, 1885.

MICHAEL A. PONZIO

CONTENTS

PROLOGUE
500 A.D.

England and Ireland in 500 A.D.

Geography Legend

500AD	Modern
Aquae Sulis	Bath
Corinium	Cirencester
Dintagel	Tintagel
Dumnonia	Devon
Eburacum	York
Eire	Ireland
Glevum	Gloucester
Kernow	Cornwall
Lindinis	Ilchester
Londinium	London
Powys	Powys

PROLOGUE
500 A.D.

As the hammering of the tympanum grew louder, Pontia loomed over the man and pulled the sword out of his throat. He did not utter a sound.

Her victim was a descendant of the Irish who had immigrated from Dal Riata. The Romans called them Scotti. She was a Briton and a Roman citizen although there had been no Roman authority in Britain for three generations.

The kettledrum's frequency increased as she extracted the tip of the sword and held the weapon high. The audience clapped. Then she tossed the blade up, did a back somersault from her perch on the narrow wooden beam and caught the handle of the sword as she landed on the ground.

Pontia cast the sword to her partner, his sword-swallowing act now complete. In exchange, he lobbed her treasured crwth and bow to her. She brought the fiddle to her neck and hopped off the narrow beam, as high as a man is tall, and her fellow players removed the plank, replacing it with a tightrope. During the transition to entertain the onlookers, her partner juggled three long seaxes, the one-bladed long knives of the Saxons. The tightrope ready, she progressed along the rope, her diminutive figure keeping balance as if she were on a stroll in a garden. Sweet music issued from her crwth as she coaxed the strings with her bow. The crowd was impressed, but even more so when she sang. Her melodious voice was the pitch of a boy which to her onlookers she appeared, in trousers and a Phrygian cap.

The crowd became even more enthralled as her comrades rolled flaming bales of hay below her while she negotiated the narrow rope. Her song ended as she reached her goal, the far post. The townsfolk, the Romano-Brittonic citizens of Corinium, applauded her somersault off the post. She removed her cap and her blonde coiled tresses emerged, revealing her gender. The surprise and delight of the crowd drew greater rewards as they poured bronze coins and even a few silver coins into her outstretched red cap.

Later the performing troupe made camp just outside the west gate of the city, along the Roman road to the town of Aquae Sulis. Roman monuments, tombs, and mausoleums lined the road. The leader of the troupe counted the take. "Pontia, it's the most we have made in months!"

"Of course we prospered!" said the young woman. "We are the trivial players, the ludii trivialness: noble Roman street performers!"

"There you go again. We aren't Romans, we are Britons. Most people around here are Britons–I am Scotti," he replied. "The Romans left many years ago! Have you met anyone else in your lifetime that claimed they were a Roman citizen?"

"No, but I am a proud Roman citizen." She grasped a square, bronze ornament that hung on the leather cord around her neck. She opened the hinged locket, a rectangle half the size of her palm. "My medal is proof!" There was an inscription on the tiny diptych.

He laughed. "It is just a family treasure. No, don't imagine that you can read it."

But Pontia pretended to read the inscription. She could not read Latin but had memorized what her mother had passed on to her when she gave her the amulet. She focused on the engraving and proclaimed, "This diploma civitatis confers Roman citizenship to the holder and the descendants of Marcus Pontius Laelianus, a Roman senator and tribune of the Legio VI Victrix."

"Your mother and grandmother were named Pontia. Sounds dull. Did your great-grandmothers have the same name?"

"Huh? I don't know. I know my grandmother lived in Eburacum. It is far north of Londinium where I was born. Then only a few years after I joined the troupe, the Saxon mercenaries revolted, started raiding, and we had to flee west. Why did the governor bring them into England? Now they invite their cousins from across the sea to take our land.

"Corinium has been secure for years. The city is properly managed as I suppose the Romans did when they ruled, but I have an ominous feeling that the Saxons are lurking nearby. Do you think it is safe outside the walls? The town of Lindinis is wealthy, but it is far west, beyond the Wodensdyke."

He stacked the coins in separate piles to distribute to their fellow players. "I think it's worth staying longer. You have no reason to be scared. Besides, several years ago the Britons stopped the Saxon raiders at the dyke. It funneled the invaders to our army in wait as they came up the Thames valley through the gap. We gave them a thrashing, and they pulled back. Corinium has strong walls and we can find safety there." He laughed. "Don't you feel protected sleeping in this graveyard among your fellow Romans? This campsite is quiet and peaceful among the crypts and sarcophagi!"

Later that night Pontia was awakened by terrifying screams and grunts. If it had been a colder night and she had worn her cap while sleeping, the seaxe would have done its deadly task. As it was, her long blond braids made the Saxon hesitate long enough to avoid slitting her throat as he shouted, "Aelle! Bretwalda! There is a woman among them!"

"Bring her along, we head south to the river." As he yanked her to standing, Pontia convinced the Saxon by pantomime that she wanted her cloak, hat, and shoes. He allowed her to retrieve them. She also grabbed her prized crwth. He bound her hands and pulled on the extra rope dangling from her wrists. She had to run to keep up to her abductor and avoid being dragged along the road. Their route was lighted by the buildings on fire in the city behind them. Several times the raiders stopped to pillage houses along the road. On one stop, there was a long delay. Pontia's guard reached under her tunic. Before he could do worse, the war leader, the

Bretwalda, returned and smashed him across the head with the flat of his sword. "It is my right to have her first! Then it will be your turn, no sooner!"

Through the night they moved south until they came to the edge of a sharp valley formed by the Avon River. It was not long until the sunrise and numerous campfires lined the opposite side of the river. It appeared the Britons had organized and were expecting the Saxons.

The Saxon leader, Aelle, having fought and run all night, still had the strength and desire for Pontia. They stopped at one of many abandoned Roman country homes perched on the valley slope. He made a fire in the peristylium, a courtyard surrounded by the villa. The garden had overgrown the stone benches and covered the fountain and pool. Vines grew thick on a wood arbor which ran the length of the courtyard. He untied her hands and demanded that she undress. But Pontia ignored his command and instead played her stringed crwth, danced, and sang.

"I don't want music!" He shouted, guzzled some ale, and reached for her.

Pontia whirled her Phrygian cap and sensuously danced away from his attempt to seize her. He laughed, aroused even more. She then pulled up her tunic. With the distraction, she smashed her beloved instrument across his face and sprinted to the front doors of the house. The Bretwalda's men, however, were at the accesses, not to guard their leader, but to ogle his antics with the captive woman.

They blocked her egress and Pontia turned to face the Saxon leader. She ran to him at full speed. He stepped forward to intercept her. Pontia cut to his side, leaped up on a stone bench with her right foot and launched herself upward, using his shoulder as the next step. He tried to grab her, but lost hold. The deflection spun her upside down, but with a one-handed cartwheel Pontia landed on her feet at the top of the wooden arbor. Pontia continued along the narrow beam without the slightest loss of balance. As she raced toward the far side of the peristylium's garden she did not hesitate. *I am going over that wall. If I don't survive, it's better than submitting to that barbarian!*

She hurdled the garden wall and landed on the roof of the villa without injury. After dropping to the ground, Pontia ran down the slope toward the river. The shouts of the Bretwalda's men and the thuds of their steps energized her, but she could tell by their loud breathing that the Saxon warriors were gaining on her. Pontia gained hope when she saw campfires across the Avon River. The sun began its ascent and Pontia saw men on the bridge, but she didn't know if they were Britons or Saxons. A strong and nimble acrobat, she evaded capture by her agility, zig-zagging around trees and bushes until she reached the river bank and without hesitation, dove into the current to swim across to the town of Aquae Sulis.

After the shock of the cold water subsided, she concentrated on the rhythm of her strokes. *My mother could swim this river, so can I! As a young woman, Mother wagered a soldier in Eburacum that she could do cartwheels around the entire forum. He said he had a silver coin that said she couldn't. She won the coin and married him, a descendent of Romano-Brittonic families who had manned Hadrian's Wall. They bestowed the family heirloom, the citizen's medal, to me, their only child.*

Thoughts of the massacre triggered her to inhale and choke on water. She faltered. Her tears mixed with the river's water. *I'll cry, but I will not let the emotion drown me!* Her remorse turned to anger then to energy as she recovered and pressed on to the riverbank. Only when she reached the far side of the river, and pulled herself out, did she look back to see that the Saxons had not followed. Pontia comforted herself at one of the many unattended campfires. The warmth from the blaze and the rising sun felt good to her numb body. Pontia removed her red cap, wrung out the water, and held it before the fire, then began an inventory of herself. *Good! I didn't lose my cap, which I will need to take the guise of a boy—it will be dangerous enough just to be alone. I wish I still had my trousers.* Pontia scanned the riverbanks again and saw no one, except a group of soldiers manning the bridge, their attention to the north along the road the way she had come. She peered at her feet. *At least I am wearing my favorite shoes. My other pair would not have lasted walking long distances. How fortunate I am! Most are lucky to have one pair and many people have no shoes. I spend what little money I make on shoes rather than food. Like my mother!* These thoughts cheered her after the terrible ordeal the previous night. She unbraided her hair next to the fire, dried her tresses, and then began re-braiding them, planning to coil and hide the locks under her cap.

The squeaking and groaning of wood drew Pontia's alarm. A man coaxed a donkey as it pulled a two-wheeled cart in her direction, escorted by a pair of men on foot. Along the river behind them, smoke rose from several campfires they had extinguished. The man halted the cart at a nearby fire, handed buckets to his escorts and directed them to put out the flames. When he headed for Pontia's location, she put on her cap, and hurried toward the city gate.

The driver reined in his donkey and shouted, "Young lady. you may stay and warm yourself! You need not run! Besides, I will give you a ride into Aquae Sulis. It is a nasty place for an unescorted woman."

These fires all along the river with no one around them. It must have been a trick by the Britons to make the Saxons think the river was defended by an army of soldiers. She heard jeers from the men guarding the bridge and glanced their way. *I can always run. Yet my chances entering Aquae Sulis with this man are better than dealing with that gang of men from the bridge.*

"Are you an honorable Briton? Unlike the Saxons across the river?"

"It would be a stretch to call me honorable, but my father taught me to never force a woman."

He stopped his cart, jumped to the ground, and addressed his companions to take care of the next fire. "Remember, don't drench it, we may light them again tonight."

He turned to Pontia and smiled. She sensed the expression was genuine and friendly. *He has nice teeth! But, do I stay or run to the city gate?* She was fixated by his shoes as he approached and was compelled to say, "Those are stunning boots! Such a robust sole. And the bands of leather are decorative but keep your feet cool. I bet you oil the leather. It looks quite supple!"

The man stopped in his tracks and laughed. He was half a head taller than Pontia, lean and muscular, and had dark wavy hair with a short beard. When he caught his breath, he said, "You favor well-made shoes? These are my grandfather's military boots. My mother's father. He served in the Roman Legions but remained here when they left. The boots are a family keepsake and yes, I oil them to preserve the leather." He showed her the bottom of the sole.

"I see the hobnails," said Pontia. "You'll keep solid footing with those."

"And your shoes. They are molded to your small feet. I have never seen red shoes. They match your hat."

Pontia answered, "They are my trivial player shoes, for performing acrobatics in my show."

He looked around. "Show?"

"I was in a troupe of players. The Saxons attacked us. They killed everyone . . ." she choked, then recovered and said, "Your accent. You sound like my late friend. Are you from Dal Riata? Are you a Scotti?"

He laughed. "I adopted my brogue from my father, who was from Eire. He was from Munster, in the south of the island. Those who left Dal Riata for this land were from northern Eire."

"Eire?" asked Pontia.

"Oh, yes, the Britons still use Roman names here. Eire is the island just west of Britain. You might have heard it called Hibernia?"

"Yes, but I thought only pirates came from Hibernia. Was your mother a Roman?"

"Must have been if her father was."

"I believe I am related to the Romans, too." She showed him her amulet, opened it, and recited the inscription.

"That is a wonderful family treasure."

Pontia watched as he put out the fire. *How lucky am I? He seems like a good man, or a good liar and actor. I still must be on guard. When we get into town, there will be people around, in case he is trouble.*

They climbed into the cart as her escort convinced the donkey to haul them to the city. "We don't even know each other's name. I am Pontia."

"I'm Corb."

"Did your ancestors have a raven talisman?"

"What?" blurted Corb.

Pontia said, "I am a Briton, you are from Eire. We speak the same language, with a few differences. But we both know Corb means either raven or charioteer. Which are you?"

"I never thought about it. My name has always just been Corb. But, yes! It means charioteer! A fierce warrior! See—I am now driving a speedy chariot pulled by my war horse!" Pontia laughed. Corb asked, "So, what does your name mean?"

"I don't know. It is the female name of my ancestors' clan Pontius."

They had just entered the north gate of Aquae Sulis and to the left was the stone bridge which crossed the Avon River. Corb pointed to a plaque on the bridge's column and said, "*Pontem Aquae Sulis*. Your name sounds like the Latin word for bridge." He chuckled. "Are you named after a bridge?"

"You can read?" Pontia said.

"Of course, as you did. You read your amulet."

They looked at each other, straight-faced, then both laughed.

"Someone told me what the words mean," said Corb. "Is it the same for you? Did someone tell you what the words mean on your medallion?"

"Yes, my mother said I must memorize it, and then bequeath the medal to my children."

"That's good advice. And I will preserve my shoes and pass them to my descendants." Pontia laughed at him.

Corb glanced at Pontia and noticed she shed a few tears. "I am sorry, did you lose your family in the Saxon raid?"

She shook her head but did not answer as they crossed the old forum. Buildings on the opposite side of the plaza looked occupied and were well kept, but the remaining perimeters were strewn with debris, trash, and ruins of buildings. At the center of the forum they passed a busy outdoor market, then headed for a columned building which dominated the far side of the plaza.

"I was hoping Aquae Sulis was still an organized city, as is Corinium. Most buildings are in decay. But what is that magnificent building?" said Pontia.

"That houses the natural thermae, the hot baths. The Romans built this town and dedicated the building around the baths to the Celtic goddess Sulis and their goddess Minerva. Now you can see that the citizens have abandoned most of the buildings, but the people left here do their best to carry on a civilized life."

Corb's men departed for the barracks on his order, then he halted the cart at the baths. He jumped off the cart and turned to help Pontia, but she had sprung to the ground. A boy took the reins and led the donkey and cart away. They walked into a colonnaded portico surrounding a rectangular pool, fifty by one hundred paces, a soft bubbling sound coming from the hot water as it flowed through the large pool. Scores of people occupied the portico.

"Do these people live here?" said Pontia.

"Most of them. In the evening, they invite the townspeople in as a place of entertainment."

Corb held his arms out and a woman, dressed as an ancient Roman in flowing robes, jingling with bracelets and necklaces, about Pontia's height but twice as wide, embraced him. "Corb! Where have you been? Busy keeping the Saxons at bay?"

The woman scrutinized Pontia. "Don't tell me you brought her to join my girls? She is too skinny!"

"No, Emilia. She is my sister."

"Your sister? I thought your family was gone? Did she just pop out of the ground?" She regarded Pontia. "Where are you from dear?"

"I, uh . . . um."

Corb put his arm around Pontia. "She is still in shock after fleeing the attack on Corinium."

"Yes, ma'am. Saxons killed my friends." She did not have to act. Real tears filled her eyes.

"I am sorry." Emilia took her hand and said, "Come and get something to eat, then you can take a hot bath." She cast Corb a look of disbelief over her shoulder as they left. "Corb, your hooligan soldier-friends are eating in the hall and are looking for you."

Pontia did not see Corb anymore that evening. She spent the night with Emilia and her troupe of promiscuous employees. The next morning after she finished breakfast, she strolled along the portico surrounding the large bath. *These women were kind to me last night, especially Emilia who let me sleep in her locked bedroom. But I must find a way to earn money. I cannot expect free handouts. I wonder if I could entertain here—acrobats and music. But I have lost my crwth!*

Corb arrived. As he approached, Pontia noted he was now wearing his armor, unlike yesterday when he wore only a tunic, leggings, and a sword hanging from his belt. Over his tunic he now wore armor made of hundreds of bronze scales, each the size of a small coin. The scale armor covered his torso and metal greaves shielded his shins. His helmet had a round top, with hinged cheek guards and a brim along the back to cover his neck. He also had a black eye and a few bruises on his face. Pontia exclaimed. "You definitely look the soldier today! And your armor—Did you inherit this from your grandfather?"

Corb appeared irritated. "Yes! Well, just the armor. But right now I must take you to see the magistrate. Remember, you must insist we are siblings! Come on!"

"Wait," Pontia said as she grasped his arm. "Does your black eye have something to do with this visit? I need to know what is going on!" He kept walking as she followed, hanging onto his sleeve.

"My men—I am a cavalry officer," Corb continued as they walked briskly. "Last night my men insisted you were a prisoner and a spoil of war to be shared. They wanted to come here last night to get you, but I . . . um . . . persuaded them to wait for the Praetor, the magistrate, to review the issue."

"What? I am a free person, not a captured slave! Who is the magistrate?"

They arrived at the stables. Corb vaulted onto a horse and then held the reins of a second mount. With her agility, she duplicated his act. Corb said, "The magistrate's name is

Ambrosius Castus Aurelianus, one of the last of the Romano-Brittonic nobility. He is the military commander of the three allied cities of Guenet: Aquae Sulis, Corinium, and Glevum. Contact with Corinium has been lost, and he needs to know if it is due to these Saxon raids, or worse, an invading army."

"Corb, do you know Aurelianus well? How will this turn out?"

"He is firm, but just. And he will swiftly decide your fate."

They rode through the city with a troop of soldiers. The other men had scale armor like Corb's, but instead of a double-edged sword, they possessed the shorter single-edged seaxes. They were armed with spears and round shields. The troop exited Aquae Sulis and crossed the bridge over the Avon River. Pontia rode beside Corb. "Pontia, emphasize your Roman ancestry. When Aurelianus found out my grandfather was a Roman, he treated me as a countryman."

The group climbed to the top of a wide flat-topped hill which rose high above the river valley. A fortified camp of ditches backed by low wooden palisades surrounded a score of tents. Corb and Pontia dismounted in front of the largest tent. A red flag mounted on a pole at the entrance waved in the breeze. The chi-rho symbol of the Roman Church was painted on the flag. This location, Sulis Hill-fort, afforded long-range views of the enemy approaching from any direction.

Corb nodded to the guard at the entrance and asked him to let the magistrate know of his arrival. A squad of mounted soldiers arrived, dismounted, and one rushed into the tent. Within a few moments, the rider exited and galloped away with his troop out the camp gate. The guard opened the tent flaps and gestured for Corb to enter. As they went into the tent, Pontia slipped her amulet out from under her tunic so it was in sight. Several men were leaning over a round table studying a map. The robust three-legged table fascinated Pontia. The top was a thick slab of yew wood and polished to a brilliance, displaying an eye-catching grain. Carved into the tabletop were the Greek letters chi and rho. One of the men turned to face Corb and Pontia. He wore a blue tunic over gray trousers. Pontia noted his boots were made of fine quality black leather and had closed toes. Behind him across the tent was armor mounted on a stand which she assumed was his. There hung a vest of solid bronze, and scale armor to cover the arms and strips of armor that gave protection below the waist. The helmet was like Corb's but had a nose guard and the top was fitted with a bright red horse tail.

"Welcome, Corb! Good job in Aquae last night," said Aurelianus. "Your campfires must have fooled the Saxons. There have been no reports of any of the enemy trying to enter the city." He rested his right elbow in his left palm and pinched his well-groomed beard in thought. "The problem is we know nothing about Corinium. I sent scouts to the north. They cannot get through to the city. The riders I sent east reported only small groups of Saxons.

"I find it hard to believe you were brawling last night. That is not like you. Was it about this woman?" He paused and glanced at Pontia's ornament hanging from her neck. His eyes grew wider. "Young lady, is that a citizen's diptych?"

"Yes, Praetor."

"Hmm. You address me by my Latin title. *Potes hoc legere Latine?* Do you read Latin? Can you read the inscription?"

"No."

He seemed disappointed. "The only people with whom I can speak Latin are monks and priests. Humph! You probably were given it as a favor, or worse, stole it, huh?"

"No, sir!" She lifted her chin and stretched to her full height. "It reads: 'This diploma civitatis confers Roman citizenship to the holder and the descendants of Marcus Pontius Laelianus, a Roman senator and tribune of the Legio VI Victrix.'"

Aurelianus snickered. "You showed great pride as you recited the dedication. Can you say anything else that would convince me you are truthful?"

"Yes, I am Marcus Pontius Laelianus's descendant. My name is Pontia."

"I doubt you could have made that up. That was the Roman custom, for the daughters to be named the feminine version of the family name. Do you know anything else about your Roman ancestors?"

"Unfortunately, no."

"I wish I had more time to tell you about the stories my family passed down to me," said Aurelianus. "Pontia, you are free to return to Aquae Sulis with Corb. I will issue word to my men that you are under my protection."

He turned away, done with the issue. Pontia said, "Thank you, Praetor. I heard you mention the confusion about Corinium. I lived there for years until just nights ago when my companions were murdered by raiders. They seized me and brought me south. I escaped and made it to Aquae Sulis. They must have been Saxons. I am sure the whole city was destroyed and taken."

"Pontia, do you remember anything they said? How many men did you see?

"Ten or twenty. But I heard shouts from many more men nearby. The whole city looked to be on fire! It was terrifying and confusing. They were moving fast, and it was dark."

"Did they address any of their leaders by name or use any words such as cyning, a war chief?"

"No, they called their leader Aelle."

"Aelle! Aelle Bretwalda?"

"Yes, Bretwalda was his other name," said Pontia.

"Bretwalda is the title of their ruler, the highest king of the Saxons in Britain. He was a mercenary for the Romans, but then he led the Saxons to revolt. Very crafty and he lusts for battle. He personally leads his men, but not for small raids. What you have told me is very valuable, young woman."

He turned to the other officers in the tent and shot out commands to send messengers to the city of Glevum, to the Kingdom of Powys, and to south of the Wodensdyke for reinforcements. They quickly left to carry out their orders. Aurelianus said, "Corb, you should return to Aquae immediately, ensure all the walls and gates are secure, and increase patrols along the river. I will come to the city to review your preparations as soon as I am able." Corb and Pontia were turning to leave and the praetor added, "Corb, I would have fought for her, too. The praetor took Pontia's hand and kissed it and said, "Thank you, fellow citizen." With this, he pulled a bronze amulet from under his tunic and read the inscription. "This diploma civitatis confers Roman citizenship to the holder and the descendants of Lucius Artorius Castus, Praefectus of Legio VI Victrix."

As they rode back to Aquae Sulis, Corb laughed, "Pontia, we both take pride that we are descendants of Romans, although I am also proud of my father's clan from Eire. And Aurelianus is what I imagine that the best of the Romans were like. Intelligent, tough, but fair."

"And proud to be a Roman citizen," said Pontia. "His forebearer, Artorius, was in the same legion as my ancestor, Pontius."

"Yes!" answered Corb.

"And the inscriptions on the amulets show that the Romans had two or three names," added Pontia. "My father said that my name is Pontia because I am descended from the Pontius clan."

Corb added, "So, according to the inscription on the praetor's amulet, the Aurelianus is of the Artorius clan."

When they arrived at Aquae Sulis, Corb had duties around the city to bolster the defenses. He left Pontia at the baths. Emilia, the manager of the brothel, heard Pontia had experience as a street player, so she invited her to perform that afternoon. Pontia described what props she would need, but told Emilia she would be more inspired if she had her crwth to play music while she sang. There was no crwth available, but Emilia obtained a flute.

Near sundown, Corb arrived to see the portico around the bath crowded with animated spectators. There was the usual warming up of prostitutes and their clients around tables, but most had their attention on a familiar young woman on the tightrope, as she alternated melodies on a flute with songs. Every few steps she would pause, set her feet firmly and spring, flipping and landing on the taut rope. She accompanied the somersault with a shrill pipe from her instrument.

Corb grabbed a pint of ale and enjoyed watching the

performance as Emilia appeared. "Corb, you have brought me a valuable employee! I have not had this many customers in years. I hope I have enough ale. Are you going to let me have her?"

"What do you mean have her? I don't own her!"

"You had a scuffle with your own men over her and you defended her at the meeting with the magistrate."

"Yes, I like her. I liked her as soon as I saw her. But there is a battle looming. I cannot take care of her now. Besides, she handled the meeting with the praetor herself. She did all the talking and wooed him over."

"Oh, I know she can take care of herself," Emilia said. "I hired her. She'll get free room and board with her skills."

"Good," said Corb. "So, you do not need my approval."

Emilia pointed at Pontia. "Look, now she's doing cart wheels with no hands! It is good she is wearing trousers under her tunic. Hmm . . . I wonder?"

"No Emilia! There will be none of that!"

She laughed. "Just trying to rile you. She will be safe with me and appears to be enjoying herself!"

Several days later Aurelianus arrived in Aquae Sulis to review the organization of the city's defenses with Corb. They sat in the portico around the baths and watched Pontia's acrobat and music show. When the act ended, after she held her hat out for tips, Corb motioned to her to join them. Pontia remained standing when she reached the table. "Greetings, Praetor! It is good to see you two having some relaxation time after working so hard."

"Greetings, Pontia. Yes, but we have much more to discuss. You are quite the performer and very entertaining! Where did you learn such skills?"

"Uh . . . from my family."

The praetor added, "But I am sure, you must have also inherited your athletic ability."

"Thank you. I leave you two to discuss military matters," Pontia said.

She departed, and Aurelianus said, "You have found a unique woman, Corb."

"Uh, everyone seems to think we are a pair. I guess it is not such a bad idea."

The Praetor smiled and said, "Corb, after my inspection today, I am going to recommend we evacuate Aquae Sulis and move the citizens south of Wodensdyke."

Corb groaned. "Sir, I have repaired the weak point in the walls. And where will all the people be housed? Lindinis, the closest city, is not large enough. They would be living outside."

"The problem is not with the walls. It's that we don't have enough soldiers to man the entire perimeter."

"But the walls have worked before now," said Corb.

The praetor answered, "Yes, against the raiding parties not even numbering to a hundred. I now suspect that the Saxons have consolidated their victories in the east and are massing into an army."

Corb asked, "Have you heard anything from the messengers you sent for help from the other kingdoms?"

"Yes, King Vortigern of Powys promptly returned a message. 'We cannot help you if you insist on following an intolerant church.'"

"What does that mean?" said Corb.

"The Christians of Powys follow the ideas of the monk Pelagius, a Briton, who claims that humans are basically good. He believes people have the free will to do good works without divine aid, so you can see Pelagius denied Augustine's theory of original sin."

"What? Who is Augustine?" asked Corb. "I am not as educated as you are, Praetor, and I do not understand the fine points of religious thought. But it seems to me if one is brought up right, a person can do good by themselves." He downed some ale. "In any case, I see they do not agree with Christians under the Roman Church and this means Powys will not help. What about the kingdoms of Kernow and Dumnonia?"

"I should hear from them any day now. King Margh of Kernow has a small holding on the coast at Dintagel. Our best hope for help is from Geraint the Fleet Owner, King of Dumnonia. He helped us build the Wodensdyke several years ago by supplying laborers."

"Why can't we move your cavalry from the hill-fort to the city?" asked Corb. "The walls are stronger than the ditch and palisade on the hill. We would have enough men to defend the city walls."

"Foremost, I see two advantages that I don't want to lose," said Aurelianus. "We have the high ground at the hill-fort. Also, the top of the hill is flat and wide enough so our cavalry can maneuver against the Saxon foot soldiers. I want all the Saxons, I mean every damn Saxon we can attract, every Saxon in Britain if possible, to fight me on that hill! I will need as many mounted soldiers as possible to rid those vermin from our land!" He emptied his drinking bowl with a long draft of ale and banged it on the table.

Aurelianus glanced at Corb. "I cannot seem to get enough information from my scouts to find what the Saxons are doing." The praetor lowered his voice and whispered, "But I have just devised a way to bring the Saxons to Sulis Hill like bees to honey. A few weeks ago, two separate hoards of Roman coins—silver and gold coins, were discovered by my men buried near the Wodensdyke. I had them expand their search, and they found two more caches. I have no doubt these coins were hidden by Romans who were departing a generation ago, thinking they would return after the turmoil ended, which still continues."

Before Corb could conjure why the Praetor brought up the treasure, Aurelianus said, "We have hidden the store of coins on Sulis Hill. Now we need to find a way to spread the reports of the treasure to the enemy, so they will come to us!"

Over the next few days, Aurelianus's requests for military aid were answered. King Margh sent a token troop of armored cavalry from Dintagel to help against the Saxons. A large contingent of reinforcements arrived from Dumnonia, led by King Geraint himself. He was determined to repel the pagan Saxons to save his own kingdom from being overrun and to stem the tide of Britons emigrating from his domain to the European continent.

Corb convinced Aurelianus to change his mind on evacuating

the city, then he spent most of the day positioning large rocks at strategic points along the wall, placing long poles with hooks within reach along the parapets, and showing the citizens, including women, how to use the devices. Townspeople armed themselves with everything from farm tools to seaxes. In the late afternoon, Corb guided the allied troops from Dumnonia and Dintagel to Sulis Hill-fort. There the leaders of the Britons met to discuss strategy at the camp. They gathered in the Praetor's tent. At the center was a round table covered with maps.

"I am Ambrosius Castus Aurelianus, Praetor of the kingdom of Guenet. Gold and silver make greed rise in the most moral of men." An officer grunted as he heaved an open chest of silver coins onto the table and dropped it on the maps. "My plan is to make this battle profitable to our men, and it will test their loyalty to their families and homeland. When we reveal the treasure to our soldiers, some could turn on us, steal the fortune and be away. Or . . ." Aurelianus locked eyes with King Margh's captain then with King Geraint, "we could go at each other's throats and the winner keep the treasure." Satisfied, he lowered his stare. "But I am confident you and your men will make the noble decision to defend our Christian lands against the pagans. Today, I will distribute one silver coin to each soldier, with a promise of five-fold more when we win. There were gasps among the officers. "Yes, the hoards were huge. So, with this, I recommend we announce these plans now and within days we will see Saxons coming to Sulis Hill."

The leaders all swore to the Christian God to uphold Aurelianus's proposal, although half of them were pagans. Then the Praetor and the leaders left the tent to announce the design to the allied troops. He directed one of his men to blow the carnyx, a bronze trumpet, to assemble the troops. The long, s-shaped horn was as tall as a man and the sounding end was crafted into the head of a snake. One of Aurelianus's officers brought out the round table for the Praetor to stand on to address the assembly. As Corb witnessed the praetor among thousands of Britons he remembered a conversation he had once had with Aurelianus. He said his family had owned only a few books. One was Caesar's commentary on the wars of his conquest of Gaul. Julius Caesar, according to the Roman tradition, gave an inspirational speech to his men before each battle. He was known to be skilled in rhetoric and stirred the legionaries to their best efforts.

Aurelianus began. "Britons! Free Britons!"

The men responded with hoorahs, cheers, and shouts.

"For generations, the Saxons, the Angles, the Jutes, and the Frisians have invaded our lands. We must stop these German incursions! Before our memories, even before our great-grandparents' memories, the Romans invaded. Yes, we fought and lost, but in the end, we absorbed the Romans and became a better society. Look around you now, most of us are part Roman and part Briton. Over time the Romans brought us a good life. Cities, better farms, roads . . . but the legions are gone. We are on our own. The Germans only bring us death and destruction. And they want to destroy the Church."

There was a wave of jeers and protests among the men.

"Will you defend your wives?"

"YES!"

"Will you defend your children?"

"YES!"

"Will we remain free? Are these reasons enough to fight?"

"YES!"

Aurelianus paused. "I have recovered a huge treasure of silver and gold coins that the Romans buried. God has sent this fortune to set off the Saxons' greed and bring them to us. It will be a hard fight—AND WE WILL WIN!"

A roar followed from the men.

Aurelianus had several men hold up the chest of money, as he held up a handful of silver coins. "Today, come forward and receive your first piece, and each of you will receive five silver pieces after the battle is won."

There was silence, then cheers erupted.

Word of the riches traveled fast to the Saxon settlements. Within several days, Aurelianus's scouts reported that hundreds of Saxons had pitched their camps four or five miles east of Sulis

Hill. The Praetor kept them under surveillance, as more joined them daily.

Corb sat alone at a table drinking ale. He watched Pontia finish her act and she departed for her room. The noisy conversations of men drinking ale were prevalent this evening as usual, and Corb was pleased to overhear that the main subject was the treasure on Sulis Hill. Corb swigged his ale. Mmm. *This is the best ale! Made from fresh barley right here in Aquae. As they say, the women make the best ale in Britain. Made by Emilia, the expert alewife herself. But, no! He snickered out loud. Emilia isn't anybody's wife! But she is a master brewer!* Corb downed another swallow. *I miss Pontia. I have been so busy preparing the city for the expected siege, I haven't talked to her in several days. What if the Saxons attack tomorrow? Or tonight!* He finished his drink and headed to the rooms at the back of the bath complex.

Pontia's room was at the end of a long hall. A feeble amount of light was produced along the corridor by a single oil lamp on the wall. Below the lamp sat a huge man on a small stool leaning over and whittling a piece of wood. Corb heard bumps, groans, and a few giggles from the rooms that lined the hallway as he approached the guard. The man looked up and smiled. "Captain Corb! Or should I say Centurion? You pride yourself as being one of the last Romans in Britain. I haven't seen you in these halls for months."

Corb stopped and slapped the man on the shoulder and laughed. "You have a good memory. But you know, we can revive the prosperous Roman days of old."

"How's that? Beat the Saxons?"

"Partly. Being Roman is a state of mind more than of blood."

"How?"

"Build and maintain the cities and roads, then commerce will follow. Keep the peace, then people will work and prosper. Support the Church."

The guard said, "That is much to think about." Corb moved to continue to the end of the hall, but the man stood and blocked his path. His hulk almost reached from wall to wall. "Emelia said no one goes to Pontia's room."

There was a familiar jingling of bracelets and necklaces behind Corb. He looked behind him but saw nothing. Then the guard said, "But for you, Captain Corb, I am sure the young lady welcomes you."

Corb knocked twice at Pontia's room, but his third rap was silent, as the door swung open before he could contact the wood. "It's about time you showed up!" said Pontia.

The next morning there was a loud pounding on the door. "Corb!" They had slept into the late morning. Pontia recognized Emilia's voice and opened the door. "Aurelianus has ordered all the cavalry to Sulis Hill," Emilia continued. "I'll let you two lovers say your goodbyes." She departed down the hallway.

As Corb dressed, he said, "I have done my best to prepare the city's defenses and I hope the treasure will lead all the Saxons to us instead of the city. The boulders are precariously set upon the walls, so be careful if you push them down on the Saxons, they could tilt towards you. Also, when you use the poles to push their ladders back, you will need help, work in pairs." They embraced in silence for a long moment. Corb turned to go.

Pontia said, "We should agree upon a place to meet, in case we lose the battle and the city falls"

"Yes, the place we first met. Draw an arrow on the boulder in the direction you make off. West means Dintagel, south Lindinis, and north Glevum." As he hurried down the hall, he said, "None of that will be necessary, we will win, and we will be together again!"

Pontia could barely hold herself back from chasing him. She felt a welling of tears coming and retrieved the seaxe given to her by Corb. The common knives were used for everything from cutting leather for shoes, to skinning goats, to defending a peasant's homestead. The single-bladed knife was as long as her forearm, but it was well-balanced and felt good in her hand. It gave her a feeling of confidence and power. Instead of crying, she was energized and viciously slashed the air with the weapon, spinning, fighting an imaginary enemy.

Corb led his troop of armored cavalry across the river and up Sulis Hill. He had been gone just one day but by the smoke rising from numerous campfires on the lower slopes of the hill, he could tell many more Saxons had arrived. Halfway up Sulis Hill they were still in the woods and came around a curve when he realized his group might be the last to join. In the road were Saxon foot soldiers. *Is our camp encircled or are they isolated patrols? Does it matter? We are going through!* Corb urged his horse into a gallop and shouted for his men to follow. The Saxons were carrying axes, spears, and round shields with one-bladed seaxes hanging from their belts.

Against enemy foot soldiers the Germanic warriors would have swung axes and stabbed with their spears but against a mounted attack they threw these weapons. Corb raised his shield. A loud clanging followed as a projectile slammed into his defense and a metal crash sounded on his right greave. As he peered over his shield, Corb saw the enemy, only a dozen soldiers, part and flee into the trees. *It's good we charged through, if they had had time to draw back into the woods, they could have hit us from the sides.* Corb and his men arrived in the Britons' camp without injury or further incident.

The camp was located in the center of the large meadow on the flat-topped hill. The number of Brittonic cavalry had swelled and most were camped outside the small fortified base. Ringing the meadow were the camps of the Saxons, only a few hundred paces away. Contingents of mounted Britons patrolled the perimeter of their encampment surveying the Saxons, although none of them appeared organized to attack. Corb left his men and reported to Aurelianus's tent.

The Praetor stood in discussion with his officers and King Geraint. "Corb, you made it! You are probably the last to get through what is turning into a siege. A group of horsemen just arrived from Powys, against the wishes of their king." Aurelianus laughed as he said, "I think they are more interested in the treasure than the differences in theology!" He was in full armor and seemed heady and ready to fight. He made room for Corb to gather around the table with the other cavalry leaders. On the table was a charcoal sketch of Sulis Hill-fort and the locations of the Saxon camps on a sheet of parchment. Aurelianus's reckoning from the reports of his scouts indicated the Saxons had surrounded the Britons' encampment, with the highest concentration of troops on the north and east sides, where the slope was the least steep.

"The Saxons have just blocked the road to Aquae Sulis with downed trees." Aurelianus continued, "This is the second day of the arrival of large groups of the enemy. There have been a few skirmishes in the open meadow that only ended when King Aelle himself came out of the woods and disciplined his warriors to return to their camp. It appears we are both waiting for more Saxons to arrive before we fight. I want to deal them a final blow and Alle wants to overwhelm us with numbers. As close as our frontlines are, it will be hard to avoid battle for the next few days, but so far, everything is going according to plan.

He pointed to the sketch. "Here you can see the Saxons are camped inside the woods on the edge of the meadow. We must draw them out to take advantage of our mobility on horseback. I predict they will emerge from the forest in their shield wall formation, but not come too far into the meadow, so they can use the trees as defense against a cavalry attack.

"We cannot charge right into their shield wall, that would be suicide. We should send a feint to their center and send our wings to out-flank them, then push them out into the grassy area." Aurelianus looked up and his men nodded in affirmation. It was a good plan.

Corb woke the next morning to the sound of loud guttural shouts. *The tongue of the Saxons! The enemy has overrun the camp!* He shot up from his blanket, grabbed his sword, his seaxe bouncing at his belt, but when he raced out of his tent, he realized the voices were from thousands of Saxons, still hundreds of paces across the meadow at the forest's edge. The enemy hurled challenges to single combat and lone warriors stood in the meadow shouting obscenities and waiting for an adversary. However, they were not forming ranks or attacking and the Brittonic leaders ordered the men into their armor. Then the soldiers took turns standing by at ready as others hastily ate wheat porridge. They prepared for battle.

As Aurelianus had predicted, the Saxons came out of the woods and formed a wall, their round shields held side by side without space to penetrate. The Britons, all mounted, carried out their leader's plan. The Brittonic cavalry attacked at three places along the Saxons' line. Aurelianus led the charge to the center, the chieftain from Dintagel led the charge to the right wing and King Geraint toward the left wing. The praetor did not trust his new allies to back him up in a crisis and positioned Corb and his men as reserves. King Alle the Bretwalda had prepared well. The flanks of the Saxons wheeled and anchored the ends of their shield wall at the woods, which prevented the Britons' charge from encircling them. Aurelianus halted the assault at the enemy's center, seeing the flanking cavalry did not dislodge the Saxons from the forest edge. After only a few clashes at the wings and minor skirmishing, the Britons retreated to their camp.

Aurelianus regrouped and directed the army back to the hill-fort. Corb joined him in his tent. His prior elation for battle turned to anger and irritation. He called the rest of his captains to his tent. Before all the officers arrived, a verbal message from the Saxons was delivered by a scout. He addressed Aurelianus: "Magistrate, King Alle the Bretwalda of the Saxons challenges you to man-to-man combat."

As his remaining officers filed into the tent, Aurelianus, his eyes wide in bellicosity, shouted, "Who has the longest spear among you?" There was silence. Aurelianus stormed out of the tent. His officers looked incredulous that he would accept the challenge. He grabbed the long spear stuck in the ground, flying the flag of the Roman Church, and vaulted onto his horse. Corb shouted to the stunned officers, "Mount up and get your men ready! Now!" They ran as Aurelianus rode to meet King Alle who waited in the meadow midway between the Saxon and Briton lines. The Saxon king was shouting in his Germanic tongue, walking back and forth, swinging a huge ax above his head. Aurelianus continued forward with the flag of the Church waving above him, its golden chi rho symbol announcing they fought with Christ as their God.

The mass of Saxons let out a shout in unison that resounded across the field. The Britons responded with loud volleys of encouragement for their leader. Aurelianus reined his horse to a stop twenty paces from Alle. He flipped over the spear and wrapped the flag around his forearm to secure the lance to his arm. The Saxon continued to pace back and forth screaming like a wild animal, with mane and hair flying in all directions. In contrast, Aurelianus appeared calm and stoic with trimmed hair and a neatly cropped beard. Then the noise from the warriors stopped.

King Alle quieted, inspected the ground, and used his long ax to draw an imaginary line on the ground. He looked up and saw that Aurelianus had spurred his horse forward, aiming his spear at the Saxon warlord. Horse and man crashed into their mutual adversary. As his spear pierced Alle's shield, the Saxon was knocked to the ground. With the impact, the Praetor heard a loud pop in his right shoulder accompanied by intense pain. He fell from his mount. *I can tell the spear didn't go deep enough to kill him. And with my right shoulder dislocated, I will be dead.* Aurelianus tumbled forward, and his injured shoulder slammed into the ground, suddenly relieving his suffering. King Alle lay stunned on his back. The spear was imbedded in Alle's shield that lay across his chest, still strapped to the king's arm. Aurelianus stepped on the shield and tried to extract the spear without success, making King Alle groan in agony. The spear was stuck, but Aurelianus realized his weight had driven the spear point into his enemy. The Bretwalda, the King of the Saxons of Britain, was dead. A hush spread over the battlefield. Then, the outraged Saxons charged across the meadows. The Praetor vaulted onto his horse and with his sword cut down several Saxon warriors moments before his cavalry arrived. Then the entire Briton cavalry line crashed into the unorganized Saxon army. With no shield wall, the Saxons were vulnerable, and the mounted Britons slaughtered them with their stabbing spears. Thousands of Saxon foot soldiers were killed on the field or caught fleeing by the Briton cavalry.

Corb continued to hold his men in reserve if any of the Saxons headed toward the camp. The main battle had become a rout and isolated clusters of the enemy were fleeing in all directions. A hundred Saxons emerged from the woods and rushed across the meadow toward the road to Aquae Sulis. Corb shouted, "Follow me now!" as he spurred his horse into a gallop. His mounted troop hurtled ahead to intercept the enemy. He saw Aurelianus approaching with a troop of cavalry and charged the Saxons to trap them between the Briton forces. The enemy on foot and in the open meadow were slaughtered by the mounted assault.

Aurelianus directed his men to form a perimeter and continue to watch for stragglers. "Good work, Corb!" the Praetor said. But he suddenly looked with alarm over Corb's shoulder. Just over a mile away in the valley below, Aquae Sulis was under attack. "We have killed thousands of the enemy here, but there is much still to do, and I cannot leave the battle field. The town, however, needs help now! Take your troop and go."

Corb called to his men and kicked his horse into a race to Aquae Sulis. *I should have convinced the praetor to stay and defend the city!* They reached the bottom of the hill, burst out of the woods and rode across the bridge. The citizens were putting up a stiff fight. A few Saxons had scaled the walls, but were overwhelmed and thrown back, outnumbered by the determined townspeople. The citizens continued to topple the attackers' ladders by pushing them off the wall with poles fitted with cross pieces at the end. The t-shaped contrivances kept most of the enemy from reaching the top of the walls. Bodies littered the ground. Other Saxons were dragging themselves away with injured limbs. As Corb raced along the river to the battle, he saw Pontia and another woman wield one of the poles and tip a ladder from the wall, sending a pair of the enemy crashing to the ground. *She is determined! I love her even more!*

As Pontia and her partner pushed a ladder back from the wall, she noticed Corb and his men approaching. She was distracted by his arrival and the end of her pole became entangled in the ladder's rungs and she was pulled over the wall.

Corb pushed his horse and bellowed, "No!" The stone wall was almost three times the height of a man and Pontia clung to the pole, which pulled her down headfirst. Her years of acrobatics produced an intrinsic cat-like response, as she flipped over in the air, landed on her feet, and bent her knees to take the shock. But her momentum was not spent, and she continued stumbling forward. She rolled onto her right shoulder and stood up. From afar her recovery appeared flawless, but her right shoulder was in excruciating pain and she froze, holding the shoulder with her left hand. Now she stood among scores of Saxon soldiers and nearby warriors converged on her. Corb was in the lead and raised his spear. *I've never hit a target this far way, but I can't wait to get closer.* He swung his right arm in a large arc over his head and released the spear.

Pontia's small stature and her focus on her injury made her appear to be easy prey. A Saxon pulled a tether from his belt and approached Pontia, intending to bind her. She turned her left side toward him to hide the seaxe hanging on her right. Pontia evaded his grab, seized her knife with her left hand, and slashed his hand and neck in one fluid motion. She heard a grunt and turned to see an enemy soldier impaled by a spear. Next, the thundering hooves and the screams of men resounded as the Saxons were trampled by the Brittonic cavalry. People atop the parapets jeered and hurled obscenities at the enemy.

Dreng opened his eyes. It was dark. *Where am I? The battle! Am I alive or in the afterworld?* Then he heard men speaking the Britons' tongue. *Yes, I was running, I made it to the woods, but something knocked me in the head when I was looking behind.* He felt his swollen forehead, not realizing the imprint of tree bark was visible. *There are no longer any Saxon campfires, so we must have lost the battle.* He looked across the meadow to the top of Sulis Hill. The Britons' hill-fort looked occupied given the number of campfires. At the edge of the trees Dreng saw a glint of metal reflecting the campfire light. Thinking it was a sword or knife, he crawled to it, knowing he would need a weapon. It was a bronze amulet on a broken chain. He snatched it, crept downhill, and fled east toward the Saxon settlements.

Over the next few days Dreng avoided being detected by the

Brittonic cavalry hunting for Saxon fugitives. During that time, he thought about the king of the Britons that killed the once invincible Bretwalda, the high king of the Saxons. Their king must be very powerful! Not only did he defeat King Alle by hurling himself through the air like an eagle, but he then slayed ten warriors, no it was twenty warriors, by himself. Dreng was obsessed with these thoughts as he made his way home. He was not the first survivor to return to his village. The people were already telling great tales of the King of the Britons. They asked, who was he, what was his name? Dreng showed the amulet to the local war chief, the cyning. He accompanied the cyning to question a Christian monk the Saxons had enslaved years earlier. Dreng, wanting to be important and cover for his failure to fight to the death in battle, said, "Cyning, I forgot to tell you, but this was worn by the King of the Britons. As I told you before, he killed our Bretwalda and a hundred of our warriors. When I challenged him, I was bashed unconscious. When I awoke, it was night. But I remember this amulet falling from their king during the battle."

The monk opened the diptych and read the inscription. The Latin words were mostly gibberish to the Saxons, but one word sounded familiar. Dreng said, "Yes, their king flew like an eagle from his horse to smite our Bretwalda! That word, yes— Artorius! an eagle, Artor, Arthur. Now I remember, his name was Arthur, King Arthur, the Eagle!"

Now a few days after the battle, Corb was pleased with his assignment. Aurelianus had appointed him to command the garrison in Aquae Sulis while the praetor took his army north to recover Corinium from the enemy. The Saxons were calling their defeat on Sulis Hill the Battle of Baden. They referred to the city of Aquae Sulis as Baden, their word for Bath.

With the Saxon threat diminished, the city returned to everyday life and drudgery with a few entertaining diversions. Day by day, Pontia's act became more popular. One evening, however, Corb noticed Pontia looked tired after one of her performances. As they relaxed later in her room, Pontia said, "My

Tribune! You are going to be a father!"

Corb hugged her and said, "Pontia, I am very happy! Now with the Saxons pushed back, our girl . . . or boy, will grow up in a safe land. If the child is a girl, I know you will name her Pontia."

"If the baby is a boy, he will be MacCorb, son of the Charioteer!"

"But our child must inherit your amulet, so his Roman name will be Pontius Divittus MacCorb. Divittus, after my grandfather."

Aurelianus's leadership stabilized the frontier against the Saxons and led to three generations of peace for the Britons. The long period of freedom from war became threatened when over the next century, thousands of Saxons immigrated from across the sea to join their brethren in Britain. Concurrently, the alliance among the Britons of Powys, Dumnonia, and cities of Guenet had deteriorated. With these advantages, the Saxons conquered the three allied cities of Guenet. Many Britons chose to cross the channel to follow earlier emigrants to West Francia. So great a number of Britons had moved to the continent that the region they settled became known as Brittany. Aurelianus's victory had become legendary; it was a story of a man named Artorius, in German Arthur, dubbed King Arthur, who had won a great victory over the Saxons at the Battle of Baden Hill.

Seventy-seven years after the battle, a Briton couple, their meager belongings in wool sacks over their shoulders, fled a renewed Saxon advance. That morning they had left Isca, a port city where the old Roman road ended, and they now followed a trail westward across Dumnonia. Both trod along for miles in silence, then Aine spoke quietly as she adjusted the head scarf that shrouded her blond hair. "It seems proper to avoid disturbing the spirits of this desolate moor. The treeless land is ghostly."

"The man in Isca said this place is called Dartmoor," said her spouse, Macorbmac. "It is only inhabited by mining folk, but we haven't seen one person all day. Are they all underground, or . . .

maybe behind the rocks?"

"You may think you are funny, husband, but you are scaring me, and making me think a phantom will jump out from behind one of those huge boulders."

"Just trying to break the monotony, sweet Aine. My *Anya*. It will take us two more days to get to South Town, the next fishing village, where there will be a boat that will take us to Brittany."

"You have said that at the last two towns and there were no boats going across the sea," said Aine.

"Then we will search all the way to Pensans, the Holy Headland, the farthest western reach of Britain, to find one," said Maccorbmac.

"I am hungry and all we have to eat is a half a loaf of bread and only enough money for fare across the sea. Let's hope the next place has a boat to Brittany."

Two days later Aine and her husband arrived at the River Plym and followed the south bank. "We should reach South Town in about two miles," said Maccorbmac.

Within the expected time, the couple arrived at a village that was located on a promontory overlooking a harbor. There were several wooden flatboats, one of them containing a heap of rocks, plus several small craft docked below on the waterfront. "Hmm, I do not see any large boats that would travel the sea," said Maccorbmac.

Aine pointed. "Look at the building next to the river, where the smoke is rising. By the sounds it could be a metalsmith's shop. Let's ask the people there."

They found a path with switchbacks, negotiated the rocky cliff down to the harbor, and arrived at the busy workshop. Laborers crushed rocks and other workers tended fires melting the pulverized ore in an open-sided shed. The pair watched several minutes, then a man crushing ore halted, tilted his head back, and shouted over the noise, "Livyow!" The laborers stopped their work. He put down his hammer, removed a dusty leather apron, and smiled as he approached Aine and her husband. "We don't see many travelers here."

"I am Maccorbmac and this is my wife Aine. Is this South Town? We were told there are boats that will take us to Brittany."

"No, this is Ictis. All we have here are ore boats and our skin coracles. That explains it. You must be more of the emigrants fleeing the Saxons." He pointed across the harbor. "South Town, er . . . it is called Sutton hereabouts, is over there. Come eat livyow with us, tell me about what is happening in the east, and I will ferry you over to the quayside where the ships to Brittany dock."

As they followed the man to an adjacent house, a woman who had also been working in the shop joined them. "I am glad Deorsa asked you to lunch, we don't see many married couples on our side of the harbor. They live in Sutton. I am Eirinn."

"You said 'lunch' but your husband said 'livyow'"? asked Aine.

"Yes, I am learning all forms of Gaelic. Livyow is used in these parts," answered Eirinn.

"And I have not heard your name before—it sounds like you are saying "of Eire," said Aine.

"Yes . . . I am so used to it, I don't think about it, but you are right, that is what it means—and I am from Eire!" she laughed.

They sat down to hot soup and bread. "I am sorry those people told you to follow the south bank of the Plym," said Deorsa. "I don't mind rowing you over to Sutton. Crossing the harbor will take very little time, about the time to walk a half mile. Otherwise, if you walked all the way around the harbor, you would have to backtrack to the river ford and tramp a half a day to reach Sutton."

"We are very grateful, sir," said Maccorbmac. Are there some chores we can do to repay your kindness? And what were you doing with the . . . rocks?"

"Yes, um . . . rocks. The rocks are called ore, tin and copper ores. The miners float loads of them on the flat boats down the river from Dartmoor. We make a good living crushing and smelting ores to make metals. We sell the tin and copper ingots to Isca, where they combine them to make bronze. Much of the bronze is used to make armor for the Brittonic King of Dumnonia." He paused to join the others slurping their soup.

"Was it peaceful in Isca? Any word about Saxons?"

"Isca is still held by the Britons. I do not know how far the Saxons have advanced from that direction, but our home was Lindinis, which fell months ago."

"I am sorry." Deorsa looked at his wife and said, "We will have to use all of our negotiating abilities if the Saxons take over, and we would have to prove to them our skills are needed. I suppose then the Saxons would be our customers."

"We have worked the metal from the earth our whole lives," said Eirinn. "As have our ancestors as far back as we know."

"Since Roman times?" asked Aine.

"Well before the Romans, during the time of the Druids. The craft is in our blood. We love it—we both love . . . rocks!" The group laughed together.

Deorsa rowed the couple across the harbor in his coracle, a skin covered, oval shaped craft. Maccorbmac expressed their gratitude and they said their farewells. The couple walked along the docks of Sutton, where tied up were much larger hide covered ships, thirty or forty paces long, used for fishing and to cross the sea. These currachs were sailboats used by the mariners of Britain, Eire, and Brittany. Maccorbmac called out, "Hello! Is anyone home!"

A fellow appeared out from under the covered aft, merely a tent of stretched leather over wooden hoops, and laughed as he said, "Yes! This is our home." He was wearing loose trousers that ended just below his knees, a shirt overlaid by a leather vest, the pockets brimming with tools and knives. A blond woman followed him as she parted the entry flaps of the cabin. She looked out of place with her colorful dress and styled hair. Her husband added, "Are you looking for passage to Brittany? That is our specialty!"

"Yes, yes! So, it is true. We were told we would find a boat to Brittany in South Tow . . . um . . .in Sutton," the young man answered.

The boatman's wife said, "We were just about to have codfish. Come join us."

The young man wrinkled his nose, but answered, "Uh, yes,

sir . . . well it does smell good cooking. Thank you, um, for your generosity."

The sailor said, "Oh, you may have not eaten codfish before. Don't worry, my wife has made green sauce using parsley and a little mint. It will cover the fish taste.

And, our names . . . I am Addy and . . ." he held out his hand, "my wife Nesta. Yes, this is our vocation. We are ferrymen for Britons fleeing the Germans."

"You are a German yourself," said Nesta. "Are they fleeing you, my husband?"

"She is just jesting, sort of jesting. I am from Mercia, the kingdom of the Angles, a German tribe. Yes, I am part Angle and part Briton by birth, but I fell in love with my wife here, the Princess of Powys. And now I am all Briton by heart. She left all her extravagant lifestyle for me! Except when we are in port, like now, she dresses up again and fixes her hair."

"I am Nesta fech Farinmail," said his wife. "My father, King Farinmail, rules the Kingdom of Powys, the last of the true Britons. But my adventures with Addy and the sea far outshine a royal life."

"I am Maccorbmac and this is my wife Aine," said the emigrant. "We have bread to share. It will be good with the fish."

Another couple with two children arrived, also wishing passage to Brittany. They welcomed the travelers to join in the meal. The children, a boy and a girl, began to explore the boat and their mother disciplined them. "I don't mind them if you don't, ma'am," said Addy.

They watched as Addy stirred the pot of boiling fish. "Yes, this is the best way to cook codfish. You add salt to a mixture of part water and part ale, then boil it. Now it's almost done, you can see the froth forming at the top. I'll skim that off and we will have some nice fish to share. "And have some bread handy." He smiled at the children. "You should pick the fish meat off the bones, but if you swallow a bone don't worry. Swallow a piece of bread and the bone will go down with it." He offered the cooked fish on a wooden slab, from which they each selected a piece and ate with their hands.

Addy continued as he ate. "I built this vessel myself, learning the methods from a crusty old Briton who plied the channel between Britain and the mainland his whole life. There has been a need for ferries for generations. He is passed now but taught me well. I found many who claimed they were good shipwrights, but I sought out the best. The frame of my boat is made of willow saplings, bent to form the frame. Now willow is supple, and some boat builders are satisfied with that alone, but the best frame is built from willow which is bent when subjected to the hot vapors of boiling water. I learned that from the old-timers. And cow hides are not good enough. Well, good enough for coracles used in rivers and such, but not for the sea. I procured thick bullock hides, stretched them over the frame, and then applied pine tar."

Nesta, who had ducked inside the small leather cabin, returned in her work clothes and interrupted. "Excuse me, husband, you should be saying you had help. I assisted you in stretching the hides."

"Yes, of course, my princess, you were a great help and a fast learner. We built the boat together. Um . . . the sail is also made from hide, but a thinner cut. As you can see, there are six oars on my craft, needed when the wind does not cooperate. You, the passengers, will be required to man the oars at times so I can steer as helmsman and we can safely take you to the other side of the channel."

"What will be the fee to transport us to Brittany, Helmsman Addy?" asked Maccorbmac.

"Whatever you can afford."

"The only thing of value I have is a silver coin."

Addy responded, "Of course, your silver coin is enough." He looked over the other passengers. "And for everyone's passage."

"You are very generous Addy," said Nesta.

"That is fair," said Maccorbmac.

The captain noticed a bronze amulet that hung from the young man's neck.

"Maybe your necklace would be a fairer exchange?"

"No sir, sorry. It is a family treasure from my great grandmother."

The parents had a whispered conversation. Then the man unrolled his blanket and pulled out a seaxe. He handed it to Maccorbmac. "I see you have a knife, but your wife does not. It is not worth half a silver coin, but it's all I can give. Here, take it for our part of the fare."

"Yes, thank you," said Maccorbmac as he accepted the barter.

The young boy pulled on an oar and said, "Sir Helmsman! I want to row too!"

"Eat all of your fish first," said his mother.

After they had eaten and cleaned up, Addy said, "Now about the rowing. Everyone watch closely, and I will show you the most efficient way a sailor handles the oars! We will row across the harbor. Anyway, I need to go check my long lines since the tide has just gone out."

Addy was an inspiring teacher and so, with sail furled, they took a practice row around a calm harbor that evening. The novelty of the experience made the exertion more like recreation than work. Near the entrance to the harbor they approached Addy's fish line, which was a rope fifty paces long suspended between two wooden posts, sunk in the sand. Large hooks, each the length of a man's hand, hung from the rope. Several fish had been caught on the hooks. As he retrieved several fish, Addy said. "The fish line was under water when the tide was higher. I baited the hooks and you can see these fish were hungry enough to bite."

After he collected his catch, they rowed to the middle of the harbor and the emigrants' daughter, then their son, showed their delight steering the boat. Addy played his stringed crwth and Nesta did pirouettes on the bow to the music, on one foot, then the other, more of an athletic jig than a dance. The oarsmen stopped rowing and clapped to her frolics. After many entertaining measures, Addy and Nesta ended their piece, which was followed by laughter. "Beautiful music and lovely dancing!" said Aine.

"It is such a joy to dance," said Nesta. "I am so lucky. If I had stayed a princess, it wouldn't have been appropriate."

Addy sang a reply as he strummed his instrument, "You are my princess!"

The little boy asked how long it would take to cross the sea. Addy answered. "Young man, it depends on the tides, we must time our departure to when the tide is going out."

"What is a tide?' asked the boy.

Addy explained how the sea level in the harbor would rise and fall, then the boy asked, "But what makes the tides happen?"

"There is an old Gaelic saying," said Addy. "*Trí ní is deacair a thuiscint; intleacht na mban, obair na mbeach, teacht agus imeacht na taoide.* Three things are difficult to understand, the mind of a woman, the work of bees, and the coming and going of the tide."

CHAPTER ONE
1065 A.D.

England and
France
1060 A.D.

50 miles

SCOTLAND

IRELAND

WALES

ENGLAND

London

English Channel

FLANDERS

PONTHIEU

Dives

Caen DUCHY of
NORMANDY

Paris

CHAMPAGNE

DUCHY of
BRITTANY

Le Mans
MAINE

BLOIS
Tours

ILE de FRANCE

ANJOU

BURGUNDY

Atlantic Ocean

Saintes
Pons

Périgueux

DUCHY of
AQUITAINE

COUNTY of
SAINTONGE

PERIGORD

Toulouse

DUCHY of
GASCONY

COUNTY of
TOULOUSE

MARCH of
GOTHIA

Santiago de Compostela

SPAIN

CHAPTER ONE
1065 A.D.

The Count of Saintonge studied the formation of the hostile knights as they assembled for battle on the far side of the meadow. The knights' red and blue shields emblazoned with a gold cross were prominent as they rode out of the forest of Baconnais. These chevaliers were from Le Mans, the capital of County Maine.

The count addressed his officers and focused on his field commander, Richard, son of Pons. "The reports from Anjou were true. The knights from Le Mans fled their home county with such haste that their force does not include any infantry or archers. That is fortunate, since we had to muster quickly and did not have time to bring along our own support troops. Captains, it appears this fight will be knights versus knights. A noble challenge to our manhood!"

The Count of Saintonge had mustered his vassals a few miles north of his capital of Saintes to stop the incursion by the invaders from Le Mans. Among the loyal contingents of knights responding to his call were those from the stronghold of Lord Pons. The lord was past his prime, but his five adult sons answered the request. Simon FitzPons, the oldest of the Pons brothers, observed the knights on both sides of the meadow and said, "I sense that all the combatants on the field welcome the opportunity to enter this pure form of chevalier combat. The men are eager to fight, and the horses are restless. Our steeds' readiness for combat justifies the long hours of training we have put our warhorses through to endure the physical and mental stresses of battle."

Simon continued, "If they were on an expedition to seize territory, why did they simply pass through County Anjou to reach us? You would think they would take a castle or secure a fortified town to use as a base, this far from their home county."

"They lost their capital to the Normans who have conquered their lands," answered the count. "These knights are now rogue chevaliers. I suspect they believe the Duke of Aquitaine is too far away and weak to help us oppose them. But they do not know our will." He scrutinized Simon's four younger brothers, mounted and ready for battle.

Richard FitzPons was the second oldest sibling, his helmet with a golden plume of horsehair shooting above like a rooster tail. The next eldest was Osborne with his signatory green tassel. Both men wore their hair short. Richard maintained a short beard, but Osborne was clean shaven. Mounted on an impatient stallion, reflecting his rider's temperament, was Drogo, the bright red panache on his helmet whipping in the wind with his long dark hair. The fourth sibling, Gauthier, sat quietly on his warhorse, his long blonde hair and blue strands of horsehair wavering in the breeze. For years, the brothers had used the personal colors to identify themselves in battles.

The count continued, "With the sons of Lord Pons leading the knights, we will stop these scoundrels. The Duke of Aquitaine will reward us for defending the county and duchy. Take your positions."

Simon and the Count of Saintonge remained in the rear with several knights and squires in reserve as reinforcements. Across the large meadow behind the enemy's main force was another group of mounted knights, who appeared to have the same rearguard function. The count decided to take the role of aggressor and ordered Richard to begin the battle.

The count's remark about the Pons brothers had distracted Richard momentarily. *Yes, we four younger brothers have defended our county for years, and Simon no longer enters in the fights, commanding from the rear. And because of the law of primogeniture, Simon inherits the castle and manor from Father Pons. Drogo returned from Sicily because of his love for the family, and we will soon go there and seek our own fortunes. I tolerate taking commands from Simon because he is our older brother and because Father, too old to fight, stays out of the field. There are only a dozen knights at the Pons stronghold. When the four of us leave, they will be vulnerable. But Father approved when we told him we wanted to go to Sicily.*

Richard freed himself of distracting thoughts and shouted to the knights of Saintes and Pons to rein their mounts and move forward at a slow gait. Richard led one of their four squadrons; the other three were each led by one of his brothers. Several years prior the Pons brothers had reorganized their battle formation in the way of the Normans. Drogo, always restless, had travelled to southern Italy and had been employed as a mercenary in the Norman County of Aversa. He then joined the Norman forces who had crossed the straits from Italy and invaded Sicily in 1061. Drogo had fought in the battle that freed Messina from the Arabs. There he learned the Norman cavalry tactics that coordinated around the conroi, a flexible and unified cavalry unit which included from 15 up to 50 knights. In their sea invasion of Sicily, the Normans had organized small conrois of twenty knights each, the number that could be transported along with their steeds by each horse-transport ship. Such cavalry units were effective only when the members had trained together for a time that they were used to each other's movements. The Pons brothers already met these criteria and readily adopted the system. Drogo directed their blacksmiths to fabricate *hauberks*, the coat of chain mail that a Norman knight wore, which protected the legs as well as the torso. He also recommended to replace the round shields of the Pons knights with longer, almond-shaped shields that added protection to their legs. The shields were fitted with two enarmes, so it remained attached to his arm, even when a knight relaxed his grip. The crest of red and yellow diagonal stripes of Lord Pons's banner was prominently displayed on their shields as they advanced to battle.

Richard's squadron formed the left flank, Drogo led his men

in the center slightly forward, with Osborne's group taking the right wing. Gauthier and his men held the rear to engage the enemy if they penetrated the front line or outflanked them.

The two forces were equal, there being about forty knights on each side. Both groups increased their speed to a trot. The knights of Maine spread into a wide line to outflank the diamond shape formation of the County Saintonge knights led by Richard. He watched Drogo lead his men toward the center of the enemy line. *He needs to shift the position of first contact to one side or the other or we could be outflanked on both sides.*

The brothers had fought together for years and as if his younger brother read Richard's mind, thirty paces before he crashed into the enemy lines, Drogo veered to the left. Richard, his troops staying with him, and Osborne's knights all tracked with Drogo's change in direction. The knights were firmly secured to their steeds by stirrups and saddles that were fitted with both front and rear elevated cantles. This fusing of horse and rider created maximum impact. Drogo's shift of their diamond formation avoided being outflanked on their left. Richard glanced back to see Gauthier react to Drogo's move and dash to the right and cover Osborne's flank. The enemy's straight line was pierced by the wedge led by Drogo as well as by the dense formation of Gauthier's men. Both squads then veered back and attacked their opponents from behind as Richard's and Osborne's troops engaged the enemy head-on. Fighting in two directions, the Le Mans knights were overwhelmed and in less than an hour, a score of the knights of Le Mans were either killed or unhorsed and out of action.

Richard called a halt to the fighting when several of the enemy knights dismounted, laid down their weapons, and knelt in surrender. He signaled his men from pursuing a few scattered knights on the fringes of the battle as the remaining Mainieres surrendered. The enemy reserves near the woods had fled and had not joined the battle.

Richard left several knights to secure the prisoners and, with his brothers, accounted for their own knights and ensured first aid was given to the wounded. The hand of one of the Pons knights had been cut off and a tourniquet had been applied. Another had been impaled by a spear. His fellow knight had cut off part of his own tunic and stuffed it in the man's wound. One other was alive but paralyzed with a broken back. A fourth had his leg crushed from falling under his horse. Another had a broken leg. "Simon, use spears and make a travail," called out Richard, while he held the cloth against the knight with the spear wound. "It will be rough, but at least you can drag him to the Abbey of Dames, where the nuns may be able to save him." The chevalier who lost his hand rode back to Saintes with a comrade directly to the forge to have his wound cauterized.

Simon and the count joined Richard. "Good, I sent a rider back to the city to bring carts for the wounded as soon as I saw we defeated them," said Simon.

"Thank you, brother."

Simon pointed south along the road. "There are the carts now!"

The wounded from Le Mans were also attended to. Those that surrendered were disarmed and retained to assist the cart drivers to move the injured to the nunnery in Saintes, the capital of County Saintonge. With these tasks under way, Simon returned to the village of Pons with escorts to report the results of the battle. The other four FitzPons brothers rode along with the caravan of wounded and decided to stay overnight. They would encourage and pray with their wounded comrades, who would remain at the nunnery to recover. The soldier whose leg had been crushed had not survived the amputation and the brothers planned to return his body to the village of Pons.

As the entourage approached the Abbey of Dames, across the Charente River from the town of Saintes, the Arch of Germanicus, an ancient remnant of the former Roman city, loomed ahead as an entry to the bridge and city.

The abbey's cloister was crowded with pilgrims staying overnight on their long trek to Spain. They had been moved outside due to the space needed indoors for the injured soldiers. As they crossed the abbey, Richard saw a pilgrim scratching an image of a scallop shell on the courtyard wall, next to an earlier unsanctioned rendition of the ancient Christian symbol of a fish. He thought defacing the wall was disrespectful, but he was eager to see his men and ignored the act. Gauthier found the knight that had taken a lance in the stomach lying next to his comrade who had lost his hand. Both men were bandaged and appeared drowsy, barely acknowledging the FitzPons brothers. They stood by observing as a nun sat in attendance. "Sister, how are my men? They look worse than when they were taken from the battlefield."

The nun wore an undyed habit, which proclaimed her poverty and identified her as being of the Benedictine order. Her woolen scapula draped over her shoulder and covered her head, hiding what little hair she may have kept as the custom was to have it cut short. "I made a poultice with jusquiasmus for each of them. The herb will help their pain but makes them very sleepy, which explains their appearance."

Gauthier asked, "I have seen very few men survive these wounds."

"With God's will they may live. The good Lord guided me to clean the wound with vinegar wine. I then spread honey on the wounds and bandaged the herb poultice in place. I will be changing the dressings every few days."

"Sister, we have used vinegar to cleanse, but I did not know about using honey. Where did you discover using honey as a medicine?" asked Osborne.

"The fact that honey helps heal a wound has been passed down for generations. We also discovered another use for honey to help close a wound, from a codex written centuries ago in the Roman times. It states that if you cook the honey, and put it on the wound, it agglutins, no the Latin word is—agglutinates, the wound."

She showed them to a nearby table and opened a book to the front page: *De Medicina – Aulus Cornelius Celsus, Book V.* She flipped a few pages and read: "'The following agglutinate a wound: myrrh, frankincense, gum Arabic,' we don't have any of those, but there, see we have honey—it says use cooked honey." She flipped a few more pages and read: "'Honey mixed with lentils or with horehound or with olive leaves previously boiled in wine holds in check putrid flesh, prevents its further spread.' We used lentils. So this book confirms the healing properties of honey."

"Where did you find such a book?"

"Our Lord guided monks to preserve the manuscript for many centuries. I was told a Benedictine monk from Paris had visited Italy, copied the book, and brought it back to the monastery of Saint-Germain-des-Paris. Then a copy was made there and brought to our abbey."

The nun studied Gauthier and his brothers. "Sir, are you a FitzPons? One of the sons of Lord Pons?"

"Yes, we are four of his sons, his younger sons. I am Gauthier FitzPons." He introduced his brothers. Each young man bowed his head as Gauthier announced their formal name: "Richard FitzPons, Osborne FitzPons, and Dreux FitzPons."

The nun's eyes grew wide. "Then it is your sister, Sara, who will be coming to Saintes to be the Countess's lady? Please tell her the sisters here in the abbey look forward to meeting her."

"Yes, it will be soon, at least within a few weeks. We will be escorting her." The men started to leave. Gauthier turned and said, "Excuse me, sister, for not being appreciative. Thank God he sent an angel to nurse our men!"

The nun lowered her gaze.

The brothers bedded outside with the pilgrims in the cloister garden. Before they fell to sleep Gauthier whispered to Osborne, "I know we decided to go to Sicily, but Father will be vulnerable with only Simon at the castle with so few knights. I have decided to stay home." Osborne was tired and said, "I have a plan which will solve the dilemma. We will talk about it in the morning."

At first light, three of the FitzPons brothers sat at the community tables to have a breakfast of pottage, a thickened soup of carrots, leeks, onions, cabbage, beans, and oats. Richard overslept and joined them when they had almost finished eating. As Gauthier thanked the sisters for the meal, he said to one nun, "The pottage has an unusual taste. It is very good!"

"You probably tasted the saffron. A few years ago, a pilgrim gave us a donation, as many are able, but then asked me what else he could do for the abbey. Saffron flowers are grown far to the south, but the herb is available through trade with the Muslims in Spain, so I asked him to bring some back when he returned from Compostela. He did, and I have since asked other pilgrims passing through to obtain herbs and spices not available here."

"Sister, I have a suggestion for the benefit of the abbey," said Drogo. "It will help bring in funds to care for the pilgrims and the sick."

"Go ahead, Sir Dreux."

"The saffron is very valuable and small quantities would sell for significant coinage, yes? Ask the pilgrims to bring back more than you use yourselves. Sell the surplus to nearby nobles and landed gentry. They would be pleased to know the profit is for the Church."

"Thank you. I will discuss this idea with the abbess." The nun looked at Osborne lying on a nearby bench. "Is he sick?"

"No," laughed Gauthier. "He always eats too fast and then wants to lie down after his meal."

Before they departed the abbey, they visited the injured knights from the Pons barony. To their relief, the wounded knights' conditions had not worsened, and they were more alert. The nuns had graciously bound up the deceased knight with a woolen shroud. The brothers procured a two-wheeled cart to transport the body and his weapons to the village of Pons. Their squires were given the responsibility to drive the cart and meet them in Pons to return the knight's body to his family.

Shortly after leaving the abbey, they passed through the Arch of Germanicus and crossed the river to the city of Saintes. As they rode past the remains of an ancient Roman amphitheater, Osborne suggested a way to persuade Gauthier to go to Sicily with them. It would require the help of the Count of Saintonge. They soon approached the count's castle. "It looks like they used the same quarry for the stone to build this chateau as the Romans did to erect that amphitheater," said Osborne. "But, wait. Yes, I see . . . they must have taken the stone from the amphitheater to build the chateau." Osborne looked down at the pavement. "At least they didn't steal the stones from the road. Otherwise the trip home would take forever."

Although their visit was unexpected, the Count heartily welcomed the brothers. "Your prowess on the battlefield was extraordinary! Well done, knights! Thank you for your loyalty and leadership. What brings you to call today?"

After Richard explained their original plans to join the Normans in Sicily, he asked. "Sire, I believe we captured about a dozen knights from Le Mans."

"Yes, and it is interesting that you mention them," said the count. "County Maine has been conquered by the Normans. Perhaps that was why these knights fled and subsequently attacked us. The customary method is to ransom captured knights; the noble families in Le Mans certainly have been disposed and cannot pay a ransom. What can we do with them?"

Richard looked at Osborne to disclose his plan. "I have a proposal, sire," said Osborne. "It will relieve you of the burden to feed and house the knights—at least those that are willing to pledge fealty to my father. They will bolster our defenses," he glanced at his brothers, "when we depart for Sicily."

The brothers spent the next several hours questioning and interviewing the hostages. Eight of the knights agreed to pledge loyalty to Lord Pons. Of those, Richard would obtain Simon's counsel in the decision to accept four of them. The count agreed the prisoners could remain in Saintes until Lord Pons agreed on the plan to integrate them.

The FitzPons brothers headed south on the Way of Tours, which was one of the four main routes that French religious pilgrims took to Spain. The road began in Paris, 300 miles northeast of Saintes, passed through Tours, and joined other paths in the Pyrenees of southern France. It took the most faithful and determined pilgrims two months to walk the 900 miles from Paris to reach Santiago de Compostela near the Atlantic Ocean in Spain. There they revered the relics of Saint James, Christ's brother.

Drogo said, "Ozzie, are we going north to Pons?"

Osborne made a good show of trying to sound irritated. "What, are you still unable to figure directions?"

They laughed and looked at Drogo, who made the devilish smile he used to show when they were boys and he was ready for mischief. He kicked his horse into a canter and shouted, "Let's go!"

As his brothers matched his pace, Richard said, "At least he isn't trying to veer in front of our mounts and unhorse us like he did when we were boys learning how to ride!"

"Gauthier, that was a good idea to stay last night and support our wounded," said Richard. "As a boy, you were angry at everyone and everything. You had a scowl all the time, too. Back then I would have never thought you would turn out to have so much compassion."

"I watched you, brother. You were older than us and at times had to stop us from seriously harming each other when we fought. Drogo always needed to be doing something and when he was bored, he would fight Ozzie and me, but you knew just when to step in."

"Yes," Richard laughed. "And I remember the time you got mad and hit Drogo in the head with a rock. He still has the scar above his eyebrow from that."

"But now we're men and . . ."

"And Father," Richard interrupted, "told us to always remain allies, love each other as brothers, and talk about our differences so they do not fester. And there are always going to be differences."

They continued to ride along the low plateau which overlooked the Seugne River valley to the east. As they approached the village, the huge oaks of the Baconnais Forest blocked the view of the houses, but they could see the donjon, the tower that served as Lord Pons's inner keep and citadel, soaring above the trees. Richard recalled that the Pontois, or villagers of Pons, called the tower Aiguille de Pons, the Needle of Pons. As they entered the village and slowed their horses, the three-beat gaits echoed along the paved street and among the stone houses. Richard enjoyed returning to his hometown, but his preferred entry was from below in the valley. From there, the views of the lofty tower were more inspiring.

At the center of the village Richard and his brothers continued through the castle gate into the bailey, the open area inside the walls. They met with the family of the deceased knight and expressed their condolences to his relatives. The family was loaned the cart and helpers for the soldier's burial. Richard informed the relations that they would be contacted by Lord Pons, who would be most honored to attend the funeral. Richard knew it was not necessary to hurry and report the battle to their father, since Simon had returned the day before. Richard suggested, however, after they handed their mounts over to their squires, that they notify him of the status of the injured.

Several days after the battle, the Pons family sat in the castle hall waiting for Lord Pons to join them for the evening meal. Lost in a rare new book, he was late and rushed down the twisting staircase to the hall, the way barely visible in the dim light. At the bottom step, the door to the hall was open and he was about to cross the threshold but stopped abruptly. He recalled a trick his sons used to play on him years earlier. *Gauthier started his game of hiding behind this same doorway when he was about five. He did surprise me, but after his initial ambush, I became wary every time I passed through the door, and I foiled his frequent attempts. So Gauthier then recruited Drogo and Ozzie. They planned more elaborate traps and fooled me, but over time I learned to thwart their ambushes. But perhaps this time my intuition is wrong. They have not tried this mischief in years.* Pons flicked his hand across the threshold to spring their trap. No response. He removed his surcoat, dangled it, then flung it through the doorway, but nothing happened. He waited. Gauthier appeared from behind the door and laughed, "You guessed right, you caught me!" He turned to go, but Pons remained behind the threshold. "Father, what are you doing? I heard you come down the stairs and set my trap, but you discovered me. Come, we are all at the table and the food is ready."

"You can't fool me," said Pons. "Your brothers are hiding on both sides of the doorway."

"We haven't done that in years," Gauthier declared with a

dismissive laugh. "Do you feel well, Father?"

"Come and eat, dear!" Pons's wife Mini called out from the hall.

I am over forty, and lately I have been forgetting names and unable to recall where I put things. Perhaps this intuition just is my imagination. He stepped over the threshold peering down, to improve the peripheral vision above the back of his head. Detecting movement, Pons dropped sharply to one knee and avoided the clutches of Osborne and Drogo who had pressed themselves against the wall on each side of the doorway. As their father hammered their midsections, they both grunted, which turned to laughter. He yelled, "What treachery!" Pons joined in their mirth. When he gathered his surcoat and joined his family at the table, Mini shouted, "God's bones, what is going on!"

At last the family sat together for their evening meal. Lord Pons always took advantage of the time to ply his family with history and give advice. The servants had cleared the platters of venison and vegetables and the family relaxed beside the warmth from a large fireplace, enjoying wine spiced with cinnamon. Father Pons held up a sheet of stiff parchment. "I have informed you over the years what this record affirms." As he waved the document the prominent title could be seen displayed in capital letters, DE FAMILIA PONTIUS. "This will is written according to the laws of Francia adopted from the Romans and Franks. Property is passed via primogeniture, to the first born." He glanced at his eldest son, Simon. "This is not news to any of you."

Pons's wife Minuet said, "Husband, as you spoke earlier, Frankish law seems to have dominated in the northern counties and duchies of Francia. Enlighten your children about the differences in the law in Toulouse, where our cousins live."

"Yes, Mini. It seems the laws passed in the southern counties are a meld of Roman and Visigothic, not Frankish. There, women can own land and thus if the first born is a girl, she can inherit, according to primogeniture."

Sara smiled. "I have never had any desire to be a landowner nor a ruler. And I prefer to gain the skills to manage a royal household, and then be a valued and honorable equal for marriage.

How time passes! I have only one more week to prepare for my move to the count's chateau!" Sara looked about the table. "And I have my brothers. That is the best inheritance."

Mini's eye misted. Her husband was quiet for a few moments and appeared pleased. He then continued, "You can read the will in its entirety if you wish. I know Sara is very skilled at reading and writing. My sons, having attained knighthood, one of the requirements was to learn how to read and write. I hope you have kept up your studies." He looked at his wife. "Mini?"

"Husband, Sara and I have ensured that your stubborn sons, who as they grew up preferred to fight and spar each other, are also quite literate in Latin."

Pons said, "Sweet Sara. Our only daughter, and despite growing up with five brothers, has become a lovely young woman, even mothering her siblings!" He laughed. "But that is family. It may be impossible for us to avoid becoming separated. Sara will be in Saintes and three brothers plan to join the Normans in Sicily, as Dreux did. But he came back. What we must do is never let anything divide our hearts!

"Today I want to talk of succession. Simon has already assumed lordship of our village, castle, and donjon. Soon our home will be half empty with Sara and three sons leaving for Sicily." Mini shed tears as she gazed at her family around the table.

"Sons, I want you to seek your own fortunes and do not expect you to remain here. I will be asking my cousin Lord Maurice in Perigueux if any of his sons or nephews who have attained knighthood, or are training as squires, will come to Pons and join our knights. We will be able to trust our cousins."

Gauthier said, "Father . . ." but was cut off as Lord Pons began one of his ramblings.

"And one part of the Bible I don't like is when Cain kills his brother Abel. That's not how it should be! Not in this family! And our ancestors, the Romans, have the same story! Romulus kills his twin brother Remus! Family is everything!"

"Father . . ." Gauthier again tried to interrupt, but this time his mother intervened.

"Husband, we are all sad with the children departing. Your son Gauthier wants to say something."

Looking on, Richard worried his brother was going to announce his parting as well and further upset their father, but instead Gauthier asked. "Father, how do you know we have Roman blood?"

Lord Pons calmed, "Why look at our written family name. Pontius is an ancient Roman name. But it is pronounced Pons in our vernacular. Language and especially names tie the generations together. Children, do you remember when I told you how our family arrived here in our village?"

"Tell us again, Father," said Dreux.

"Even if a person of Francia does not know much history, it is common knowledge the Romans lived here, evident from the roads and the bridges we still use. We cannot ignore the ruins of great structures, such as the aqueducts and amphitheaters in the towns we now live. Centuries ago our ancestors departed Italy and intermarried with Gauls and Visigoths. The name Pontius was mostly forgotten, except in the vestiges of spoken and written language. Pontius orally became Pons in Occitan and French, as both languages evolved from Latin. A century ago, Ramon Pons the Count of Toulouse, along with his wife Garsinda, founded a monastery in honor of Saint Pontius of Cimiez. Pontius was a Christian, martyred in the third century for preaching Christ's words. Ramon believed he was descended from that very Pontius."

Richard saw that the timing was now right for his brother to state what he originally was going to disclose. *It is like when we are in battle, we can read each other's intentions.*

Gauthier said, "Father, four of your sons will be departing. I have decided to join my brothers." He explained the plan to recruit the knights from Le Mans. "This is why I have decided to go." He laughed. "Besides I have been defending my brothers' backs since we have been knights. I can't stop now."

"I see you have a detailed plan for recruiting the new knights," said Simon. "We should also have the priest talk with them to ensure their faith is strong. The priest might also discern any insincerity. As Father wishes, I will still recruit our cousins from Perigueux to maintain family leadership in the cavalry troop."

"Well, this is something your mother and I must steady ourselves about," said their father. "But we want you to find your own fortune and life, even if it is halfway across the world."

Mini's eyes were still misty, but she was also smiling.

"Remember the stories I told you about when I fought the Moors in Spain?" said their father. The family waited in silence. Richard glanced around the table. *We all want to hear Father recite his quest again, although we all probably know it by heart.* Father Pons continued, "Before I was married, I also left home to find adventure. I fought in the Reconquista, the war to expel the Muslims from Spain." He went on to describe the hardships and battles and again came to advice he had repeated many times over the years. "Be patient and don't let anger control you. Don't forget all your training and just rush at the enemy. When I was young, I was a nervous and anxious fighter. I used to carry two daggers and strap a second sword on my saddle. I thought direct attack and brute effort would overcome the enemy. But I finally learned that patience and timing will win. Thank God it was before my reckless habits killed me."

He ended with a warning. "Sons, the battles you have fought in your young lives have all been noble, that is—to defend our home, our domain. The horrors of wars when invading another land will pressure you to do terrible things. Don't let the fear change your heart. Think for yourselves and avoid joining the evils of the mob."

"We hope to experience such a grand venture, Father—and remain Christian men," said Gauthier. Then he looked at Drogo. "Tell them the other news."

"Yes, when we talked with the prisoners from Maine, they told us King Edward had died and Harold Godwinson was crowned the King of England. William, Duke of Normandy, claims he is the rightful king and has declared he will invade England. He has sent couriers across Europe entreating knights to join his army. We have decided to answer his call and enroll."

"Well, I must write a letter of introduction for you to Duke William," said Lord Pons. "Drogo, recall that on your way here from Sicily you stopped in Toulouse and met our distant cousin, Guillaume IV, the Count of Toulouse. There you discovered that he had married the niece of the Duke of Normandy. I shall include that in the letter, that we are related by marriage. It should help." He looked at Drogo. "What was her name, son?"

"Her name was Emma, Father. She is the daughter of the duke's brother, Count Robert of Mortain."

"So, Mother, we will not be as far away. England is closer than Sicily," said Drogo.

Osborne rolled his eyes and said, "You are getting better at geography, brother!"

The following week the FitzPons brothers and Sara departed their home village of Pons. Simon accompanied them along with his knights. In Saintes, with the help of a priest, he planned to interview the captured knights from Maine. The twelve-mile trip north was on the Way of Tours, a good road and mostly level, so Sara chose to ride sidesaddle rather than in the family's two-wheeled carriage. Her horse trotted beside Richard's mount. "Simon told me for the last two years you have replaced him as the leader on the battlefield. Do you think you will be a captain when you join the Normans?"

"All my brothers lead during the battles, depending on the situation. That is, except Simon, who has stayed in the rear since I was designated by Father to be lead knight. We have adopted the way of the Norman cavalry, so I hope that will help us all to gain promotion to officers in their army."

"Simon described your formation in the battle near Saintes and he said Drogo was in the front and started the attack on the enemy."

"Yes, that did happen, I initiated the approach to the enemy and he modified the tactics as needed. His decisions were sound, or I would have signaled to retreat. I want his position as center and front. The only way I can direct Drogo's fervor is to maintain a battle position where I can keep a watch on him."

"How about Osborne? What position does he prefer?"

"Ozzie wants to be on the right wing. And he also shows leadership, taking the initiative at times during battle by adjusting to what our opponent is doing. Ozzie's great passion in battle encourages others as well. At times he has charged ahead of us, leading the knights on the right flank and we follow. We trust each other to make the right decisions, and then we keep form and support each other."

"And Gauthier. I know he is the defender. He directs the reserves and reinforcements."

"Yes, his vision of the battlefield and what is about to happen is excellent. His timing is impeccable, and he is patient, only committing the reserves when it is the right time and place."

"You have talked of your brothers' strengths and desires, but what about you, Richard?" asked Sara. "What would they say about you?"

"I don't know," he laughed.

Sara said, "Maybe that you are always late?"

"What!" Richard's brows furrowed.

Sara smiled, "Except when it really counts, when it is important—then you are most punctual!" Richard calmed.

"And, you are *celui qui est parti avant,* the one who has gone before," Sara continued. "The one who never gives up. I remember when you injured your knee in a skirmish with some raiders from Anjou. The next day when they attacked our borders in force, you rode into battle, leading the conroi, even though you were in great pain and had to be helped onto your mount."

Richard was quiet in his thoughts. *I can't remember details of that fight, except after the battle I recognized that I had been worried that the injury would be my . . . our, failure. The fear drove me to excel.* He smiled to himself as Sara hummed a familiar song. *I may never see her again, but I will remember her by this pleasant tune.*

Sara slowed her horse to talk to Osborne. "You seem to be the most excited about joining the Normans."

"Yes, I am looking for adventure, but I will miss you, Sara."

"But it doesn't mean forever, brother. I will miss your

enthusiasm and your creativity. Remember when you suggested that your brothers wear different color plumes?"

"Yes. It was so we could find each other on the battlefield."

"*Of course!*" laughed Sara.

"Hmmph! But thank you, sister, for making the dyes."

Sara laughed. "Will you continue to wear your individual colors after you join the Normans?"

"Yes."

"In case you lose your horsehair tails and need to color new ones, do you remember how we made the dyes?"

"Let's see . . . the red for Drogo's crest was made from the madder roots. Gauthier's blue came from the weld plant . . . the leaves."

"No," Sara said. "The plant for the blue dye. . . here is a hint, the name of the plant sounds like weld, but is also another name for the color blue."

"Woad! Yes, woad leaves make blue. And we used weld to make yellow for Richard, then mixed woad dye with the yellow dye and made green."

"On our first try we ended up making a nasty looking yellow-green!" said Sara.

Osborne laughed as he said, "And it looked like goose turd!"

Sara added, "But remember we ended up using onion skins to make Richard's color, to make a golden yellow.

"I know you will safely guide your brothers to Normandy, you study maps and have a good sense of direction. What did we call you when you were younger?"

Osborne frowned and didn't comment.

"Oh, yes," laughed Sara. "it was *remember boy!*"

They rode in silence for a while, then Osborne said, "When we leave, I will also miss my time tramping in the woods. It is beautiful and peaceful in the Baconnais Forest: the valleys, the streams, and the wildlife."

Drogo galloped alongside, startling Sara. "Dreux, it wasn't that long ago when you would have raced by and obstructed your brother's horse! You never did that to me. Don't start now!"

He didn't say anything, and it was difficult to determine if his smile meant he would be pleasant or make trouble.

Sara said, "That look is charming, but deceptive!"

Osborne sniggered, "There is nothing charming about that face!" And rode ahead.

Gauthier, riding rearguard, caught up to Sara. "What was that about?'

"Dreux being Dreux."

"You mean Drogo being himself, yes." said Gauthier.

"We were reminiscing about when we were much younger," added Sara.

"You were always coordinated, especially using your hands, even when you were very little. Mother said you were the first to pick up a stick and copy Father practicing his sword, so your brothers called you the *hand man.* That was your sobriquet."

"Now as adults, Osborne and Dreux have cognomens, but you and Richard don't," said Sara. "After you conquer England, do you plan to be known as Walter, the English version of your name?"

The disgusted look on Gauthier's face was a shock, but he laughed as he said, "I'm NOT a Walter!"

CHAPTER TWO

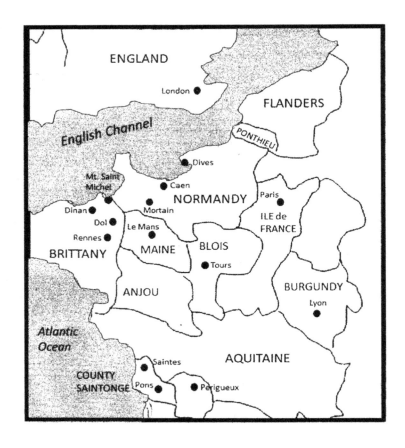

CHAPTER TWO

Their farewell in Saintes was less emotional than their departure at the castle in Pons the previous day. The brothers knew that Sara was happy to be more independent in her new role as the lady-in-waiting for the Countess of Saintonge. Four additional knights from Saintes joined them in their expedition. Departing Saintes, the party now included eight knights from County Saintonge and an equal number from Maine who had been captured in the battle. The FitzPons brothers planned to use the eight knights from Le Mans as hostages to help them pass safely through County Maine on their way to Normandy. They proceeded through the old Roman arch, then passed the abbey and the field where the battle had been fought just weeks earlier. The captives' weapons were kept out of reach, packed on two extra horses with the supplies. Within several miles they came to an intersection where a road followed the pilgrims' route from Paris. The milestone pointing north to the city of Tours read: TURONORUM $\overline{\text{CL}}$ PASUUM. Osborne said, "We will take this road north to Tours. It's 150 miles to the city."

The fifth day after leaving Saintes the knights entered Tours, the capital of County Blois and located in the broad valley of the Loire River. Walls surrounded the center of the city, including the Chateau de Tours and the Basilica of St. Martin. Entering the basilica, they prayed with pilgrims passing through on their way south to Compostela. There they paid homage at St. Martin's tomb. Richard read aloud the Latin inscription carved on a stone tablet at the tomb. The throng of illiterate pilgrims, for the most part quiet out of reverence, became totally silent and listened. As Richard read, they contemplated the images on the stained-glass windows that depicted scenes of St. Martin's life. "Saint Martin of Tours. Born in Pannonia in the year of our Lord 316. Died 397. He served as a Roman legionary in the, um, equites, uh. I am not sure of that word. I know the word equus is horse and eques means knight."

A voice from behind him said, "You are getting close, young man." A priest stood nearby. "The word equites means cavalry. Please go on, you are doing very well."

Richard continued. "Yes, he served in the Roman cavalry. After twenty-five years of service, his Christian faith and objection to taking human life compelled him to refuse his military pay and go into battle unarmed. This led to his discharge from the legions. He became Bishop of Tours in 371, converted druids to the Faith and defended the Church against the Arian heresy. Bishop Martin founded monasteries in Liguge and Marmoutier.

"Father, forgive me. I was reading it for the benefit of the pilgrims."

"That is fine, son. I also do the same to supplement the stories. Most pilgrims cannot read and only know the stories told by the images. I believe you are knights, yes?"

A few of their party nodded.

"Are you headed to go on crusade with Duke William?"

"Why, yes!" said Osborne. "What do you mean, crusade?"

"Oh, perhaps you haven't heard. Pope Alexander has not only given his blessing for what he considers William's religious crusade but has gifted him a consecrated banner!"

"I fought in Sicily," said Drogo. "And the Pope also issued such a banner to Count Roger for his crusade against the Muslims. It was the Banner of St. Peter."

With this surprising new information, the group mounted to

depart, and Osborne said, to no one in particular, "The inscription said Saint Martin was born in Pannonia. Where is Pannonia?"

"If *you* don't know, don't ask me," said Drogo.

The FitzPons brothers and their charges left the city and crossed the Loire River. Carved on a pillar at the entrance of the bridge was: PONT D'EUDES-COMTE DE BLOIS 1034 A.D. Richard said, "This rather impressive bridge is only thirty years old. Most of the bridges in Aquitaine are much older, built by the Romans."

Osborne asked, "Richard, where is Pannonia?"

"I do not know, Ozzie, but we will be crossing into County Maine within a few days, the homeland of the Le Mans knights. I recommend we get to know them better. Their cooperation will help our passage through the county."

"A couple of the Le Mans chevaliers told me they were going to volunteer for William's army." said Osborne.

"Hmm, when we stop tonight let's discuss this with them," added Richard.

They rode on at a trot. "St. Martin had remarkable faith," said Osborne. "He wasn't a coward, served in the legions all those years, and when he decided not to fight, he didn't even arm himself. But I can't understand why he wasn't punished for not fighting."

Richard said, "He was either brave or senseless."

They covered more than half the distance to Le Mans and then camped for the night alongside a small stream. Sharing a skin of wine, they sat around their fire and ate bread and cheese they had bought in Tours. Richard glanced at Osborne and then directed his question toward the knights of County Maine. "Tomorrow we will reach Le Mans. You don't seem threatened about returning to the city."

A couple of the knights shrugged.

Richard continued, "I am puzzled. You fled the Normans, but a few of you have said you will now join the invasion of England."

Lambert, one of the Le Mans chevaliers, spoke. He was tall and lean with blonde hair and moustache, both generous in length. "The FitzPons brothers, knights of Saintonge, and the knights of

Maine have much in common. We all must leave our homeland to gain fortune. We are knights, but pawns in Duke William's game."

"Well expressed," said Richard. "Yes, I understand. I have seen the game of chess, though I do not play, but I understand what you mean. We are pawns, mere foot soldiers, until we prove to William we are worthy to take on the responsibility of a knight."

Lambert said, "After the Normans took over in Maine, we volunteered to go with his army to England. One factor in his decision to accept us was that we were already organized as a troop and had much experience fighting together. There were two reasons we invaded Saintonge. Duke William sent us to test your county's defenses as well as to see how well we fought. We failed."

Richard asked, "Your reserves that fled the battlefield . . . did they report to William?"

"Yes," said Lambert. "They were Norman observers. You are strong fighters and were well organized on the battlefield when you defeated us. It appears you have already learned some of the Norman tactics. I propose we work together to convince William we can help him achieve his goals: to assume his right as king, and to conquer England."

Richard glanced at his brothers as he said, "If all of us work together . . ." He sensed from the expressions as consent to continue. "A proposal: knights of Le Mans, you will not interfere with our travel across your county and will ensure we get to Normandy. When we cross into the duchy, we will give back your weapons. Then I will propose to Duke William that all of us will fight for him as one conroi. If we are tested, together we will meet the challenge and you can have a second chance."

Richard stood and addressed all the knights. "I observed your piety in the attendance at St. Martin's Basilica. The Pope has given William his approval and St. Martin is the patron saint of the cavalry. On that, do you all swear by St. Martin to my proposal?"

The knights stood and shouted, "*Mon Dieu certainement*! Certainly, Holy God!"

The next morning, they continued north, stopping in Le Mans

to buy food. Next to the shop was a tavern. Gauthier bought a round of ale for their entourage. Osborne took a long draft from his mug and said, "Richard, the men are more talkative and social now. Is it the ale or because we have sworn to be comrades for the same cause?"

"Perhaps a little of both, but it is good." He turned to Lambert and raised his cup. "*Sante!*"

Lambert put his arm around another knight and said, "My brother, Lothar!"

They toasted. "*Sante!*"

Lambert smiled as he grabbed another one of his comrades and pulled him over. "My other brother, Leufred!"

They saluted. "*Sante!*"

"So, we are four brothers FitzPons, and you are three brothers?" said Osborne.

Lambert continued smiling, "No, we are not really brothers, we just grew up together and always fight for each other."

"That's how I will remember your names. I'll think of you as the "L" brothers! Lambert, Leufred, and Lothar!"

After a second round, they departed the city and rode north. Richard asked Lambert, "When you were accepted into the Norman army, what kind of standards did they require?"

"When we sought to join his army, we were awarded an audience with the duke . . ."

Richard interrupted. "William himself interviews knights who wish to join him?"

"Yes. And before you can see him, his men will determine if you have the necessary equipment to be considered a knight. You must have a long hauberk, a tall shield, helmet, sword, a lance or winged spear, and a trained warhorse."

"What else can you tell me, Lambert?"

"When we heard about the Pope's approval of William's plan to invade England, I was thinking it was only rumor. The duke publicly emphasizes piety, but I do not think his faith is deep. It is a show, so he can fight under the Pope's banner. I believe you are pious, but if the duke asks what is your allegiance, answer 'to God first,' then to him. It will impress him. Also, the Normans believe they are superior to all other knights of Francia. And one more thing, almost all the Norman knights are cleanshaven. They look like monks!"

"During our journey, I heard some of your men call the duke, 'William the Bastard.' Is that common and does it make him angry?" said Richard.

"People of his realm who are not Norman typically refer to him by that name, because his father Robert never married William's mother. The duke had a violent and dangerous childhood and adolescence because of the frequent assassination attempts on his life. Calling him a bastard makes him angry, but he is most enraged and ruthless if you insult his mother. She was the daughter of a tanner and once when William had a city under siege, the defenders jeered, waved tanned skins from atop the walls, called his mother a lowly tanner's daughter and a *puterelle*, a woman of ill repute. He broke the siege, found the soldiers who had insulted his mother, and had their hands and feet cut off." Lambert gulped some ale. "Richard, where did you learn the Norman cavalry tactics you used in your fight against us? Those skills will be an advantage in your quest for William's approval."

"Drogo served for a year with the Normans in Sicily," answered Richard, "and returned to train us in their methods. We also replaced our shields and armor with Norman designs.

"Now we will reorganize into a conroi made up of the sixteen knights in our party. There will be four squads, each led by a FitzPons. You are one of eight knights from Le Mans. A pair of your knights and a knight from Saintonge will be in each squad. We will make time to train together every day on our journey to William's capital in Caen."

After several more days of travel, the FitzPons conroi arrived at the city of Caen. They were detained and questioned at the Porte sur la Ville, the gateway to the town. The entrance was reinforced by two barbicans, large fortified gate towers. Richard submitted a written declaration signed by his father stating that they were knights of the Lord of Pons of Aquitaine and were present to swear their allegiance to Duke William. They waited a few hours before they were granted permission; then they continued to the castle of Chateau de Caen, located on a hillock in the center of the city.

William's squires appraised their equipment to determine their qualifications, and Richard was informed that only two knights of the group would be permitted an audience with William. Richard asked Lambert to accompany him since the knight had already been through the questioning.

In the receiving hall, three men, who appeared to be nobles, were seated behind a large table. A man sat at the end of the table with quill in hand. Sheaves of parchment were piled around the scribe. Richard was certain the noble in the middle was the duke. William wore a long tunic, had a robust, thickset body, and reddish hair with a receding hairline. He was cleanshaven and had short hair like his knights, except for a small moustache. The other two men who vaguely resembled William were also cleanshaven with short hair. All three appeared close in age. The man on William's right wore fine clothes and a white cone-shaped hat. Richard had seen high ranking clergy before. *He is wearing a miter so he must be a bishop..* The man on William's left wore a military tunic of roughly spun wool. The duke spoke. His voice was strong, rough, and baritone. "Welcome knights of . . . let's see, although people think I am uneducated, I can read . . . Pontius Dominus . . . Lord Pons, in French! I see the list of names on the roster you submitted, Sir Richard filius de Pontius . . . Sir Richard FitzPons. One of you is Sir Richard FitzPons?"

Richard knelt and then stood. "I am he, Duke William."

"I recognized Sir Lambert with you," said the duke. Lambert also briefly knelt. "Lambert, your task was to return here with news of your victory in Saintonge. But that did not happen." William laughed. "By all appearances it could be that you won and brought back Richard, a captured knight of Saintonge. But I am puzzled, you are instead the captured?"

"We were defeated," said Lambert. "They engaged Norman tactics and the strategy of the conroi."

William guffawed. "Sir Lambert, my brother Robert told me everything. I was simply jesting."

Lambert continued, "I and my fellow men of Le Mans have since joined the knights of Pons to form a conroi which will serve you well, Duke William."

"Hmm," William paused in thought. "Pontius, Pons—your father's name is not Norman nor even Frankish. That is a Gallo-Roman name, but then, you are from Aquitaine.

"Sir Richard, how would you know of Norman tactics?"

"My brother Drogo served with your countrymen, under Count Roger of Sicily."

"And tell me, why is the Norman cavalry effective?" asked William.

"Calvary charges have the best success if the knights are in formation, disciplined, skilled, and equipped with the best armor, said Richard. "In addition, their horses must be trained to endure the stresses of head-on charges. All of these principles must be met."

"And you can verify your conroi meets all those standards?" asked the duke.

"Yes."

William continued, "Tell me, Sir Richard, where is your men's first loyalty?"

"To God."

"And do you and your knights pledge your earthly loyalty to me?"

"Yes, sire."

William quietly conferred with his brothers. There were nods, and his brother Robert said, "The world is a small place! In this letter, your father writes that you are related to me by marriage. It is true. My daughter Emma married your cousin Guillaume, the Count of Toulouse. I wonder how she is? Have any of you been there recently?"

"Drogo will be pleased to give you details about his visit to Toulouse, where he met your daughter Emma."

Robert's eyes grew wide as he said, "I shall certainly engage him later in conversation. I thank you!"

"Sir Richard, your conroi is welcome to join the French division of our army," said Duke William. "Report to the squires who brought you here. They will assign you a place in the barracks and take care of your horses."

As they left the building Richard asked Lambert. "So that was Robert. Who was the other man with the duke?"

"He is Robert's brother, Bishop Odo. And they are both half-brothers to William. Robert is the Count of Mortain, and the other is Bishop Odo of Bayeux. Robert was William's lead commander when he conquered Maine and he was with the group watching us in our battle against us at Saintes."

The FitzPons conroi joined a wing of William's army formed of primarily Frankish knights from northern France. They adopted the Norman method by attaching a gonfalon, a swallow tail banner, to Richard's lance. The gonfalon was emblazoned with the diagonal stripes of red and yellow representing the Pons barony. Where Richard went on the battlefield, the conroi could see the gonfalon to follow. The Norman knights remained apart in their own division. Each division included infantry and archers, primarily crossbowmen. The Norman cavalry was known for its effectiveness in battle and showed superior tactics against other mounted foes, but William recognized a disciplined and organized infantry could stop a charge by even his knights. His strategy, already proven effective in several battles, was to disorder the enemy army with his infantry and archers, then follow with a mass cavalry charge. Normans had also used the tactic of feigned retreat to break up enemy formations, once versus the army of the French king and another time against the Arabs at Messina. In these battles, the Norman cavalry had withdrawn as if they had been repulsed, but then had turned on their opponents when the enemy's formations became drawn out and vulnerable.

Due to their familiarity with Norman tactics, Richard and his brothers integrated into the French wing without difficulty, drilling with the French knights during the next several weeks. The training had become routine and one day as they ate the midday meal in their barracks, an announcement was made that the army was going to head west within a few days to fight in Brittany.

Richard gnawed his bread he had dipped in his stew as he watched Lambert eagerly spoon a thick pottage of grain and pork into his mouth. "Comrade, will we eat this well on campaign?"

"I doubt it," answered Lambert, after he guzzled the rest of his ale. Then he grabbed a pitcher of water and refilled his mug. He grimaced when he swallowed some of the water.

"Why the face? There's nothing wrong with that water," said Gauthier.

Lambert answered. "I know, it is pure, but water only tastes good after sweating for hours in my armor. Besides I do not find it as hearty to the palate as I do ale."

"Since we are rationed only one mug of ale per meal, I drink water first, then follow with ale," said Gauthier.

Lambert's expression hinted his intentions. "Hmm. Good idea, friend." He grabbed for Gauthier's mug. "Give me that, I'll try your idea!"

Gauthier reacted faster and quickly downed his ale. Drogo held his mug close to his chest, with an exaggerated mien of fear that his would be stolen. Osborne's mug was empty as was his bowl. None of their group was surprised he had eaten fast and was now napping on the bench.

The horseplay avoided, Drogo asked, "Why do you think the duke is going to war with the Bretons? You'd think he would be preparing to go to England. There are many ships to be built."

"I've learned much talking with the Norman knights in the last few weeks," Richard answered. "The word is that William wants to weaken and then dominate the neighboring realms, so they will not be a threat when he departs for England with his army. Rumors say that he married Matilda, daughter of the Count of Flanders, to make a political alliance with a county to his northeast. Years ago, he defeated King Henry of France to the east of Normandy, and Henry's son Philip, now king, is too weak to oppose William. Lambert, you experienced firsthand his invasion of Maine to the south. According to the babble around the castle, William sent a warning to the surrounding counties including Conan, the Duke of Brittany, to stay out of Normandy. Conan responded that he would attack as soon as William departed for

England. Thus, we are now heading west to Brittany."

"William's plan makes sense. When he subjugates Brittany, all his borders will be safe," said Lambert. "But Conan is a fool to proclaim he will invade Normandy once the duke departs!"

Lambert looked around the table at the FitzPons brothers. "Friends, stay aware and be ready for surprises. William used me and my men as fodder when he ordered us to attack Saintonge without the proper support troops. You may not get a second chance like us. Whatever happens you will have me and my men's backing. William is very shrewd, he plans well, and everything he does is a part of his master plan, even if it doesn't make sense at the time."

The Norman army marched west from Caen and approached the monastery of Mont Saint-Michel. As they crossed the River Couesnon, the boundary between the duchies of Normandy and Brittany, many horses and men became mired in quicksand at the crossing. This obstacle slowed the army's progress. William had sent scouts ahead to Mount Dol, a fortified village built upon a huge granite outcropping rising above surrounding marshes. Dol was home to a group of Bretons who favored William and were in rebellion against Duke Conan. The scouts returned just as the army was at last free of the quagmire. With them was Sir Rivalon, the leader of the rebellion, and a handful of his men. They had barely escaped hours earlier when they had lost the Mount Dol stronghold to Conan's army. William's scouts had ventured close enough to observe the enemy, but had gotten lost in the marsh. They were able to return when Rivalon, hiding from Conan, had found them wandering and guided them back to the Norman army.

With Rivalon's knowledge of the area, William ordered the army to move ahead to Dol. When they were within sight of the massif, they camped in the patchwork of dry areas within the marshlands. Scouts assisted by the Bretons determined several routes to surround and enter the village, but it was late afternoon and the assault on the village had to be delayed until the next day. As the sun set, the Norman soldiers ate cold rations and gathered around campfires. Some of Rivalon's men camped near the

FitzPons conroi and shared a campfire. "What am I seeing on top of that rocky hill—they call it Mount Dol?" said Drogo. "It's ghostly looking!"

Osborne answered. "It's just a big rock. Don't worry about it. The vapors rising from the rock are just spooking you."

"I think that rock looks like a penis as tall as a house," laughed Gauthier.

"It's a menhir. A rock left by the ancient ones," said one of Rivalon's knights. "I have seen many in Brittany. You must not have any in Saintonge? The Druids left them as warnings. There is a legend about this menhir. Whenever a person dies, this menhir, the tallest one in Brittany, sinks a little farther into the ground. When it fully submerges, it will signify the end of the world."

Gauthier said, "What? Our grandfather told us a story once about the end of the world. He said the priests announced the world was supposed to end—that is, with the second coming of Christ, in the year 1000. But the world didn't end, so then the soothsayers assumed it would not be 1000 years after Christ was born, but 1000 years after he died, in the year 1033. Grandfather did not live to see that year, and we had not been born, but the year 1033 came and went and the world is still here!"

Osborne said, "All this superstitious talk is giving me a headache. Go to sleep!"

In the morning the signal horns summoned the men to attention. There would be no breakfast. As the men collected their gear and readied their horses, Gauthier said, "I thought those horns were only used to drink ale, not wake you up and annoy you." After much organization using Rivalon's intimate knowledge of the swamplands, they reached Mount Dol. Duke Conan, however, had fled.

The scouts discovered that the enemy had escaped to the south, and the Norman army followed. The knights of the French division, commanded by Count de Eu, were ordered to ride in the vanguard of the army, followed by the Flemish knights provided by William's father-in-law. The infantry and archers were next, and lastly the Norman cavalry. The army moved at a fast clip and the infantry had a hard time keeping up. To catch the Britons retreating south toward Rennes, the capital of Brittany, Count de Eu led his knights ahead and left behind the rest of the army. As they urged their mounts ahead in a brisk canter, Richard recalled what de Eu had told the conroi leaders: *On the lower half of Duke Conan's shield is the image of three castle towers in gold upon a field of red. The top half is a white field covered with an ermine pattern, common among the Bretons. And a handpicked group of knights, his bodyguards, have the same pattern on their shields.*

A few miles north of the city, believing that the French would catch them before they reached the walls, the Bretons halted their march and formed a defensive line at the far side of a meadow near the forest edge. Behind the foot soldiers were archers and the mounted knights of Duke Conan. Count de Eu halted his cavalry and discussed options with his officers, the captains of the conrois.

"We should wait until the rest of the army arrives, said the count. "Then our infantry and archers will create a diversion for the knights to outflank the enemy." He ordered a pair of scouts, lightly armored and fast riders, to return to William to report his plan. Within less than an hour, the scouts returned with the duke's orders. "Duke William and the infantry are still far down the road. William's orders are to engage the enemy and don't let Conan reach Rennes. The city is a stout bastide, protected by massive stone fortifications."

Count de Eu measured his officers and said, "We will charge the Breton lines."

Richard surveyed the other conroi leaders. *They seem edgy, but not from fear of battle. Are they as uncomfortable with this strategy as I am?* "Count de Eu," said Richard, "charging without support troops will put us at risk from their archers. This strategy contradicts Norman tactics."

Count de Eu riled at the effrontery. A junior officer barely twenty years old questioned not only his command, but one dictated by William. He stared at the line of the Breton foot soldiers and then back at Richard. Then the stern lines in his face relaxed. With a forced smile he said, "Sir Richard, the skills of your training are to be applied when ordered to do so. You are new to the Norman army, so I will pardon you. If William said attack, that is what we shall do!"

The count shouted orders to the captains. "Advance with widely spaced conrois." As the captains joined their men, Count de Eu called to Richard, "You will lead your men ahead of the first line of knights."

Richard returned to his knights and announced their dangerous role. There were twenty-four knights in his conroi: the four FitzPons brothers, the four knights from Saintes, eight Le Mans chevaliers, and eight freelance knights from parts of northern France, who had no loyalty but to those who hired them as mercenary soldiers. Lambert's eyes were wild. He shouted. "My men and . . . " he laughed, "and the L brothers are ready!"

Drogo silently tightened his saddle and checked his weapons. Gauthier looked infuriated and said, "This charge against the archers is a crazy idea. I bet they would not send the Norman knights to do this. It makes me mad, and I am even more enraged by our position out front. What does that accomplish? I tell you what it accomplishes, it makes me fighting mad!"

"We joined, now we have to fight," said Osborne. "Come on, let's ride!"

"This is your test, FitzPons brothers, and my second try, to prove we belong in the Norman army," said Lambert.

Richard agreed. *It seems as if the count is sending us ahead to be forfeited, but we must fight and survive. We are knights!* As the conrois were assembling for the charge, Richard saw a troop of Breton knights galloping behind the enemy lines and heading north. He pointed. "Those riders are Duke Conan's bodyguards. I can tell by the pattern on their shields. Conan must be among them. He is trying to escape again. If there is an opportunity, we must capture the duke." He looked over his knights and yelled. "Stay with your squad leader!"

The French knights charged, with Richard and his conroi in front. A storm of arrows broke the assault. Repelled by the archers, the French knights retreated in disorder. During their withdrawal, Count de Eu did not see Richard split off in another direction. His brothers and most of the FitzPons conroi followed him into the forest. A handful of Richard's knights did not go with them and returned to the French division, regrouping for another charge.

The FitzPons conroi sped on through the evening, racing north on the road to Dinan. Within half an hour Richard could see the rear guard of the Breton contingent ahead. They could not gain on them, however, but matched their pace. After two hours of pursuit, they approached a castle and fortified town. The castle was built strategically on the side of a steep hill with stone fortifications and towers, although many of the palisades were constructed of wood.

Richard reined his horse to a stop just outside the town walls as the gates closed. As the enemy urged their horses up the steep hill to the Chateau de Dinan, he again saw the distinctive image of Conan's coat of arms on the knights' shields. One of the riders had a plume on his helmet and wore a cape with an ermine pattern. He was certain it was Duke Conan.

At Rennes the battle continued as William arrived and reinforced Count de Eu. They scattered the Breton army, but most of the enemy escaped to the city. They lined the parapets atop Rennes' formidable walls and prepared their defense.

The next morning, William ate breakfast with Robert and Odo. "It is very unfortunate that Conan reached Rennes," said the duke. His body was not found on the battlefield. The Breton prisoners that were interrogated revealed he is in Rennes. A siege will be necessary. It is not the city that is important, but we must capture or kill Conan. The Breton resistance will collapse without him."

"I have sent out parties to obtain food supplies," said Odo. "And they will be on the lookout for Conan in case our prisoners lied."

"Not likely Brother Odo, your methods are very convincing. Most likely the siege could take weeks or longer," added William. "And, Robert?"

"Our men are cutting trees in the forest now to make ladders, battering rams, and enough wood for a siege tower," Robert answered. "The stone walls are well built, and we don't have the men with the skill to dig under the foundations. I ordered a conroi to return to Caen and bring an engineer and sappers. They will be here in a week."

"What about the deserters?" asked Odo.

William's eyebrows raised. "Deserters?"

"Yes, Count de Eu informed me that several knights witnessed most of the FitzPons conroi leaving the battlefield after the first charge. A handful of the French knights in their troop refused to follow. They don't know where the FitzPons brothers went."

"I had confidence in Sir Richard and I am greatly disappointed," said William. "But we have more pressing tasks at hand to subdue Brittany so we can get on with the invasion. Our position is favorable. We have Conan trapped in Rennes. There could be thousands more Bretons ready to fight, but without Conan's leadership, they will not unite. His capture is the key."

A squire called out at the tent entrance. "Steward! Count de Eu requests a word with the duke!"

William motioned to bring him in. With Count Eu were a pair of knights that had fled the battlefield with the FitzPons conroi.

"Deserters!" Odo stood and cried out.

William held up his hand for his brother to sit. "Count de Eu. Let these men speak for themselves." One of the knights appeared less shaken than the other and reported. "Duke William, we followed Conan to Dinan and observed him enter the castle keep. Our conroi has monitored the gates all night. Conan is still in the chateau there."

"What! . . . but how do you know it is Conan? He is in Rennes."

"We chased a troop of knights yesterday when they fled the battle. Their shields had Conan's coat of arms displayed on them—the three towers and the ermine pattern. This morning Sir Richard sent us to notify you, Duke William."

William, Odo, and Robert regarded each other, but no one spoke. After a pause, William addressed the couriers, "Wait outside the tent with Count de Eu."

William left forces at Rennes to maintain the siege and ordered the rest of the army to break camp and march north. An hour before the sun set, they reached the town of Dinan, where the knights of Richard's conroi were monitoring the castle gates. The Normans and their French and Flemish allies camped around the castle and set up posts to block escape and prevent reinforcements from reaching the city. Richard's men were relieved from their monitoring of the town gates, and Count de Eu escorted him to William's headquarters. As they crossed the camp, Richard wasn't sure what to expect. *Will I be accused of desertion? If we had not followed them, Conan could have escaped.*

De Eu and Richard passed through the encampment of Norman knights surrounding the headquarters. He recognized William's tent by the banner displaying the Norman coat of arms, two yellow lions on a red field. The duke's tent was pitched between two other large tents, one was Robert's, flying the red and white striped banner of the County Mortain, and the other was Bishop Odo's, which had a cross on the entrance flap. They entered Bishop Odo's tent. Other than a cot and several three-legged stools, there was only his armor and battle club. Richard recalled that Odo had said bishops were not to shed blood. Like William, Odo was disciplined, ate sparingly, and was in robust health.

"Sir Richard, Count de Eu, join me and have some ale."

The men shared deep draughts of the ale. A squire refilled their mugs and left. De Eu and Odo did not speak for a long minute, which made Richard uneasy. *Is this a trap while I am away from my brothers and relaxing with ale? No! They would have had me arrested already.*

Odo smiled. "Richard, do you believe in justice?"

"Yes, Your Excellency. Um . . . do you mean as in the Bible?" *What did the Bible say about justice?* "As 'an eye for an eye, a tooth for a tooth?'"

"You know scripture from the Bible. Good. Remember Jesus said, as written in the Gospel of Matthew, to refute the eye for an eye concept and 'turn the other cheek.'"

"In the world of a knight, that would lead to failure and death," said Richard.

"Granted. Then we should return to the first rule, an eye for an eye . . . in our world, yes?" Odo said. "What were Count de Eu's orders?"

"To charge the Bretons."

"Did you follow the orders, wholeheartedly?"

"No, I protested."

"And what was Count de Eu's next command?"

"To lead the charge against the Bretons."

"Did you do that?'

"Yes."

"Yes, you did," Odo looked at Count de Eu, who nodded. "And, along with all of our knights, we were driven back by the Breton archers. There was a second charge, but your conroi, at least most of it, was not present. Where were you?"

"In pursuit of Conan."

"And was that successful?"

"Yes, we trapped him in this town."

Odo stood up, swallowed a mouthful of ale and banged his mug down on his stool. He grabbed his club in one hand and used it as a walking stick as he paced. "When you objected to Count de Eu's command, which was also William's command, it demoralized the other captains of the conrois. That is punishable by flogging and demotion."

Arguing with him about tactics is useless. Richard answered with an even voice. "Yes, Your Excellency."

"When you left the field of battle, it appeared you were running away! Do you know the penalty for desertion?"

"Execution," answered Richard, his voice barely betraying his anxiety.

"Yes, and what method do you think Duke William will order? You are not a heretic, so you will not be burned, unfortunately. Hanging would be a better example for the army. But you are a knight, so if approved by William, you may be given the privilege of a beheading."

"If you must order execution, that is most honorable," Richard was surprised that vocalizing the threat helped him steady himself. *Stay calm. Be patient. Listen. There will come the right moment to defend myself.*

"I think the reason you went to Dinan was to join Conan and to warn him!" sneered Odo. He pounded the end of the bludgeon into the ground. "Treason is rewarded by stringing and quartering! Do you think that is justice, Sir Richard?"

Events from the recent months, the farewells with his sister and parents, the skirmish near Saintes, the battle with the Bretons, and the pursuit of Conan, all flashed before Richard. *I've got to try something. I am going to die anyway. Mother said, "It's always darkest before the dawn."*

"Bishop Odo, my father told me when I was a child, 'The world is not just, but in our family, there will be justice.'"

"Yes?" said Odo. Richard imagined a prolonged "s" which made him think of a snake hissing.

Richard continued. "I trust fellow knights in battle as they should trust me. Knighthood is a brotherhood. They are as my brothers and therefore my family, and so the Norman army is now my family. I ask for a fair judgment from Duke William."

Odo huffed in aggravation. "Then let's get back to the Bible's judgment. So you have lost one eye due to disobedience." He held up a finger. "You lost a second eye from failure to join in the second charge because you left the battlefield, without orders to do so." He held up a second finger.

"You have recovered one eye by leading the first charge," he folded one finger. "And a second eye by ensnaring Duke Conan." He folded the second finger.

There is hope. Richard took a breath.

Odo leaned his mace against his cot, and moved toward the entrance. Count de Eu stood. "You do not have to come," said Odo. "William's decision will be swift."

De Eu followed, however. As the tent flaps parted, Richard saw that there were armed guards posted outside. Richard stood to think. *Will they involve my brothers? No, knights are too valuable, I was in command and I am being made the example. Unless my brothers' reactions could put themselves in danger. And I must get them to tell our parents that I died in battle.* His thoughts were interrupted when Count de Eu returned without Odo. With a stern face he said, "William declared you are even. By the rule, you lost two eyes and got them back, but in the Norman army, you must be above being level. You must excel.

"Again, you disregarded my orders and left the field of combat, but you had a legitimate reason and it contributed to our objectives, to capture Conan. However, the captains of the conroi heard your dissent and the troops saw you leave the battle. They will remember that. To compensate for insubordination, William has a special mission for you and your conroi."

As Richard returned to his men, he felt his anger rising. He knew, however, that showing his rage to his men would be contagious and counterproductive. Instead, he composed himself before he joined them at the tents. His absence was not unusual, as Count de Eu had frequent meetings with the conroi captains. A few of the men had left the campfire and retired to their blankets. The FitzPons brothers and their comrades from Le Mans were gathered around the fire in quiet conversation.

Richard began, "Brothers." The men regarded Richard with curiosity. "We have the burden of another dangerous trial." Groans from the men followed.

Richard continued, "It could be worse. We were accused of desertion." The FitzPons brothers stared at him, pondering his statement.

Drogo spoke. "But we trapped Conan . . ."

Richard interrupted. "Yes, yes, but let me continue . . . the world is hard," said Richard. "But we have the opportunity to rise above a simple existence. If we meet this new challenge, we will accompany the duke to England, and we will become landowners." Richard looked at his brothers. "Father did not give us horses or armor, we worked and bought them ourselves. We earned our knighthood. One more push against what you might deem as injustice is what I ask of you!" Richard explained what their role would be in breaking the siege of Dinan.

Before sunrise Richard rekindled their campfire to chase the morning chill. He poked a stick into the ashes as he waited for his brothers to join him. *My mind has been churning all night with ways to succeed and survive. Count de Eu said our task would be to set the palisades on fire, an extremely dangerous mission, but he also said the army would be in support. I need to shove the fear to the back of my mind, stay calm, and work with my brothers to plan this. And they can't accuse me of being late this time!* Richard laughed out loud.

"What's so funny? asked Gauthier as he stumbled out of the tent. I thought we were on a suicide mission today?"

Richard remained silent, knowing Gauthier was never in a good mood in the morning. Ozzie had followed Gauthier out of the tent. Richard threw his brothers each a hard biscuit. "Ozzie, remember when we explored those caves in the Baconnais forest?"

He mumbled as he ate. "Yes."

Drogo and the rest of the knights appeared. They passed around biscuits and a skin of diluted wine as they added more wood to the fire.

Richard continued, "We made torches out of pine branches and they burned for hours. But the Bretons are sure to have water ready to put out fires."

"The torches are made with lots of resin," answered Osborne, "which may resist a little water, except if completely drenched. But we can just make a bunch of torches. Some will stay afire, and some may be extinguished."

"We should make teams of two," said Drogo. "Last night you said William will support us with archers, but the Bretons also have archers. When we charge the walls, one man will hold a shield and one will carry a torch."

"Bring an extra shield to cover the torch after you place it against the wooden walls," added Gauthier. "That will keep the water from extinguishing the torch."

"Yes! We are awake now! We are thinking!" shouted Richard.

"I'm going to the woods to collect some pine branches and resin. Anyone coming?" said Osborne. The knights from Le Mans followed him.

Richard conferred with Gauthier and Drogo. "There are only ten or eleven of us. If we work in pairs, we would only be able to set five fires."

"Instead, each man could carry his shield and a torch. That will be at least ten fires," said Gauthier.

"Then what happens if some of us get hit by arrows?" said Drogo.

"We go back to working in pairs, but each man will carry a torch and a shield," answered Gauthier.

"But stay within sight and watch out for each other, added Richard. "With arrows and spears flying at us, we'll need to make it as simple as possible."

Osborne and the others returned with bundles of freshly cut pine branches, each the thickness and length of a man's arm. They split one end of each branch into four sections, placing a rock at the juncture to keep the split sections apart. The men had also collected pine resin that oozed from tree trunks and filled the split sections with the sticky substance. Cat tail fluff was added to help light the torch. During their work, Richard departed to notify Count de Eu that they would soon be ready. In a short time, Richard returned with the rest of their conroi, the knights who had refused to accompany them when they pursued Conan. Ozzie, looking disgusted, stood up from his work on another torch. "Hey, are they here to say goodbye, then bury us?" he asked Richard.

"No. Make more torches. They are joining us!" answered Richard. "I told them it was our punishment, not theirs, but they insisted on helping us."

The latecomers helped their comrades in fashioning more torches.

The keep of Duke Conan's castle was a stone tower located on the side of a steep hill. Approach to the castle was blocked by wooden palisades at the bottom of the knoll. To reach the walls, an attacking force had to cross wide meadows. The knights of the FitzPons conroi assembled about one hundred paces from the palisades. With flint and steel, Osborne started a campfire. Like the other knights readying to run, he did not wear his hauberk. The shirt of chain mail reached to mid-thigh, and the weight as well would prevent them from running effectively. They retained their padded vests worn under the hauberk and donned their helmets. They each carried a shield and had a sheathed dagger at the belt. Duke William and his half-brothers arrived on their warhorses and halted about fifty paces further back. Behind them was the Norman army, in orderly ranks of thousands of men and horses, punctuated by shouts of the officers, clanking metal, and the snorts of horses. In the front lines were the archers, followed by the infantry, and behind them the mounted knights. Officers barked their last commands, at which the straight lines lost their disciplined form. Infantrymen set their shields on the ground and the knights dismounted. Squires were among them and held the horses.

Count de Eu rode forward leading ten companies of crossbowmen, 500 archers, whose job was to drive the enemy defenders from the palisade battlements. William said something to Robert who shouted, "Count de Eu!" When the count looked back, William held up two fingers and Eu signaled all but two of the companies to return to the army ranks. The remaining archers continued forward. Richard looked back at the commanders and Norman knights. "The army is at ease and William just took away most of the archers that were to support us. It appears he has broken his word and will abandon us to our own devices. The army will not charge with us." He surveyed the knights of his conroi and directed his comment to those who had not joined him in the race to Dinan. "This foray is *our* sentence, men, not yours. You can still withdraw." They shook their heads.

Osborne raised his unlit torch above his head and yelled, "God's Bones, let's go!"

Richard shouted, "*Dieux aide*! God aid us!"

They all repeated the battle cry.   *DIEUX AIDE*!

"Very well," added Richard, "the crossbowmen are pelting the enemy now and have cleared the walls as best they can. Light your torch. Stay with your partner. Every man is going to return!" The FitzPons brothers lined up in the center, the Le Mans chevaliers on the right, and the rest of the knights on the left. "Spread out! *Allez, allons-y* ! Come on, let's go!"

Behind them, outside of earshot, Odo turned to the duke. "William, you were against their execution, yet this undertaking may be their death penalty. Did you tell de Eu the army was going to charge with them?"

William did not answer.

"What do you think is going through their minds?" asked Robert.

"Planning, strategy," William said.

"They don't appear to be overwhelmed by fear," Robert added.

"I remember your own description of their battle in Saintonge as well as Count de Eu's comments about their maneuvers near Rennes," said William. "They showed bravery in both instances."

"Yes, but they disobeyed orders when they fled to Dinan. Beheading would have made them an example for the ranks. Yes, in front of the whole army. We should have been done with them and charged the walls already."

"Their success and perhaps their courage are due to their trust in each other and in their brothers' decisions," said the duke as he glared at Odo, then Robert. "We might learn from their example."

William continued, "We are in Brittany for one reason. To eliminate the Britons as a threat while we invade England. And what better way to preserve our army to fight the battles against the English than to let this event take its course?"

Richard and his conroi sprinted to the walls, each man carrying a flaming torch of pine resin. The long shields were effective protection against the enemy arrows. As Gauthier burst ahead, he had a flashback to his youth, to the races with the other children of the manor around the village. He was fast, faster than all the others, except he was always third or fourth behind his brothers. He had once told his mother, that if it wasn't for his brothers, he would have won every time. *But this isn't a race to the walls, it is a race of survival. I pray my brothers make it back!*

Gauthier began running a crooked pattern after he passed the groups of Norman crossbowmen still fifty paces from the walls. Half the archers were reloading their bows as they crouched behind shields, as the rest of the archers were loosing bolts. Peering over his shield Gauthier headed toward an area they had cleared of defenders. No arrows impacted his shield, but several bolts pierced the ground close by and he heard the zip of a few overhead.

Then a staccato of zips and a one-two, THUNK! THUNK! jarred his shield. He cut to the side and heard several more arrows knife through the grass behind him. *God's bones. Where are our archers!* His anger fueled his run. He cut again and was thirty paces from the wall when there was a loud clang as the top of his shield slammed back into his face. Another missile bounced off the top of his helmet. *They're throwing stones?* He tripped and looked down as he stumbled forward, a burning pain at his groin. On the ground was one of the heavy objects that had hit him. It looked like a stone axe, made of a stout stick with a fist sized stone strapped to the end. He regained his balance and made it to the wall. He was about to set his torch at the base of the palisade when he felt water and quickly pulled the torch under his shield, keeping the flames alive.

Osborne was thirty paces away, the flames from his torch climbing the wooden palisade. He gestured for Gauthier to join him in their dash back. Gauthier wedged his torch in the space between wall planks. Suddenly a body tumbled from above and hit the ground near Gauthier. An arrow protruded from the man's shoulder. He looked at Gauthier with surprise and reached for the handle of a stone missile that lay between them. Gauthier was quicker, and he seized the crude weapon. The man drew his dagger and lunged as Gauthier blocked the thrust with his shield and smashed the enemy's forehead with the stone club. He threw away the bloody club, slung his shield across his back, and bolted to join Osborne. As they ran back Gauthier had trouble making speed, with the pain in his groin.

Osborne said, "He wasn't fast enough to beat the *hand-man.*"

"Go ahead, I'm hobbling," said Gauthier.

"No, we all get back, besides, I can't go any faster, I turned my ankle, we'll stay together as planned."

Two knights from the FitzPons conroi did not make it back alive to the Norman lines. A knight from Maine and one from Ponthieu succumbed to arrow wounds as they were carried from the field.

The Norman army watched the walls burn. With no reinforcements, Conan surrendered and was taken prisoner. William was extremely pleased with the FitzPons feats. Not only had their "desertion" from the battlefield at Rennes led to the capture of Conan, but their incendiary mission had reduced Dinan's walls to ashes. Thus, William had avoided a siege that would have lasted for weeks and could have cost many casualties to his army.

The resistance in Brittany crumbled within a few weeks and the Breton-Norman war was over. With the subjugation of the duchy, all of Normandy's borders were secure and conditions were set for William's invasion of England.

CHAPTER THREE

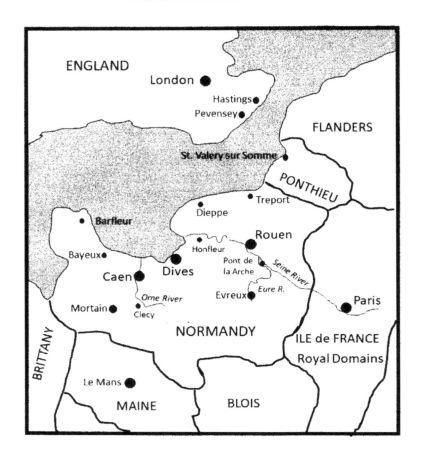

CHAPTER THREE

William led his army through the major towns in Brittany and demanded the fealty of the Breton nobles. He proclaimed that any men enlisting in his army would be paid as a mercenary and in addition, any knight who fought for his cause would be granted land in England. Thousands of Breton knights and foot soldiers pledged their service and William created a new division of the army consisting of Bretons and recruits from Maine. The Flemish and French wings were combined into one division and the Norman knights remained a separate third division. Garrisons were stationed in Brittany to train newly enlisted knights in Norman cavalry tactics. Proficiency in the crossbow could be achieved in less than a month, so William recruited Bretons to train in the weapon, increasing his number of archers.

It was early spring of 1066 and the shipbuilding effort had barely begun. Foot soldiers had been conscripted to help build the ships at ports on the English Channel, including Barfleur, Caen, Dives, Dieppe, Treport, and several ports inland along the Seine River. The Norman and French-Flemish knights returned to William's capital city of Caen for continued training. William visited Barfleur to review the construction of his flagship. After their change of fortune, the FitzPons brothers were among the two score chevaliers accompanying William and his entourage.

They arrived in the town of Barfleur late in the afternoon. William and his half-brothers were quartered in the mayor's house. A score of Norman knights were billeted near the duke and the FitzPons conroi camped at the edge of town along the road, guarding the landside approach to the seaport. The FitzPons brothers and their comrades gathered around the campfire, having finished their meal. Lothar commented, "This wine is a pleasant change from our usual ration of ale. Is it because William favors wine and now we are prestigious guards of the duke?"

"I would rather have ale," Leufred stated. Lambert agreed.

"Crude northerners drink ale. I imagine the duke chooses wine to be like us sophisticated knights from Aquitaine," said Drogo.

"Ale is the drink of men!" said Lothar. He stood up and towered over Drogo.

Drogo raised to his full height, then went up on his toes to press his forehead against Lothar's. "So does that mean you are implying wine is the drink of women?" His voice was filled with challenge.

Lothar leaned his forehead into Drogo's and growled, "Yes!"

Watching Drogo's lightning movement, Richard recalled their childhood and how his brother had always challenged his siblings to wrestle when they were boys. Drogo had Lothar in an arm bar and choke hold. "In that case, let's be friends!" He pecked his friend on his bearded cheek and released him. The men laughed as Lothar shoved Drogo back with comic disgust.

"Wine or ale, one or the other, let's drink to our promotion from liver eaters to steak eaters. That beef stew was excellent!" said Osborne.

"Yes, we are the heroes of Dinan," said Gauthier, "and have been elevated from *rifle et rafle* to *le meilleur amis de Duc*, from riff-raff who pick over dead bodies to the duke's best friends!"

Suddenly Lambert's mien turned sober. "Men, be aware. Don't become too self-possessed! William is a conniver. Our fate could flip like a coin."

His comrades quieted. Then his solemn look became a grin, "But now let's celebrate! We have run the gauntlet. We have survived the test and are now favorites." He toasted with a skin of wine. "*Sante!*"

"And everyone here—we are all knights—will be landowners soon!" Richard said. "Landowners and thus suitable for marriage to beautiful noble ladies!"

The next morning was cool, but the sun cast an agreeable warmth. A herald arrived at the knights' campsite with orders that William expected the FitzPons brothers at the shipyard. They left their conroi and arrived to see William, Count Robert, and Bishop Odo reviewing the construction of a longship of Viking design. A fourth, younger man that Richard did not recognize was present. Nearby were several other ships under varying stages of assembly.

The sons of Pons dismounted, handing the reins to the squires. The duke was without armor and in the chill of the maritime air, he wore a blue surcoat over his tunic. He sipped wine and handed the jug to Robert, who said, "I see you still enjoy your wine in the morning, brother."

William noticed the arrival of the FitzPons brothers and called out in his booming voice. "Comrades, your actions at Rennes and Dinan inspired me to invite you here today. I believe your talents can help us solve the many problems we have had in preparing our fleet on time."

Richard introduced his brothers to Duke William, Odo, and Robert. William said, "I invited a new member of my court to see the ship building so that he might become inspired and fashion a poem honoring our immense undertaking. This is Pont de Dinan, Conan's former bard, now in my employment."

Pont bowed, the glint of a metal object noticeable as it dangled from his neck.

Count Robert gestured. "Duke William's wife commissioned this longship, being assembled to Viking specifications, to be his flagship. Those smaller versions of the same design are to transport troops and supplies."

"Yes, the ship is a gift from my sweet Matilda. What a strong and intelligent woman!" exclaimed William. "She just bore our eighth child and she governs while I am away fighting!"

"You sound lonesome, brother!" said Robert. "We need to get you to Caen so you can work on your ninth child!"

As they inspected the work, Richard noted a wooden sign in front of the flagship. He read the inscription aloud, "*Mora.*"

"Yes, the flagship was christened *Mora* by my wife. With this name, she captured the regal spirit of the ancient Viking kings, from whom I am descended. The Mora Stone, in Sweden, is where Nordic kings have traditionally been consecrated. I am related to four English kings through my Great-Aunt Emma, two of whom were Viking. Therefore, I should rightfully inherit the monarchy. Harold Godwinson has stolen the crown and is a pretender. Matilda learned much of our family history from Emma when they lived together in Flanders. She has inherited the role of keeper of family lineage and history and maintains the records."

"May I comment from the point of view of a Breton, Duke William?" asked Pont.

"Yes."

"Although I speak French like the Normans, my native tongue is Breton, a Celtic language. *Mora* harkens back to the Breton word *mor*, which means sea. The people of Brittany are descended from the Britons from across the channel. Our people remember the stories of our ancestors fleeing Britain from the invading Saxons. It has been many generations, but the thousands of Bretons accompanying your invasion force can imagine they are returning to their native lands."

"If they prove strong enough, spoils go to the victors!" said William. "The choice of the *Mora* as the flagship illustrates how perceptive Matilda was in selecting the name. I recall she said the Flemish are descended from a Celtic tribe called the Morini that lived on the same coast. In that Celtic dialect, *mori* meant sea. They were the people of the sea. Through her dubbing the flagship *Mora*, she has brilliantly woven together the Franco-Normans, the Bretons, and the Flemish, the three realms undertaking the conquest."

"God has sent you a woman who possesses talents which complement your own," said Bishop Odo. "And as I watch this immense flagship rise, I recall a verse from Proverbs: 'She is like the merchants' ships, she bringeth her food from afar.'"

William added, "'The heart of her husband doth safely trust her,' also from Proverbs."

"Very good, brother! I didn't think you read much of the Bible."

"Another doubt at my piety and literacy!" His booming voice was noticed by the laborers, who wisely kept working despite the outburst. "I have built two abbeys, donated great sums of money to the Church, and I am still considered ungrateful to God? Today I will show the importance of God. You are my superior in religious matters. But you were appointed by me and you are also my secular vassal. I order you . . . uh, request, you perform Mass this afternoon. I will halt all work on the ships, so the men can attend."

"No, no, you took insult when none was intended, William. Do not stop the construction. I know we need every hour to finish."

The three brothers examined each other in silence.

Then Odo said, "That is a good notion, Duke William."

They paused as squires brought cheese and bread. The tension relieved, the men enjoyed the repast and the pleasant day.

"I see a score of other longships being built," said Richard. "They are the same type as the *Mora*, yet shorter."

"Those ships will be used to transport soldiers and supplies for the invasion," Robert answered. "Hundreds more of them will be constructed to add to the two existing fleets already secured by William." He pointed to a ship beached on the sand. "That ship is from the Norman fleet he inherited from his father. It was pulled from the water to use as a model to build the new longships. In addition, Count Baldwin, William's father-in-law, has loaned the duke a sizable fleet, over a hundred ships, which has just returned from a raid on the English coast."

William said, "Drogo, I have been told that you served with Roger De Hauteville in Sicily."

"Yes, sire. For one year."

"Why did you leave? They are still fighting in Sicily. It will take years to complete the conquest and plenty of adventure is left!"

"Sire, I foresee your invasion of England to be the greater adventure!"

"Yes . . . hah . . . a strategic answer! There are Normans who have returned home from Sicily and are in Caen constructing horse transports. You may see one of your former comrades-in-arms."

"Yes, sire. When the Norman army crossed the straits from Italy to Sicily, each ship transported twenty knights, their weapons, and their horses. Thus the conrois were organized into twenty knights to match the transports and were ready to fight as a unit when they landed on the beaches. Will we be reorganizing into smaller conrois as well?"

William looked at Robert and answered. "An intelligent observation, Sir Drogo."

They walked through a workshop open to the elements save for a good roof and watched the carpenters using wooden mallets and wedges to split huge oak trees. Other workers were using adzes and axes to form the oak beams into an inverted "T" shaped keel. Robert introduced the master shipwright to William and Odo, who explained the work. He pointed to a keel being trimmed and hewed to shape. "Each keel measures twice as wide as a man's hand, five hands deep, and twenty-five steps long. One beam is needed to construct these ships. The flagship *Mora,* however, required two of these beams end to end to fashion its keel."

As the men continued discussing the keels, Gauthier lingered a moment with the shipwright. "I can see these longships are quite extensive and the *Mora* is twice as long as these," said Gauthier. "Can you be more precise? What is the length of twenty-five steps? How long, say, in French feet, in *pieds*?"

"Of course," said the shipwright, seeming pleased someone was speaking the language of his trade. "So you know the *pied*. A 'step' is two-and-a-half *pieds*. Using the French measure, the standard longship is about fifty *pieds* in length and eighteen *pieds* wide at the middle."

In the boatyard, there were longships in various stages of

completion. As they surveyed the construction, the master shipwright commented, "After a keel is set, the hulls of the longships are formed by overlapping the planks. We can use either oak, ash, elm, pine, spruce, or larch for the planks. William's flagship, being a large and prestigious ship, has hull planks made entirely of oak. The planks are tapered at each end, so the wood can be bent to shape the bow and stern. Iron nails are used to join the planks at the overlap. Each overlap is stuffed with hemp or animal hair soaked in pine tar. Then nails are hammered into the outside of the hull until they are flattened, to rivet the planks together."

"I see wooden pegs being used on several of the ships to join the planks," said Robert.

"Yes, sire, when there is a shortage of nails, the erstwhile method is used. Holes are drilled in the planks using a twist drill, and the planks are joined by inserting wooden trunnels soaked with linseed oil. The trunnels hold the ship together just as well, but it takes more time than nailing the joints."

"We are building so many longships in such a short time that the trees are newly cut. Is that a problem?" asked Robert.

"No, sire. In fact, green, damp lumber is preferred, which allows us to bend and shape the planks without cracking the wood. Seasoned wood needs to be soaked before it can be bent, anyway. God has blessed the Pope's approval of this crusade by providing us with this abundant natural resource. We couldn't build the ships in time if we had to season all the timber. There is one drawback using greenwood, however. Ships made of greenwood age faster than seasoned wood."

William and Robert both frowned.

"No, the channel crossing will not be affected," said the shipwright, "I am talking about the ship lasting perhaps two decades, instead of three."

"Very good," said William, appearing relieved.

"We are fortunate our Lord has sent you here with your expert knowledge," added Odo. "Shipwrights from all over Europe have responded to our call to build this great fleet in so short a time. Your accent? Is it Nordic?"

"That is correct, Your Excellency. Bishop Odo, I am from Daneland and have the honor to preserve the shipbuilding skills of the ancient Vikings."

"And your services are much appreciated!" William said to the shipwright. "Normans are descended from Danes. The first ruler of Normandy, Rollo, was Danish, but now few Normans know how to build ships."

"Do you know how many ships, beside the duke's flagship, you will build here?" asked Odo.

"Uh . . . let's see," he looked out in the harbor and counted, "We have completed ten ships, the other twenty anchored here are from the Norman fleet. We have ten under construction now and orders for fifty more ships."

Odo smiled. "Good. The Bishop of Le Mans and I together have funded seventy ships to be assembled here since both Le Mans and Bayeux are without ports."

Drogo stepped closer. "Duke William, may I ask a question?" he said, as he gestured the query was for the shipwright. The duke nodded.

"Sir, I understand why newly cut wood must be used to build the transports, because of the lack of time. In Daneland, did you use seasoned wood for the whole ship? And I thought you said you then soaked that wood to bend the planks. Is that right?"

"Why, yes. We always did it that way. The method has been passed down for centuries."

The following morning William and his entourage rode to Bayeux. He and the knights attended Mass, celebrated by Bishop Odo in the partially rebuilt Our Lady of Bayeux Cathedral. The original had burned a few years earlier. Odo remained in the city of his episcopacy, and William and the rest of his party proceeded onto Caen.

After two days' ride, they neared the capital city and recognized the Chateau de Caen, an immense castle that William had built five years earlier. They passed an impressive campus of buildings which included a large church. William halted his mount and addressed his entourage as he pointed to the grounds. "Those buildings are the men's abbey, Saint Etienne Abbey. My wife sends our sons there to study Latin and to learn how to read. Their teacher is the abbot himself, Lanfranc, a close friend and ally. When the Pope opposed my marriage to Matilda, Lanfranc supported me. The Pope said my wife and I were too closely related, but we are only fifth cousins! I commissioned the abbey to satisfy my penance, and Lanfranc convinced the Pope to sanction our marriage. And he is also a genius! Lanfranc built this monastery. Abbot Lanfranc of Pavia, Lanfranco in his native tongue. Yes, he is an Italian, but most capable!

"Men, we part for now. Drogo, you may reunite with your southern comrades at the shipyard. There are shipwrights here from Sicily." William laughed, "They will answer your many questions."

The duke, the bard, and his knights entered the chateau. Robert and the FitzPons brothers continued to the harbor five miles north. Richard asked, "Count Robert, Duke William is very proud of his family. I recall the duke said he has eight children?"

"Yes, that's right. I am thirty-seven and William is only a few years older, although I am yet to be married or have any children! He has four sons and four daughters. As William said, Matilda is very involved in ensuring the children are educated. The boys learn at Saint Etienne and the girls . . . there, it is in sight now, the women's abbey, Saint Trinity. That is where his daughters attend to their schooling.

"Richard, did you or your brothers leave any wives or betrothed back at Pons?"

"No, we plan to win our fortunes, then marry."

Richard dropped back and rode next to Osborne. "Ozzie, I did not have time to discuss the bard's name. It sounded like our father's name, Pons. What did you think about that?"

"To me it didn't sound like Pons, it sounded like he said *pont*, bridge," said Osborne.

"Yes, perhaps it was his Breton accent; we can ask him about it later," answered Richard.

The group arrived at the harbor of Caen. It was a scene much like Barfleur but on a larger scale. A score of longships with pointed bows and sterns were being constructed from the keel up. There were also several larger ships with round ends which were fitted with boarding ramps at the bow. Near them was a large cargo ship that was beached and being modified. As they dismounted, Drogo said, "Those big ships with ramps and flat bottom hulls are horse transports, like what the Normans used to invade Sicily."

They went to inspect the modifications of the large ships. A foreman called out, "Count Robert! We are honored by your visit. I am in the middle of a dilemma. The Sicilian shipwright has proposed an idea for which I would like your approval." They walked by several ships and approached a short, stocky man who was shouting orders to workers in strongly accented French. As they drew near, Osborne said, "What language is the shipwright speaking? It sounds like a mixture of Latin and French!"

The stout man, with dark curly hair and moustache, turned to them and exclaimed, "God's bones, I am doing the best I can. You Northmen can work on ale. I need good wine to think!

"Oh, um . . . I did not see you, Sir Roberto, I mean Comte Roberto, *bona die!*"

"*Bonjour*, Maestro Ponziu!" said Robert.

Osborne laughed as he whispered to Richard, "Now I hear Latin, French, and something else!"

"What is your proposal, Ponziu?" asked Robert.

The Sicilian waved his arm at the big ship on the beach. "Instead of building the horse transports from the ground up, we will have enough by modifying existing cargo ships. We can add boarding ramps and stalls with horse slings to them. They are large enough to carry *venti equi*, uh, twenty horses, and men."

"I approve of your idea, Maestro Ponziu."

Robert turned to the FitzPons brothers. "God has sent this man to help us. Although he is not a Norman, and not a warrior, his skills are valuable." Ponziu, standing behind Robert, rolled his eyes and shrugged, his hands quite animated.

Robert continued addressing the FitzPons brothers, "After

listening to your questions today on shipbuilding, I agree with William that your services will be best used preparing the fleet. The work I ask you to do may be humbling, that is, considered beneath a knight."

"I need a calm, patient man to work here with Ponziu. Although he is very brilliant, he is rather emotional and spends a lot of time complaining and not correcting." The Sicilian looked disgusted, turned around, and hammered nails into the hull.

"I find satisfaction working with my hands," said Gauthier. "I will follow his instructions, be his assistant, and stay with him. I will be his hands."

"Good," said Robert. "I have promised 120 ships to William. There are vast forest reserves in my domain of County Mortain which can supply the wood, but I need a man to do a better job organizing the selection, felling, and delivery of the timber to Caen."

"I can find my way through any forest," said Osborne. "Give me woodcutters, enough carts and oxen and I will deliver the wood."

"Agreed," answered the count. "Also, we are having problems getting the proper wood to the right shipyards and need improvement in the accounting."

Drogo suggested, "While I have been listening to the shipwrights, I have thought of several ways to improve construction."

"Let's discuss your plans tomorrow, Drogo," answered Robert.

"Another problem," the count continued. "Many of the new ships built at the Seine ports have leaked."

"I will take care of those ships." said Richard.

Over the next few months, Gauthier followed Ponziu from ship to ship in the Caen shipyard, as the thickset man belched out commands and corrections to the carpenters and workers. Gauthier learned how to use the carpenters' tools and joined them in the work. The adze, the axe, and the draw knife were his mates. Gauthier was also learning the Sicilian's use of words. He found that when Ponziu mixed his native dialect with French, he could still understand him, while his speech baffled the other workers. The man's speech was like the written Latin that Gauthier had learned from his mother and sister in Pons, except the s's and m's had been dropped from most words. The Latin *longus* for long became *longu*, the Latin *altum* for high became *altu*, and so forth. But it did not occur to Gauthier that the Sicilian's name had also evolved from Latin in a similar way, until one day, the shipwright wrote his name on a vessel ready for launching. He chalked the name PONTIUS on the bow of the ship, indicating it had passed his inspection.

Osborne was challenged but enjoying every hour. He followed the game trails in the forest of Mortain, looking for choice trees to cut for ships' keels and planks. With him was Mathieu, a serf who for years had been guiding Count Robert through his domains, hunting red deer and boar. The men trekked for hours without talking, enjoying the companionship and solitude. They moved efficiently on foot without mounts, and marked the trees to direct the woodcutters later. Working down both sides of the Orne River from Caen into County Mortain, the pair designated thousands of oak trees to be felled. Osborne had verified Drogo's number of trees required for building fifty new transports and modifying fifty cargo ships to transport horses. He drew a map of the Orne River Valley on parchment, adding the location of the trees they had tagged. Mathieu never had seen a map but declared he didn't need one to remember where the trees were located.

One morning Mathieu awoke but chose to remain warm under his blanket, drifting in and out of sleep, listening to water cascading in the Orne River. With permission from the manor foreman, they had slept comfortably in a barn at the village of Clecy. The river's soothing effect was interrupted by footsteps as Osborne returned with a handful of eggs and a small loaf of dark bread. His water skin hung full on his shoulder. "Wake up, Mathieu! The manor lord had the kitchen maids prepare us a breakfast." He threw a couple eggs at him which bounced off

Mathieu's head.

"What are you doing! But what is this? They didn't break!" said Mathieu.

"Yes, it's new to me, too, but they boiled them and see"— he peeled back the egg shell and took a bite. "They are solid inside, and tasty! They also filled my skin with ale!"

As they wolfed down the novel food, Osborne said, "I heard in the village that we should explore southeast and follow the Cance River, where there are old stands of oak."

Mathieu spouted, "No! I mean, no, I'm familiar with that area, it's, uh . . . too rocky and the valley is too steep."

They ate in silence. Osborne had only known Mathieu for a few weeks, but suspected evasion in his companion's voice. Mathieu added, "I know the Cance. We can't float logs to Caen from there because it flows the wrong direction. Also, the land is too rugged for oxcarts to pull the logs to the Orne."

"I sense there is something wrong, my friend," said Osborne.

"I will be honest. We can't go there. Count Mortain would not allow it."

"The villagers told me a majestic cascade is to the southeast. Do you mean the count would forbid us merely to see the waterfall?"

"Yes, the site is supposed to be kept secret, only for Count Robert's enjoyment. The area around the Grande Cascade is only for his own hunting pleasure."

The next breakfast the men shared was at the base of the Grand Cascade. "Of course, it should never be logged, it is too magnificent," said Osborne.

"I agree. And Count Robert would not let that happen. It will be safe even though very few can enjoy it. How tall are these waterfalls?"

Osborne pointed to several tall oaks about as high as the cataracts. "I believe those trees are eighty *pieds*."

"*Pieds*?" asked Mathieu.

Osborne held up his hands a distance apart and said, "This distance is one *pied*."

"Someone has big feet!" said Mathieu.

Osborne asked, "Have you climbed to the top of the cascades?"

Mathieu nodded and began the ascent. Osborne raced him to the top.

While his brothers were absorbed in their assignments, Richard journeyed to Pont de la Arche, a port on the left bank of the Seine River. The Count of Evreux had promised eighty ships for Duke William's invasion. His town was located upstream on the River Iton, south of the river port. Over the next few days, Richard spent hours at the port asking questions and listening to the shipwrights, the carpenters, and the laborers. The immediate area near the Seine had been logged many years earlier, but Pont de la Arche was an advantageous location for a shipyard. Although the town was small, it was at the juncture of two large rivers, and workers were available from the city of Rouen, a few miles away. Richard had learned that trees were cut at locations inland, then the timber was floated down the River Iton to the Eure River, and then to the port on the Seine. The Count of Evreux had also provided the funds to hire the workforce. During a brief visit to the shipyard, he had complained to Richard that out of the twenty ships launched so far, only half were seaworthy.

Richard consulted the shipwrights. A few wrights thought the leaks were due to warping from use of the green lumber. The shipwrights and carpenters advised to simply continue construction and then return the leaking ships to be repaired. He concluded this was the best plan considering the rigorous schedule. He then arranged for the foremen to conduct detailed inspections when each new ship was launched. Over the next two weeks, most of the new ships needed repairs.

The leaks were being repaired and Richard was pleased with the progress, but standing on the dock one morning when studying the activity of the shipyard, his thoughts drifted back to seasoned wood. *All the seasoned wood available has already been used at the shipyard. Because it would take months to dry wood to build the ships from seasoned wood, the ships could not be completed by the end of the sailing season. When a ship is made of green wood, it dries, cracks and warps which causes the lower hull to leak. But if the ships are built quickly and put in the water . . . and they are . . . the part of the hull under the water line does not dry out—does not crack—does not warp. So that means the upper part of the ships built of green timber are drying out, warping, and distorting the lower hull, which then leaks. Yes! Use green wood solely for the hull that will be under the water line and use seasoned wood for the parts of the ship that are not constantly wetted. I wonder if Drogo has this same problem?*

At the shipyard at Dives, Drogo surveyed the inventory of seasoned wood. *William said he will need 700 ships to transport his army across the channel. He has collected just over 200 ships, including the Norman and the Flemish fleets. The inventory of seasoned wood is enough to build about 100 ships, so 400 ships must be made from green wood. Although fifty to seventy trees are required to make one ship, the resources are available, and it is just a matter of cutting and shipping the timber to the shipyards. The nobles insist on using the seasoned wood first because they will make more profit. But Ponziu said ships made of green wood will warp and crack when they dry out and cause the hull to leak. Here at Dives, so far, we have only made modifications to the cargo ships, such as the boarding ramps, and have not found any leaking problems. I don't know what we will do when we run out of seasoned wood. I need to go to Caen and talk to Robert.* The next morning, Drogo sent a messenger to Caen requesting an audience with Robert. The courier returned the same day with the count's consent. Before Drogo left Dives, he gave instructions to the shipwrights to not use any of the seasoned wood. Since they were still modifying cargo ships to use as horse transports, it would not delay progress.

Drogo began riding at daybreak the following morning and completed the trip to Caen before midday. He met Robert at William's castle. They shared a pitcher of ale as Drogo explained his dilemma. "The master shipwright said the green wood is very pliant and easy to bend and shape, but he is worried the ships' planks will warp and then leak."

"Yes, I recall he said it would not be a problem, that those ships made of green wood might last twenty years rather than thirty. That is not a concern."

"Yes, sir, that is correct, but I am talking about a short term problem. The ships could leak days after they are launched or when we are crossing the channel to England. There may be a connection with the leaking ships built at Pont de la Arche. I would like to ask my brother Richard about his experience before I deplete the seasoned wood."

"You may, but do it quickly," answered Robert.

"Count Robert, another idea?"

"Proceed."

"We should make sure that blacksmiths are located at each shipyard to supply enough nails, rather than fabricating the wooden trunnels. It will speed up construction because it requires extra time to drill a hole before inserting the trunnels."

"Yes, yes! I will correct that right away. And, Sir Drogo, a fortunate coincidence. One of my knights is escorting his sister to Rouen, only a few miles from your destination. They are leaving tomorrow by ship to Honfleur, near the mouth of the Seine River. It is a day's sailing from here and then another day's ride to Pont de la Arche. I will add your name to my letter for room and board at the Abbey of Notre-Dame de Grestain. The dispatch will also grant you horses for loan to complete your journey."

In the morning Drogo was delayed and boarded the longship just as it was casting off. The young man and woman on board smiled and said, "*Bonjour* Sir Dreux!"

"Bonjour. Please do not be formal, call me Drogo. I am sorry, Robert did not tell me your names."

"My sister is Trinette and I am Morry."

The ship sailed out with the tide, left the estuary at Dives, tracking east along the Normandy coast. Initially, the three passengers remained seated, then tentatively stood, testing their balance on the open deck. Drogo approached the pair, grasping rigging and the ship wale to keep his balance as he made his way. The young man had the air of a disciplined knight, unlike, in

Drogo's opinion, the rough characters that had been scraped from the bottom of the barrel to enlarge the invasion force. Morry wore a gray woolen tunic covered with a surcoat, with dagger at his belt, his long coat flapping open in the wind. He was of average height, about eye level with Drogo, but appeared taller upon approach, due to his soldierly bearing. His sister was petite and attractive and wrapped in layers against the chilly wind. Her tunica, surcoat, and overcoat were in subdued but pleasing colors. Her hair was covered with a scarf which swathed around her neck and draped down her back. Drogo shouted above the wind and the flapping sails. "Lady, you look warm and bundled up in this chill. And sir, you appear as if the cold blows right through you without a care!"

They both laughed and the three almost forgot they were on a sailing ship as they traded stories and family history.

The men were welcomed at the monastery and Trinette was housed at the nearby nunnery. Robert had told Drogo that the abbey had been founded fifteen years earlier by his father and mother, now both deceased. His mother, Arlette, was also the mother of Robert's half-brother, Duke William. Because of the great class differences, the duke's father had not married her, but he arranged her marriage with his close friend who was rather prosperous, so she had enjoyed a comfortable life. Arlette was buried at the abbey. The next morning the three travelers laid flowers on Arlette's grave and said prayers as Robert had requested. Drogo then departed for Arch de la Pont.

During his ride he recalled his conversations with Morry and Trinette. He sensed Trinette's enthusiasm to train as a lady-in-waiting. *Many noble women look forward to a life of comfort and ease, but Trinette seems eager to learn the complexities of managing a manor, the education of her future children, and even governing when her husband could be away. I recall Father saying, 'Marry a woman who can educate your children and can manage your accounts.' And Morry is a gentleman. He is one of William's knights and possesses their lofty martial skills, but he does not project the conceit and arrogance I have seen in other Norman chevaliers.*

By late afternoon Drogo arrived at Pont de la Arche and after a short reunion with Richard, the brothers surveyed the shipyard, and then shared some wine to further discuss the use of green wood. Richard had learned that the first ships built at Arche were made entirely from the site's limited amount of seasoned wood. None of those ships had leaked, unlike the more recent ships made entirely from green wood. Drogo and Richard arrived at the same conclusion: the green wood in the upper section of the hull, above the water line, dried out and warped, causing the leaks. They decided to use fresh cut planks for the lower hull which would remain under the water line and use seasoned wood for the upper part of the ships. Drogo hurried back to Dives and shipped Richard enough seasoned wood for the topsides of his ships. He began to implement the new methods of construction at Dives and recommended the other shipyards do the same.

At Pont de la Arche, Richard stood on the wharf to observe another ship being launched. A foreman shouted at the men on the beach pushing and dragging the boat into the river. Along the river shore were nine more identical longships being built. Because the ships were being hastily constructed, none were fitted with carved dragon heads. The Normans would not protest this loss of tradition. Across the generations, these former Vikings had not only lost their shipbuilding skills, but had forgotten their superstition that the dragonhead was needed to protect them from the evils of the sea.

Another longship was returning from a test sail on the river. Sailors rowed the ship upstream as other crewmen lowered the detachable mast before it passed under an impressive stone bridge made of twenty-three arches. The lengthy bridge was required to cross two parallel rivers near the point where the Eure joined the Seine. Centuries earlier, a wooden version had been erected at the same place, its bridge deck low to the water surface to block Viking ships from reaching Paris. It had been fortified, and towers had been located at each end. Over the centuries, the structures had deteriorated, but the bridge had been rebuilt. Longships could only pass underneath if their masts were lowered. The crew secured the incoming ship to the dock and fixed the oars in place. Richard's attention was suddenly diverted. He was surprised to see a young woman jump from the docked longship onto the wharf. She had on a gray woolen tunica overlaid with a woad surcoat, both almost reaching to her ankles. The image reminded him of the last time he had seen his sister in traveling clothes, also less ornate, but more practical than a lady's usual dress. The woman's head was covered by a simple coif, the color of her tunica, and tied at her neck. Her dark hair hung in a long braid down her back. As Richard admired her hair, she retrieved a long scarf from her pocket, also the color of her tunica, draped it over her head, wrapped it round her neck, and tossed the end over her back. The resulting headrail now only exposed her face.

She noticed Richard staring. "You are Sir Richard? Forgive me. On the ship, only the coif would stay on my head. The wind on the river is brisk today."

"No apologies necessary," Richard bowed slightly. "You know my name, lady?"

"My father and I have today joined your inspection crew."

She is an inspector? Quite out of the ordinary for a woman. This young woman is very attractive, and her confidence stirs me.

She met his gaze. An awkward silence followed, then a man with a dark moustache and Mediterranean complexion joined them and put his arm around the young woman. "Daughter, how was your first inspection?"

"Papa! This is Sir Richard. He is the knight managing the ships."

"Well! Very good, Sir Richard," said her father. "I am Froila Alejandro Vermúdez de Traba. My daughter, Amicia, Amicia Vermudez Perez de Traba. Please join us for the noon meal!"

As Richard strode along the wharf with the pair, he noticed men setting up a canopy. By the time they reached the shelter, a table had been positioned under the awning and containers of food had been removed from a cart and placed on the table.

Two nobles arrived, escorted by a handful of knights. The two men dismounted and joined Richard and his new acquaintances under the pavilion. Richard recognized the older of the pair as Count Evreux. "I see you have met Sir Richard FitzPons," said the count. "Sir Richard, my son Guillaume." The two young men traded respectful nods. "And please, all of you enjoy the food," continued the count. A servant handed each of them a wooden bowl with pieces of cut pork, vegetables, and bread, which they ate using their hands. Pitchers of ale and wine were placed on the table as they ate heartily standing about the table.

"Thank you for this delightful meal, count." said Vermudez. "I know the drink of choice in Normandy is ale, and I appreciate you arranging for wine. To the duke's expedition! With God's help, the duke will be crowned King of England. *Salud*!"

The group toasted, "*Sante*!"

Count Evreux laughed as he said, "I have heard that William is collecting barrels of wine to take on the invasion. Perhaps because the ale spoils too fast? But he is himself partial to wine."

He turned to address Richard. "Your plan of accounting and tracking repairs is increasing quality and the production rate, Sir Richard."

"Thank you," answered Richard, "all those involved have cooperated to make it possible. My brother just visited and with his help, we will be making improvements."

"A very humble answer," said the count. "We should achieve even greater production with Lord Vermudez here now guiding the shipwrights. He has been building ships his entire life in Caruna, the main port of Galicia."

"Galicia? The county in Spain where the Cathedral of Santiago de Compostela is located?"

Lord Vermudez answered, "Yes, but Galicia is now its own kingdom. One year ago King Ferdinand died, and his three sons divided his realm into separate domains: Castile, Leon, and the former county of Galicia, which was elevated to the rank of a kingdom."

Richard said, "We are very fortunate to have you here, Lord Vermudez."

"And my daughter Amicia is very capable. She has learned

shipbuilding since she was a young girl. That's what my family does in Caruna, build ships. She is an expert in selecting materials, fabrication, and workmanship. She helped me build the bucius anchored just downstream of the bridge."

"That explains the origin of that ship," said Richard. "It seems to be a sturdy cargo ship. That sort of merchant ship is referred to as a cog here in the north. But no, you did not sail it from Galicia, did you!"

"Yes, we did, and it was the most exciting adventure of my life!" exclaimed Amicia. Richard enjoyed her enthusiasm. *Her excitement pulls at my heart, and what a beautiful smile.* She continued, "We had to load it with lumber as ballast. The ship is flat bottomed, and we needed the extra weight in the rough seas. Besides, now the lumber can be used here in the shipyard."

Vermudez laughed, "We didn't need the lumber, your trunks of clothes were enough ballast!"

"Father!"

"The ship is Amicia's dowry," continued Vermudez. "Guillaume and Amicia are betrothed."

Richard's heart sank. *That is unfortunate.* "Uh . . . my, um, congratulations, Sir Guillaume and Lady Amicia." He found it difficult to acknowledge their relationship.

He barely heard Vermudez add, "And Count Evreux compensated Amicia for the bucius, er . . . the cog in silver to cover the dowry, then donated the vessel to the invasion fleet."

Amicia smiled as Guillaume said, "It is no small miracle that we ever were brought together. I believe God has sent her to me. My father and Lord Vermudez bonded in friendship and camaraderie years ago. As a knight, Father traveled to Spain, joined in the Reconquista, and fought alongside Lord Vermudez."

Count Evreux gently clasped Vermudez's shoulder. "We have not seen each other in over ten years, but we are still like brothers. I pledged to help Duke William and promised eighty ships. There were not enough shipwrights, so I chartered a littoral ship—the pilot was not a sailor of the ocean like Vermudez—so we sailed from port to port staying close to the French coast. I found one shipwright in Bordeaux and another in Bayonne that would join the cause, but my real objective was to hire Vermudez!"

"A very intriguing story!" said Richard. "A toast to your engagement. *Sante!*" He forced himself to smile.

Work continued six days a week in the shipyard at Pont de la Arche. Richard interacted often with shipwrights and foremen, including Amicia, who was constantly escorted by a man about her father's age whom she called Tio. He did not speak French, but was very polite. Richard enjoyed being near her, although he continually reminded himself she was already promised. As they worked, he tended to drift to personal conversation after shipbuilding discussions, and she joined spontaneously. Richard's respect for her increased as he observed her incessant demands for better work from the carpenters and laborers.

Nobles had bestowed several merchant ships to the invasion fleet. Richard dispatched these to Dives to be converted to horse transports. After Amicia and Richard discussed plans to retrofit the dowry ship, it was also sailed to Dives to be modified as well. As they watched the ship cast off into the Seine River and begin its journey, Richard asked, "Your father sailed this boat here. His crew is working here. You will remain here in your new home in Evreux, but how will your father and the crew get back to Galicia?"

"They will return by the pilgrim's way, Saint James' Way. My father always desired to walk the long journey as penance."

"Compostela is in Galicia, but you have not been there?"

"Yes, we all have, I mean our whole family has walked the route to the cathedral, but the journey was only forty miles from our home. It was not the great effort undertaken by most pilgrims."

"I used to see many pilgrims traveling through my hometown," said Richard.

"Where is that?"

"The village of Pons in County Saintonge. You sailed right by and did not wave!"

Amicia seemed puzzled, but then laughed. "I have a sister and a brother in Caruna. I am sure my father misses the family and my mother," said Amicia. Do you have any other siblings?"

"Yes, I have four brothers and one sister. My sister is in Saintes and should be married by now. Three of my brothers are working at other shipyards. Ozzie is happily trekking through the woods finding the biggest trees for the keels. I know Gauthier is finding satisfaction working with his hands and Drogo is shrewdly figuring ways to reduce costs. It is like a game to him. We are going to England with the duke and will fight alongside each other in the same conroi.

"So are you all knights?" asked Amicia. Richard nodded. She added, "My fiancé is also a chevalier and will be going to fight. You seem to miss your brothers."

"Yes. Do you miss your siblings"?

"Very much. I have a twin sister and I miss her."

"And your brother?"

Amicia laughed as she said, "My mother told us when my sister and I were born, my older brother was disappointed because he wanted a brother instead, but that changed, and he grew to be very affectionate and protective. My sister is in good hands."

"I am also confident that my sister is safe. She is only twenty miles from home. But you are a very brave woman, being so distant from your family."

She turned away and brushed something from her face. "We should get back to work."

With a faint bow, Richard said, "Lady Amicia Vermudez, I have my brothers, but you are far away from your family. Please accept my pledge as a knight to support you in any way.

Amicia was silent.

"Uh . . . forgive me if you think that inappropriate."

"No, Sir Richard, I sense you are sincere. You will be my older brother away from home. It will be our secret."

All summer of 1066, the woodcutters, the carpenters, the laborers, and the shipwrights worked seven days per week to meet the duke's goal to sail by August. The Normans were considered a very pious nation, but the bishops used the Pope's blessing of the venture to justify working on the Christians' day of sabbath.

The *Mora* had been finished and completed her maiden voyage to Caen, under Captain Airard FitzStephen. During the passage, the banner consecrated by the Pope and bestowed to William flew on the ship's mast. The standard carried an image of a cross on a green field. The banner's fly end consisted of three pennant shaped tails.

Osborne had completed his exploration of the forest for timber and returned to Caen to retrain and sharpen his martial skills. Gauthier joined him at the stables of Chateau de Caen. They donned their armor and prepared to mount their steeds, held by squires. "Drogo said he will be here the sixth hour," said Osborne. He looked skyward. "Yes, the time is sext." The sun was at its highest point.

"Richard was supposed to return days ago. We have reassembled our conroi and been training for a week now without him," said Gauthier. "Why is he delayed?"

The two brothers rode their mounts across the field to join their conroi assembled outside the chateau. With the Le Mans knights, several chevaliers from County Ponthieu, and the four FitzPons brothers the conroi when fully attended would number twenty. As they had been organized in Saintonge, their conroi was split into four squads, each led by a FitzPons brother.

In anticipation of the channel crossing, each of the large horse transports held a score of knights, their horses and squires. The conrois had been reorganized into groups to match the capacity of the ships. The English knew the Normans were coming and had manned the coast all summer waiting for their arrival. William expected resistance upon their disembarking and the duke wanted to go ashore in organized fighting units ready for battle.

As Gauthier and Osborne discussed who would substitute for their brothers as squad leaders, Richard and Drogo arrived at a gallop and reined in their horses. The drills started with basic riding, changing speeds from a trot to a canter, then to a full gallop, while keeping the formation intact. They practiced charging at full speed, with random changes in direction, also to test their ability to keep the shape of the conroi. Lastly they practiced the feigned retreat, and ensured the first squads had enough space to turn and withdraw between the advancing squads.

The knights practiced charging using the traditional method, by first hurling a spear and following up with sword slashes. Then they employed the couched lance attack and impaled targets hanging from posts. The success of this newly developed method depended on the structure of the arched saddles. With high front and rear cantles, the knights were held firmly in place upon impact.

They finished a long day of drills and turned their mounts over to the squires for care. Osborne and Gauthier embraced their older brother. "It is good we are all together again!" said Osborne. "We are getting our touch back."

"All that carpentry grew your muscles, Gauthier. Your forearms, they look . . . um, bigger!" Richard said as he slapped him on the back. "Ozzie, are you going to join the heavy infantry after all your rambling up and down the hills of Normandy?"

"And Drogo, you always seem to be in health, even when you take a scribe's job," laughed Richard.

"How many cargo ships did you send me to convert into horse transports? Ten, eleven?" said Drogo. "We know what you were doing in the south, passing on work to others." He laughed.

"We are awarded a night at the tavern every ten days. Richard, after that practice, do you have the vigor to join us at the Broken Sword?" Osborne said.

"Brother, that is where the Norman chevaliers gather," said Lambert. "They look down on us. I would not go there if you want a relaxing evening."

As expected, the FitzPons brothers could not convince any of their conroi brothers to venture with them to the Broken Sword.

There were military rules strongly enforced by William's marshals. The soldiers were not allowed weapons while on leave in the city. The quartering of thousands of soldiers required for the invasion was taking a toll on the local resources. The duke strictly enforced a ban on harassing the civilians, stealing, or foraging provisions, activities which were common when large numbers of armed men gathered.

The tavern was crowded and the FitzPons brothers reveled in discussing their recent duties, their expectations of fighting in England, winning battles, becoming landowners, and marrying princesses. Richard invited a couple of Norman knights, both cleanshaven with tonsures, to join them at their table. They had an enlivening discussion on cavalry tactics and showed great interest to hear that Drogo had fought alongside the Normans in Sicily. After a few hours most of the clients of the tavern, including the FitzPons brothers, had consumed much ale.

A drunken soldier seemed to suddenly notice them and pointed to their table. He shouted, "We have spies in our midst! Look at their long hair. They resemble Angles . . . or Saxons . . . or English."

"Don't pay any attention to him," said Iacobus, one of their Norman tablemates. "He is always causing trouble."

They followed his advice and continued their conversation, but the Norman soldier walked up to their table and rattled it, spilling their drinks, and yelled, "You are not men, you are not Normans, to ignore my challenge!"

"What challenge?" said Drogo.

"I called you English!"

"Doesn't sound like a challenge to me."

The Norman said, "You don't understand, you see—no, no, you are jesting with me, and I don't like it."

"You want a fight! You'll have a fight!" laughed Gauthier. He stood and pulled Osborne to his feet, who swayed back and forth. Gauthier pushed Osborne ahead and said, "Ozzie will show you a trick or two!"

As the Norman knight threw a roundhouse cuff, Osborne, who was losing his balance any way, stumbled back, and the punch missed. Gauthier caught his brother and pushed him toward the Norman, who swung again. Gauthier, enlightened by the first happenstance, pulled his brother out of the way, and the Norman missed his target a second time. There were many spectators now and most were having a good laugh, except the one who started the fight.

He stepped closer to Osborne, who, now more aware, smiled

and played it like a game. He managed to duck the next punch and rolled across the floor, then stood behind his aggressor. He tapped the man on the shoulder which made him more enraged, and he swung his arm back. Osborne dropped and ducked the backhand, then circled him and jumped up behind the Norman again. Nearby patrons doubled over and cried with laughter.

Frustrated, the knight moved as if to attack Drogo, the other long-haired "Englishman." Richard, Osborne, and Gauthier all converged on the man, but Iocabus stood and stepped between them. He was a head taller than the other men and calmed the situation. Drogo bought the instigator an ale. "Lambert was right, we did not have a relaxing evening, but it was entertaining none the less!" said Richard.

CHAPTER FOUR

By the first week of August 1066, almost 700 vessels were ready to cross the English Channel. Duke William ordered that the ships be assembled at the large estuary at the mouth of the Dives River, east of Caen. Three thousand warhorses and ten thousand men bivouacked along the estuary and waited for his command to embark for England. But the northeasterlies prevailed, and until the winds were abaft the beams of the fleet, they could not sail. Of the ten thousand men, about eight thousand were milites: archers, foot soldiers, and knights who would fight in the battle. The rest were squires, oarsmen, helmsmen, smiths, carpenters, monks, cooks, servants, and others needed to support the army.

William directed his officers to keep the troops engaged by performing daily calisthenics, drills, and training. Monks were dispersed throughout the army to lead prayers. Priests were brought from Caen to offer communion. He also ensured they were well fed and received their rations of ale and wine. He even supplied entertainment, utilizing several trouveres, his own personal minstrels, Ivo Taillefer and Pont de Dinan, and others who had enlisted.

The army had been encamped for two weeks at the foot of a hillside, an immense sand dune covered with vegetation and located at the mouth of the River Dives. It was the last week of August and the wind blew from the northeast for yet another day.

After hours of training maneuvers on their steeds, the FitzPons conroi gathered with scores of other knights for dinner. They sat outside the small church in the town Notre Dame of Dives-Sur-Mur, at tables improvised from wooden planks. They shared food and drink while Ivo Taillefer, Duke William's prime minstrel, recited the Song of Roland. He was accompanied by a musician playing a vielle, an instrument which the performer held on one arm and with the other would pluck or slide a bow along its five strings. The ballad described a ninth century epic about King Charlemagne, who had been ambushed in the mountains as he retreated from Spain into France. His lead knight Roland had fought heroically, and with his knights had led a fatal rearguard battle against the Muslims, ensuring the king's escape. Taillefer finished his poetic song and received generous applause. The soldiers had no problem following the story because it was sung in the vernacular, being secular music, and was not chanted in Latin like the religious songs of the monks. The local patois was the northern dialect of French, referred to as *Langue du Oil*. When Taillefer completed his song, he repeated the war cry of Roland that had been part of the ballad. "*Montjoie!*" Many of the knights responded with, "*Montjoie Saint Denis!*"

Enjoying the fare with the FitzPons brothers was Pont de Dinan, who they had met briefly in Barfleur months earlier. Richard addressed the trouvere. "My brothers and I were interested in your name, is it Pons or Pont? Our father's name was Pons, and he said it was a family appellation he inherited."

"I am also named after an ancestor, here it is written." From under his shirt, Pont drew a chain hanging from his neck. An amulet was attached to the end. He showed it to Richard. Etched into the bronze in Latin was: "This diploma civitatis confers Roman citizenship to the holder and the descendants of Marcus Pontius Laelianus, a Roman senator and tribune of the Legio VI Victrix." Pont said, "See, P-o-n-t-i-u-s—Pont. It is the only word I can read."

"This must be an ancient Roman artifact," said Richard. "Where did you get it?"

"During my father's time, Vikings still raided Brittany.

Pagan warriors had desecrated our ancestors' cemetery and stolen relics. A Viking robbed one of our ancestors' graves and rifled the talisman. Father slew the robber, retrieved the family keepsake, and passed it to me. A monk translated the inscription for my father and he taught it to me. He was also a trouvere, no, more accurately he was a jongleur."

"I read and write Latin," stated Richard, "and my family's name is also spelled P-o-n-t-i-u-s."

"My forebears are from Brittany," added Pont. "Their ancestors traveled across the sea from Wales—the only part of the island not conquered by the Saxons. It is still free and consists of small kingdoms." He paused in thought. "I feel drawn to Wales. I will go there as soon as we finish our battles with the English. But people don't have family names now except a few nobles. How can we have the same name?"

Richard answered, "The declaration on your talisman states that Pontius was a Roman. He could have been from many places, Italy, France, or Britain. Long ago, the Romans governed the world."

"Yes, I understand. Then we are distant cousins!"

Richard nodded, then asked, "You said the word jongleur— your father juggles, is he an acrobat?"

"He passed away. But, yes, he juggled and did tricks. He also recited poetry and sang. He was a complete entertainer!"

"And you said Taillefer was a minstrel, as are you?"

"It is only a matter of words—and employment," said Pont. "A jongleur travels from town to town performing an array of entertainment. The trouvere's specialty is lyric poems and songs. When a trouvere becomes a permanent employee in court, as Ivo and I now work for Duke William, we are considered minstrels, royal minstrels," he said. "I must go now. It is my turn to perform. I will sing the tale of King Arthur."

Pont tugged at the strings of the vielle, finding a meter suitable for his song.

"Long ago Gildas the Wise, wrote of our ancestors' plight.
Then Arthur, against them he led the British kings to fight.
Saxons increased their numbers and raised a mighty horde
Four hundred and ninety years after the passion of our Lord.
Arthur with the power of Christ, twelve battles he did wage
The final struggle was at Baden Hill, penned by Gildas our sage.
Our hero slew 960 pagans, Saxon warriors of faithless nations
Freed were the Bretons after Baden, for many generations."

Pont sang more couplets of the legend that told of Arthur's background and details of the twelve battles he had fought against the pagans. He ended by singing the opening stanza once more. Both the tale of Arthur and the Song of Roland had military themes, and the knights clearly identified with them. Pont returned to sit with the FitzPons brothers, and four commanders joined the gathering. The men easily recognized Count de Eu, who led the knights of the Franco-Flemish wing.

"Being a royal minstrel," said Pont, "I have learned the background of some of the commanders. The tallest noble, other than William, is FitzOzbern, who leads the infantry in the Breton wing. He is a cousin of Duke William and was his ducal regent after the death of William's father." Pont continued, "Next to him is Robbe de Beaumont. A Norman, he commands the Breton cavalry and is also a cousin of the duke. You may have seen the fourth officer, who is standing next to Count de Eu. He is Eustace, Count of Boulogne, who is the commander of your wing, the Franco-Flemish division, with over 2,000 milites. Also, he is a fierce adversary of Harold Godwinson, the false King of England. For that reason and his generous donation of merchant ships to the invasion, he has been given this important command. His family owns many ships and has become wealthy shipping wool from England to Flanders." Pont then whispered, "Even with these qualifications, William does not completely trust him. I heard that one of Eustace's sons is a hostage in Normandy until Eustace proves his loyalty."

"Speaking of Harold, there is a rumor that he was . . . well, a *guest* of Duke William during our war with the Bretons months ago," said Drogo. "He allegedly swore upon holy relics to give his allegiance to William and professed that the duke should inherit the English crown. It sounds like puffery—how can that be true?"

Pont said, "I believe it, although I was not there. At that time, I was in Dinan with my former master, Conan. But Ivo told me that before King Edward died, Harold had traveled to Normandy intending to recover his nephew, who was a hostage. Instead, he shipwrecked on the shores of County Ponthieu and was then ransomed to William. And before releasing him, the duke took advantage to make him swear that William was the rightful heir to the crown of England."

"Ozzie, you seem disgusted with all this gabble of names and titles," said Drogo.

"Yes, it's making my head spin," his brother answered. "The talk of rivers, towns, and geography. Now that is interesting."

Their conversation was interrupted when Count Eustace stood atop a table to gain the soldiers' attention. The men quieted. "Knights, soldiers, we are ready! God has delayed the southerly winds, so we have had time to organize and train to seize what is rightfully our duke's kingdom!"

A host of the knights bellowed, "*Saint Denis mon joie!*"

"Yes, *Montjoie*! Saint Denis is my hope!" shouted Eustace.

The count continued, "This place is a fitting location to disembark for the invasion. Almost ten years ago, a few miles upriver, Duke William decisively thrashed the French led by King Henry. Lord FitzOzbern fought at that battle." Eustace gestured to FitzOzbern to take his place.

"It was the year 1057," began FitzOzbern. "King Henry joined his forces with those of Geoffrey Martel the Hammer, Count of Anjou. They invaded Normandy and our duke was outnumbered. He retreated to find an advantageous position. As Henry's army followed, his men pillaged the countryside and towns. Henry's troops became burdened with plunder, and Duke William took advantage to outdistance them, planning an ambush at the river ford. The duke kept the crossing under surveillance as his men lay in wait within a forested area nearby. William allowed the vanguard of the French army to cross, and knowing the tides, waited. About half of the enemy army had forded the estuary when the flood tide came in and split their forces in two. The Normans attacked from the rear and sides, defeating and scattering the enemy. Many of the French soldiers drowned in the waters of the incoming tide, but King Henry escaped. Since then, France has not threatened Normandy."

There were cheers of approval from the men as Robbe de Beaumont raised his arms and shouted the Normans' battle cry, "*Dieux aide*! God aid us!"

The men roared, "*DIEUX AIDE! DIEUX AIDE!*"

The songs and tales of battles had spirited the soldiers and Eustace seized the opportunity to announce a great plan for the next day. "Tomorrow our entire army will assemble in our battle formation with the Franco-Flemish division on the right wing. We will marshal in the customary way, with the infantry in the front lines. Next will be the archers who will be mobile enough to move in front of the foot soldiers to shoot, then retreat behind them, or to move to the flanks. The conrois of mounted knights will be in the rear. The center division comprised of the Normans will be led by Duke William and his brothers, Bishop Odo and Robert. The infantry, knights, and chevaliers from Breton and Maine make up the left wing commanded by the Count of Rennes Alan Rufus. All three divisions will have their own infantry, archers, and cavalry." He paused. "As many of you have heard, Harold Godwinson, the false king of England, swore upon holy relics that our duke was the rightful heir. Bishop Odo was a witness. Harold has broken his word, a holy promise, and that is one reason the Pope has blessed William's right to England. The Pope further declares that any man who perishes in our sacred crusade will be absolved of all sins!"

The three divisions of the army assembled the next day and practiced maneuvers for several hours. Afterwards the conroi leaders and officers of the archers and infantry met with their men. The officers explained that the men would meet after the midday meal near the mouth of the River Dives. There they would be notified on which ship they would embark when the fleet sailed.

Richard was still at his officers' meeting with the other conroi captains. Waiting for the rest of their conroi to assemble, Osborne and Gauthier stood on the sandy riverbank studying the ships. Many were beached, but the larger vessels were anchored near the middle of the estuary. The tide was in flood stage and the crews of three longships, each with thirty men, were rowing the vessels upstream. "I wonder which ship will take us across the channel?" asked Osborne.

"I hope it's one of those big horse transports," said Drogo as he joined them. Their comrades from Le Mans also arrived as did the French knights in their troop. "I wonder where Richard is?" He counted: "There are nineteen of us. We are all here, except Richard."

Gauthier slapped Lambert on the back. "Are you glad to be in the FitzPons conroi? Your countrymen, all the other knights from Maine, are in the Breton wing."

"I want to be here. You and your brothers are good fighters and . . . amusing to be around," laughed Lambert. He pointed at the three longships being rowed upriver. "Those ships just came in from the sea. Probably to spy on the English. They aren't waiting for the south wind."

"Most of our ships move under sail," said Drogo. "The holds will be filled with the horses, knights, and supplies to be ferried across the channel. There won't be enough room for oars and rowing crews. Those boats that went upstream were a few of the escort ships that will protect the fleet if we encounter the English navy during our crossing. Our fleet includes over six hundred other transport ships. Many are merchant vessels bought for the invasion and they only have a pair of oars to maneuver in the harbors. I worked at the shipyard. The horse transports, which were made in the same design as those used in Sicily, took longer to build than we expected, so we only had time to build twenty of them. They are fitted with offloading ramps at the bow. We also added the ramps to fifty merchant cogs, and they can only move under sail. The rest of the army will cross on the smaller longships."

Lambert pointed to an anchored vessel. "That ship is twice

the length of most of the longships and it has a full set of oars. The figurehead at the bow is a lion's head, instead of a dragon. It must be the duke's flagship."

"That's the *Mora*," said Drogo. The large ship was built in the design of the Viking long ships, with symmetrical ends. Those traditional longships had a carved dragon head at the prow and a coiled tail sculpted into the stern end. This prestigious ship, however, had a gilt carving of a child at the stern. With its left hand, the figure was holding an ivory trumpet to its mouth, and with its right hand was pointing forward. Instead of a dragon, the prow was shaped into a lion's head, the same image as on the banner of the Duchy of Normandy. The ship's rectangular sail was multicolored, and the pennant which had been consecrated by the Pope and given to William flew from the mast.

"The flagship has a long steerboard; it must be hard to guide," said Lambert. "And is there a reason all the ships have the steerboard on the right side?" Before anyone replied, Lambert answered his own question. "Yes! Because helmsmen use their strong hand, their right hand, to steer!

"Well, well, Richard has arrived!" said Drogo.

"We were admiring the ships Gauthier helped build and you inspected," laughed Osborne. "Tell us we'll sail on one of the big ones."

"Um, no." Richard pointed to a row of almost identical longships beached a few hundred paces down the river and started toward the vessels. Scattered among the ships on the beach and afloat were hundreds of small punts for ferrying men and supplies to the anchored vessels. They would also be used for the landing in England. As the men followed him along the shore, he said, "Our scout ships just returned from across the channel. Harold's peasant army, the fyrd, has finished their two months of required service, but they are still camped along the coast watching for our arrival. The English fleet is waiting at the Isle of Wight to intercept us. They know we are coming, so the duke wants us armed and ready when we land. The Norman knights will cross on the large horse transports with ramps, so they can swiftly disembark with their mounts. Each horse transport carries a twenty-man conroi, their steeds, and squires. They will be the vanguard." They arrived at the line of identical longships. "The next five ships in the line will transport our conroi." Other knights had convened in the area and were also examining the ships.

The longships were modeled after the ancient Viking longboats, with a single mast and a square sail. But unlike the Viking ships that had twenty pairs of oars, these boats had one pair of oars to navigate in a harbor. Also, because the ships were built hastily, the ends were not adorned with dragonhead figureheads and the sterns were without the ornamental tails. On one side of the hull, a section of the top planks had been removed and placed as a ramp for the horses. Hemp rope lined slots in the hull to provide a seal when the planks were re-inserted. Wattle enclosures were installed between the bulwark to provide four horse stalls in each ship.

"These ships are fifty pieds long, if I remember," said Drogo. "They will each carry four knights, our horses, weapons. So as you pointed out, it will take five ships to carry our conroi," said Drogo, "and with us being poor chevaliers, one squire for the four of us?"

Richard nodded. "Also, we must take food to last three days for the men and horses. The FitzPons brothers will sail on separate ships. Each of you is capable to lead the conroi in the event my ship doesn't make it."

The morning of September 12, 1066, was a Tuesday, and the soldiers of the Norman army at Dives awoke thinking of breakfast. The sun had just risen. It was the first hour and Bishop Odo rushed after William as he hurried down the river shore. The duke's guards readied a punt to row their leader to the flagship anchored in the middle of the estuary. "William! I know we must act quickly, but let the men eat and then afterwards we should have Communion to bless our departure."

William gazed up at the papal banner flying from his flagship and pointed. The wind was blowing north. "God is giving us a holy sign! Communion will take too long. I see the campfires are kindled. The men are eating now." He paused as he studied the incoming tide. "Spread the word that we will board the ships at the end of the second hour. As I ordered, when the gjallarhorn is sounded from the *Mora*, everyone will report to their ship."

Odo returned to William's headquarters and directed the servants to pack with haste. Pont de Dinan was returning to his tent, which he shared with Ivo Taillefer. It was located near the duke's marquee. Odo was barking out commands. "What is the commotion, Your Excellency?"

"The Lord has provided us with a holy wind. The yelling horns are about to sound to summon us to the ships!"

"St. Deiniol has answered our prayers!" said Pont.

"What?"

"I came from the Breton camp," answered Pont. "The priests held Communion for Saint Deiniol's feast day—today, September 12. Saint Deiniol was martyred centuries ago in Wales. He founded a monastery and helped the poor. The Bretons continued to revere him when they migrated to Brittany. A village a few miles from Dinan is named after him. Oh . . . forgive me, Your Excellency, you know all of this, you are the bishop and know all the feast days of the Church." There was a brief and awkward silence. "I am elated, Bishop—*Montjoie Saint Deiniol*! We must prepare for the crusade!" Pont hurriedly entered his tent.

Odo sent squires to the officers to spread the word of the departure—and to report that it was the feast day of Saint Deiniol and that God had sent this holy spirit to guide the army across the channel.

Little more than an hour later, the blasts from the gjallarhorns echoed off the hill, calling the men to the ships. It was not complete flood tide yet and William wanted to launch the fleet as the current ebbed and the wind was favorable. Horse transports had been beached. The bow ramps were lowered like drawbridges, and the squires led the warhorses into the holds. One after another the large ships were cast into the river with the aid of the rising tide.

The *Mora* was rowed to sea and was escorted by a score of longships whose crews included crossbowmen. Aboard and commanding the flagship was Captain FitzStephen who aligned the sixteen-point bearing rose incised on a horizon board. He had lined up the sun with pegs on the board that morning, as he had done every day at sunrise and sunset, expecting the wind might shift. Now over two hours after sunrise, he would have to wait until noon to recheck true north. In the interim, he knew enough of the channel currents, waves, and winds to keep the fleet on course on the NNE route chosen to England. When they arrived on the English coast, his familiarity with landmarks would tell him whether they should sail east or west to reach their goal, Pevensey Bay.

With the strong southwesterly winds behind them, the pilots steered their ships NNE, following the *Mora*. At noon the flagship's captain checked their direction with the horizon board and made minor adjustments to their heading. Otherwise, the voyage was going as planned. Three hours later Captain FitzStephen reported to the duke that they were about a quarter of the way across the channel and if they maintained the same speed, they would arrive at Pevensey in about nine hours.

Within an hour conditions began to change. The wind increased in velocity and shifted direction. The westerly wind blew the ships off course to the east as a storm overtook them. Captain FitzStephen knew the west wind would drive them toward the coast of Normandy which angled to the northeast. The *Mora* was the fastest ship, and with the fierce wind it quickly outpaced the fleet. The captain found a sheltered bay at Saint Valery Sur Somme, up the coast from Normandy in County Ponthieu. When his escort longships arrived next, William ordered them to row along the shoreline to find any scattered vessels and guide the rest of the fleet to the bay. Several ships crashed on the coast south of Saint Valery, drowning many crew members and troops. Of the fortunate soldiers who made it to shore, numerous deserted.

Gauthier, still drenching wet from the storm, was relieved as their helmsmen guided their longship into the huge estuary at the mouth of the River Somme. It was nearing dusk and he could see a few lights on shore in the town of Saint Valery. He was not cold, having warmed from his exertion bailing water for hours. Now he manned one of the two oars to guide the ship into the bay, assisted by the flood tide. Hundreds of ships had made it to port before them and had either anchored or beached along the river. *Where are my brothers?* He did not realize the helmsman had steered to the shore and he was startled by the jarring stop when they hit the beach. The squire held the horses' reins as they tried to leap over the sides of the boat. The helmsman shouted, "Hurry, put the ramp down and get the mounts ashore!" The crew helped the steeds off the boat, then the squire led them to the adjacent fields lush with grass. Gauthier made a campfire to dry their clothes and ward off the chill of the night air. His boatmates soon fell asleep, and although exhausted, he lay awake for a time, anxious about his brothers.. He finally joined them only after he convinced himself at first light he would find them in good health.

The next morning just after sunrise, the Count Guy of Ponthieu arrived from his nearby castle at Beaurain, leading his servants who were pushing carts laden with food. He was looking for his brother Hugh, a knight in the invasion fleet. Gauthier walked along the sandy shore and stopped at a Ponthievin cart to get something to eat. A man attended a fire with meat cooking on a spit. The servant handed him a piece of meat. He took a bite. "This mutton," said Gauthier, "has a different taste. It's salty."

The attendant gestured toward the meadows, where sheep were grazing with the expedition's warhorses. "The mutton is from those sheep. The tides are frequently changing the river's course, and then grass springs up in those meadows. The soil is very salty," the attendant said.

After some ale, Gauthier went on and soon came to a beached ship. A helmet with a green plume had been strapped onto the prow. He did not see anyone aboard. "Ozzie! Where are you?"

Osborne peeked over the edge of the ship's hull and laughed, then he jumped to the beach. He pounded his brother on the back and yelled, "You made it! And look!" He pointed across the estuary. Gauthier saw a teardrop shaped shield hanging on the side of a longship, embellished with the red and yellow diagonal stripes of Pons. "That is either Richard or Drogo's ship."

They heard a shout. Lambert was running toward them,

barefoot, kicking up sand. "He's smiling," said Gauthier. "I hope it means good news."

Lambert, talking between breaths, said, "My boat is beached near Drogo's. He went upriver looking for you, while I searched downstream."

"Richard's boat is on the other side of the harbor," said Osborne, "and we lost our punt in the storm." He looked at Lambert and then Gauthier. "Do either of you still have one?"

Lambert nodded as Gauthier shook his head.

"Let's get Drogo and we'll row over to find Richard."

The invasion force was shattered both physically and emotionally. Although the sailors were experienced and had dealt with what they considered a middling storm, most of the soldiers had never been at sea. Many of them had not recovered and were still shaken from their terrifying ordeal. In addition, it had been difficult to handle the horses and keep them from panicking. Men and horses had been injured, and a number drowned when frightened steeds broke out of their wattle enclosures aboard the longships. Scores of ships and their crews were missing, including the commander of the Franco-Flemish knights, Count de Eu. The next few days were full of gloom. It was general knowledge that the time was already past the sailing season. Unfavorable winds again gusted from the north. Rumors spread that William had kept secret the number of dead and had covertly buried them. The leaders denied there had been desertions and instead reported those who were missing had been injured and could not remain with the army. Many knights and soldiers openly voiced their opinion that the invasion would never happen.

William's actions over the next several days showed he was determined to continue. He sent an appeal for aid to his father-in-law, Count Baldwin, in nearby Flanders. Only a few miles north of Ponthieu, the count quickly responded and brought supplies and food for the army. In addition, several days after the storm, most of the missing ships sailed into the estuary to rejoin the fleet. To find safety from the storm, Count de Eu had led his ships into Treport, only ten miles south, which was in his domain of County

Eu. He had resupplied his ships and brought extra foodstuffs. The army, now well fed, was kept busy repairing ships and moving their vessels to reunite with their battle units and conrois. After the army was re-equipped, William continued to keep the troops occupied, ordering them to return to training.

For the next two weeks, William and his brothers prayed each day at the abbey of Saint Valery for God to deliver southerly winds. Their pleas were not answered. The duke believed in the power of prayer, so to gain the collective petitions of thousands, he led a solemn march around the harbor through the men's camps, with the monks of the abbey carrying and displaying the bones of Saint Valery. As William strode in front of the litter which held the saint's bones, he wore the ring the Pope had given him and draped relics around his neck, the same relics upon which Harold had sworn his oath. A staff flying the papal banner was carried by Odo in the procession. Officers and soldiers prayed and made contributions to the abbey, tossing coins on the doorsteps of the church.

The next day, Wednesday, September 27, the wind direction shifted and blew towards the north, convincing William that God had answered their supplications. William gave the order to board the ships. Captain FitzStephen, with a full crew and the *Mora* fitted with twenty pairs of oars, guided the flagship to the mouth of the Somme River to wait for the fleet. An oarsman atop the *Mora's* mast shouted that the last of the 700 ships had left the harbor. William delayed the fleet's crossing to avoid arriving in England while it was still dark. Then two hours after sunset, he ordered the flagship to sail north. Lanterns were hung on the flagship's mast for the fleet to follow. Each crew hung a lantern on their mast and another lantern aft.

The sail bulged northward and Richard's longship picked up speed. It was dark, and the helmsman guided the ship to keep the aft lantern of the preceding ship in sight. Richard, although near the helmsman on the steerboard side, could barely see his face, the aft lantern and the quarter moon providing little light. "You seem relaxed and confident; isn't it more difficult to sail in the night?" asked Richard.

"With the lanterns and a good helmsman like me," he laughed, "our fleet will do fine. And when we are out of sight of land, it is easier to navigate at night than during the day." He pointed at a star diagonally to the right of the bow. "Sailors use the North Star. God has provided us with a bright crescent moon and a clear night to sail."

"So that star is north. Then we are sailing northwest?" said Richard.

"Yes, that's right. Pevensey Bay is exactly northwest of Saint Valery."

"How long will the crossing take?"

The pilot studied the wake churned by the ship's hull as it glittered in the moonlight. "At this speed we will arrive in about twelve hours, a typical time to cross the channel. The duke is clever. Although the tide brought the fleet out at sunset, he had his captain furl his sails. The fleet did the same. This will delay the voyage a few hours, which will avoid reaching the English coast in the dark and we will have the morning light to clearly see the coast."

"Was it William or was it God who delayed?" asked Richard. "Perhaps it was Saint Valery?"

The helmsman did not comment.

Richard added, "Or was it Neptune?"

"Well, it was G . . . umphh! It is too dark to see if you are smiling, but I am going to assume you are jesting, Sir Richard.

"I am a Flemish pilot like my father and his father. They told me of the Roman god of the sea. You are an educated knight, unlike many that I have met who are simply mercenaries and fighters. You are a Christian, so I am thinking you have an inquisitive mind and that is why you are talking in this manner."

"Do the ancient Flemish mariners have a sea deity?" asked Richard.

The helmsman looked about to determine if anyone could hear them, as if he was afraid to continue the discussion. In a hushed tone he said, "Yes, the Celtic sailors, whether they are Irish, Welsh, Breton, or Flemish, still suspect Lir, the god of the sea, is nearby. Most sailors I know are Christian, as I am, but we are a superstitious lot and hold onto ancient thoughts."

"Do the Norman pilots have superstitions?"

"No, but they have not retained their ancestors' love and knowledge of the sea. Their ancestors, the Vikings from Daneland, are still pagans and worship their own god of the sea, Aeger."

The helmsman looked up at the mast and said, "The mast lantern blew out. Go forward and be certain the crew knows to relight it." At sea, the helmsman was in charge so Richard did not hesitate to follow his orders.

The wind remained steady through the night and within several hours most of the flotilla arrived in sight of the coast, a few miles west of their goal. Captain FitzStephen recognized landmarks on the coast and led the fleet to anchor off Pevensey Bay. It was the third hour and flood tide would begin in two hours.

CHAPTER FIVE

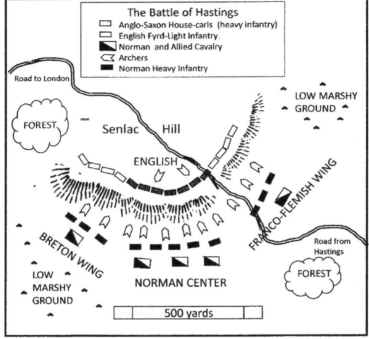

CHAPTER FIVE

Richard leaned on the upper wale of the ship and watched a score of longships being rowed into Pevensey Bay, England. It was the fourth hour of September 28, 1066, the tide was rising and would be at full at noon. A gentle breeze did not create any problems with their anchorage. The entire fleet had been in position for an hour outside the bay. Clustered around Richard's vessel were the four other ships of his conroi. Richard had raised his conroi's red and yellow gonfalon which helped his brothers and Lambert to guide their ships to anchor nearby.

Before leaving Saint Valery, William had given orders to his division commanders that the first soldiers would go ashore organized and ready to fight. The ships rowing now into the bay were his escort vessels, full of crossbowmen ready to cover the disembarkation. Not a soul was visible on the beach. Richard climbed up the mast and sat on the cross piece, the yard, for a better look. He recalled a story an old sailor working in the shipyard had told him. The veteran seaman had said the ancient Vikings would hang a cage of crows on the mast and release one when they were lost in the fog. The crow would always fly toward land, which directed them where to sail. As Richard watched the first ships beach on the sand, he heard a shout. Osborne waved from his perch on his ship's yard. His brothers had also climbed their ship's mast and were observing the archers jump ashore and spread out, anticipating resistance from the fyrd, the English farmer-militia organized in times of war.

Richard could see there was no opposition to the first landing. The oars of the *Mira* began churning and the yelling horn was sounded once. The horse transports carrying the Norman knights were rowed into the bay. The ships picked up speed, the transports hit the beach, and the drawbridges were lowered. The horses were led down the ramps by the squires and the knights disembarked fully armored and then mounted their steeds on land. However, from a few of the ships, the knights rode their steeds down the ramps directly onto the beach. Their comrades still at anchor cheered their flamboyant charge. The Norman cavalry surveyed the area and rode into the small port town of Pevensey, deserted except for stray cattle and pigs. The gjallarhorn sounded from the *Mora* three times, which signaled for the rest of the fleet to enter the bay.

Within three hours, the tide would ebb and the oarsmen would not have been able to overcome the tide rushing out to sea. Recognizing this, the helmsmen quickly guided the remaining ships into the large bay to find a place on the wide beach to unload. Men and supplies were transferred by punts from ships at anchor to the shore. The Franco-Flemish knights guided their vessels aground and used their side ramps to bring their horses to shore. The knights were then assigned to guard workers as they dug a moat and raised a mound inside the perimeter of a much larger Roman fortress. Carpenters and engineers assembled sections of wooden walls that had been pre-fabricated in Normandy and transported by ship. The resulting mound and courtyard surrounded by a palisade and ditch, a motte and bailey castle, would house the garrison at the bay. As part of the guard, the FitzPons conroi let their horses graze close by and observed the construction of the walls. Osborne read aloud an inscription in Latin at the gate to the old Roman fort, *"Anderitum Numeri Litoris Saxonici per Britanniam."* He translated, "'Anderitum Cohort, the Saxon Shore of Britain.' I recall in Pont de Dinan's song that King Arthur was one of the last Romans, leading the Britains against the Saxons. The Saxons must have been raiding these shores well before King Arthur's time when the Romans still ruled Britain.

So it means the Cohort of Anderitum built and garrisoned this fort as protection from Saxons. That is ironic! Now, centuries later with our arrival, the fort is being used as a defense against the Saxons' descendants!"

When the Norman fleet had first appeared off the coast, most of the inhabitants had fled the market town of Pevensey. The Norman army camped near the town, and the invaders seized the community's livestock. For the two nights after the landing, the aroma of roasted beef and pork from the spits of hundreds of campfires filled the air.

The third day, after reconnaissance of the area, William decided to move his army east to Hastings. He had already sent a vanguard of Norman knights who had occupied the town by riding inland, then north circling the bays and inlets to reach the village. To cover this distance by foot would take days, so the infantry and supplies were instead ferried across two bays along the coast. The FitzPons knights, as part of the Franco-Flemish wing, guarded the ferrying operations as Duke William and the rest of the knights secured Hastings. Cogs, the merchant ships that had been modified into horse transports, could hold the greatest loads and were used to do most of the transfers. When the army had crossed the bays, the knights of the Franco-Flemish wing turned north to follow the route to Hastings that the Norman cavalry had taken. The *Mora* and several escort vessels then sailed to Hastings and anchored. There was no good harbor at the village, so the rest of the fleet returned to the Pevensey harbor. At Hastings, William constructed a second motte and bailey castle using prefabricated sections of wooden palisades.

The FitzPons brothers led their huge warhorses in a thunderous canter on the road to Hastings. The villages along the route appeared to have been looted. The doors of the houses and buildings were either open or smashed off their hinges. Empty wooden crates and discarded household items were strewn all over the streets. There were no livestock or people in sight, but a few bodies of Englishmen were lying in the streets. The rest of the townsfolk had apparently fled. The Norman army, which had for weeks remained disciplined under the strict orders not to loot while assembled in France, had not waited long to begin harrying, raiding, and pillaging after they reached England.

Richard and his brothers continued eastward along the old Roman road and passed through ravaged villages. Richard soon detected the scent of burning wood. Within a few minutes he saw smoke rising above the treetops, and shortly they entered the village of Ashburnham which was on fire. They made a detour to avoid burning houses.

Richard rode next to Gauthier and said, "What luck. We did not have to fight the English fleet during the crossing nor the army as we came ashore. The few English that were captured said that the fyrd guarding the coast left two weeks ago to harvest their crops. And about the same time the English fleet withdrew to the Thames River and hauled their boats out of the water because the sailing period had ended. The English decided it was too late in the year and presumed the Normans were not coming."

"And the invasion almost did not happen. First the winds did not cooperate, then the storm, and after that hundreds deserted," added Gauthier.

"Yes, William would say the change in winds, the fyrd leaving, and the enemy fleet disappearing were miracles sent by God. The chatter is that King Harold's personal holdings are here in Sussex. Perhaps the duke has encouraged harrying," said Richard. "He wants to enrage Harold and draw the English into battle as soon as possible."

"The commanders had ordered us to bring three days of rations," commented Gauthier, "but it is good we brought enough rations for a week, because the Norman knights have done a thorough job ahead of us. The country has been wasted. Why is the duke moving us to Hastings?"

"That is where William's holy spies live."

"What?" asked Gauthier.

Richard sensed that Osborne knew and let him answer. "The Abbey of Fecamp is near Hastings and the monastery's landholdings surround the town. I learned from camp gossip that William promised the abbot more holdings if he provided guides and knowledge of the region. His monks will be envoys to Harold and I am certain they are also spying for the duke." It was a long day before they finished their journey and united with the rest of the army at the village of Hastings.

Several days later, the FitzPons brothers who were gathered around their fire trying to ward off the chill, were eating biscuits and salted pork. After swallowing some wine, Gauthier muttered, "Are we drinking wine because the duke prefers it?"

"No, I have heard it won't sour as fast as the ales," answered Drogo. "That may be why they brought along barrels of wine."

"I heard they don't drink much wine in England. So when it runs out, I hope to return to ale," said Gauthier.

"If the ales are like those made in France, you better hope it is brewed by monks," said Drogo. "I have spit out many an ale made at the taverns."

Lambert arrived in a dither and blurted, "There was a great battle in the north! Thousands were slaughtered! A monk arrived last night from London and reported that the King of Norway, Harald Hardrada, invaded with a huge army. He was defeated by the English, and now, Harold Godwinson, emboldened with victory after beating the Vikings, is on his way south with a large army."

"I have no doubt the English are on their way," said Gauthier. "Who is this monk telling us of a great battle? It sounds like garbage. Is he a spy from Harold trying to dishearten us and show their superiority in war?"

"No," Lambert said, "he was sent by the duke's cousin, Robert FitzWimark. He was the steward of the late King Edward, also William's cousin."

"That is why our duke is the legitimate king," said Richard.

"King Edward grew up in Normandy where he was in exile," added Osborne. "His steward, FitzWimark, was born in Normandy."

"Good, Ozzie! I thought you only liked maps and memorized the names of all the French counties!" said Drogo. "But royals, even when they are related, are not angels. They undermine, fight, and kill each other."

Gauthier asked Lambert, "What else did the monk say?"

"The monk also said FitzWimark recommended that we stay in Hastings within our fortifications."

"Hmm," mumbled Gauthier. "If he told us to go back to France, I would then think he was our enemy, but . . ."

"No matter, William sent the monk back with the message that he wanted to give battle to Harold as soon as possible," added Lambert.

He had barely finished the sentence when the yelling horns sounded. It was a call to arms and muster. Richard looked at Osborne. "Account for all the men in our conroi and have them ready when I return. I am going to the officers' tent to find out what the signal means."

Richard hurried away, but he returned within minutes, just as the sun was setting. "Put out the campfires and have your weapons ready. And your blankets. It may be a long night. The army is to stay at the ready. We received information that Harold is camped less than ten miles north of us and there could be a night attack. Wear your armor. We will take turns sleeping."

Drogo asked, "Hear anything else about the English army?"

"Yes, William is surprised they arrived this soon. His scouts had reported they were miles away in London just a few days ago, but apparently they traveled by horseback."

"The whole army? They have that much cavalry?"

"I was told their steeds are but ponies compared to our warhorses. If they want cavalry battle, we'll give them a good one!"

After an uneventful night, the Norman army broke camp, and at first light on the morning of October 14, 1066, marched north. William's scouts had reported the English army was camped on Senlac Hill, seven miles away. After a three-hour march, the Normans could see the English army gathered on the ridge, blocking the road. Several banners with a white dragon on a red field flew above the English army. The center ranks of the English line were King Harold's housecarls, his bodyguards, numbering two thousand heavily armored professional soldiers. Among them was the king, armed like his guards. His personal banner flew above them, depicting a housecarl with a round shield and long battle-axe. The image was popularly called "The Fighting Man." On each wing were soldiers of the fyrd, lightly armored, but most with shields and spears. King Harold had chosen the site well. The ridge was flanked by low marshy land on the east and forest on the west. Although the approach to the ridge was a large meadow, the surrounding marshy area and slope were not an ideal place for the Norman cavalry to maneuver.

Four hundred paces from the ridge, the Breton division turned from the road and marched to form the left wing of the Norman army. The Norman division took up the center, and the Franco-Flemish troops formed the right wing. The archers, armed with either short bows or crossbows, stood in the front lines, behind them was the heavy infantry arranged into companies, and the third line of troops was the mounted knights grouped in their conrois of twenty. Together the three Norman divisions formed a crescent to oppose the English army which was arrayed in an unbroken semicircular line.

The Norman supply train arrived last. The squires brought the spare war horses, carts of food, extra arrows, cross bolts, and weapons. Monks from Fecamp Abbey arrived to give last rites and to provide medical treatment. A camp of tents was set up to treat the wounded and store the supplies. Lastly, there trickled in the hardiest of camp followers.

On the left wing of the Norman army, the Bretons displayed their banner, which had a white field peppered with ermine spots. William brought the Papal banner, a green cross on a white field. Numerous red banners with the image of two gold lions, representing the Duchy of Normandy, flew over the center division. On the right wing the Flemish banners, yellow with a black lion, were prominent along with the pennants of various French counties. Like each leader of the cavalry conrois, Richard displayed a gonfalon on his lance for his men to follow him. The bright pennant was painted with diagonal yellow and red stripes representing Barony Pons.

Richard looked over the meadow, recognizing the familiar smell of horses in pasture. Not unpleasant now, he knew it would soon be a bloody battlefield and the horses' scent would be overwhelmed as the battle progressed. Horse dung, grass, mud, and blood would be churned into a mire. The odor of unwashed men was usual, but he sensed that it was altered, carrying the scent of fear. He caught his brother's eye.

"It appears the English are all foot soldiers, in the tradition of Anglo-Saxon warriors, I assume," said Gauthier. "They rode here. Where are all their horses?"

"Perhaps William is also wondering that and expects them to use their cavalry to outflank us. See, our conrois on both of the flanks are spreading out," said Richard. "Look ahead!"

Ivo Taillefer, William's personal minstrel, was riding alone toward the English as he trolled the *Song of Roland*. The Normans cheered as he charged toward the enemy lines with couched lance. Fifty paces before he reached the enemy lines, he turned his steed and raced alongside their front lines, repeatedly tossing up his sword and catching it as the enemy soldiers jeered. A few arrows whizzed by as he sped along the English army and juggled his sword. When Taillefer reached the end of the formation and returned for a second pass, an English housecarl stepped out from the battle line to confront him, but the minstrel with his lance, firmly tucked under his arm, impaled him before the warrior could get within range. Taillefer dispatched two more challengers one at a time. Then one arrow and another penetrated his armor, he faltered, and then was surrounded, pulled down, and killed.

Richard shook his head, "Why?"

"What a squander of life!" said Gauthier. "But his dash revealed the English are wanting in archers."

The gjallarhorn sounded and almost a thousand Norman and mercenary archers advanced toward the English lines. They had no armor, but they were mobile. It was unlikely the English would attack, since they would be giving up their higher ground, but the archers could easily outrun them. As a precaution, however, William had the infantry move forward, but outside of the range of the few English archers, two hundred paces for crossbows and one hundred for the short bows. The English soldiers drew closer together, creating a wall by overlapping their round shields.

The bowmen stopped their forward progress at two hundred paces, within range for their crossbows, but outside the effective distance for their short bows. The crossbowmen let fly several volleys; a cacophony of whizzing bolts and quivering bowstrings filled the air. The barrage finished ending the thudding and splintering of hundreds of arrows impacting wood. The English troops remained firm behind their shield wall, which now bristled with feathered shafts. The officers leading the Norman archers appeared surprised when they discovered that several of their men had been hit. One sounded a yelling horn twice in succession and half the archers ran up the slope as crossbowmen resumed firing into the English shield wall. The archers charged within fifty paces of the enemy. Now with all the archers and crossbowmen shooting, thousands of arrows and cross bolts impacted the adversaries' shields. The English returned fire with a much-reduced salvo of arrows, but the Normans began concentrating their fire on the sources of the enemy missiles. By sheer numbers, the Norman arrows and bolts penetrated crevices or topped the shield wall and soon the meager English counter attack subsided. The Norman archers expended all their arrows and cross bolts, but there were still no discernable gaps in the enemy ranks. The attack did not appear to weaken the English lines. As the archers returned to the rear of the army to resupply their quivers, battle horns sounded among the Norman foot soldiers who then moved forward to attack.

In their heavy armor, the infantry of the three divisions worked their way up the slope. Only a few arrows opposed their approach and did no damage. But ten or twenty paces before reaching the English battle line, the enemy pelted them with a blistering hail of missiles, hurling spears, heavy stones attached to sticks, and throwing axes. The fusillade took a heavy toll on the Norman foot soldiers, weakened their attack, and encouraged the housecarls to break from the shield wall. The fierce, mustached warriors, their long hair flying as they whirled about with their two-handed axes, cut bloody swathes through the attackers' formation. In less time than it took them to march up the hill, the Norman foot soldiers retreated, leaving many of their own dead or dying near the top of the ridge.

The English reformed into their shield wall as the gjallarhorns signaled the Norman knights to advance. The FitzPons conroi was readying to move forward. Richard punched Gauthier in the arm, the sound of metal on metal, and said, "I will see you back here soon, brother."

"I will never get used to the Norman way," said Gauthier. "A mounted charge against a shield wall? This is senseless! William doesn't even follow his own tactics. It is like beating your head on a rock thinking you will break it!"

Richard laughed. "At least it angers you into a fight!" There was a shout a few horses away as the steeds jostled, their blood stirred for the combat for which they were bred.

Osborne stood up in his stirrups above his arched saddle, his green helmet plume noticeable above the other knights. "Let's go! *Montjoie!*"

Beyond him Richard found Drogo's red crest. He locked eyes with Drogo. *That is his combat face.* They traded salutes. Richard hollered to the squires and his men: "Take a pair of throwing spears and leave your lances." He saw his brothers nod. Then he glanced about to make sure his men were looking at him. "Remember your training. Follow me and when your first spear is in flight, close in and stab with your other spear." The squires quickly distributed the weapons, just in time before their conroi moved up the slope.

There were 500 knights in the Franco-Flemish division commanded by the Count de Eu. Richard was one of twenty-five conroi captains in the division, who cooperated with each other on timing their charges and spacing their units to avoid interference from downed men and horses. They all reported to Count de Eu, who rode in the first wave to attack the English battle lines. The FitzPons brothers were in the second wave of cavalry. The knights rode slowly to conserve their mounts' energy climbing the slope, but the scene was impressive. Across the meadow one thousand paces wide, with an added 500 knights from Brittany and three times as many Norman chevaliers riding together, the colorful gonfalons waved in the breeze, representing each conrois from a hundred baronies and counties.

The lead conrois were one hundred paces from the English, the yelling horns sounded twice, and the first wave of the cavalry charged the shield wall. When they were less than fifty paces, the chevaliers hurled spears into the English formation and were met by a storm of enemy projectiles. At twenty paces most of the knights threw their second spear. Richard, still advancing in the second wave, let out a loud "No!" The knights then drew their swords and hacked at the front lines of the enemy. They had to expose their right side to use their swords, but their shields were in their left hands. And while they towered over the English foot soldiers, their own unprotected legs and the hindquarters and legs of their horses were easy targets, especially for the axes of the housecarls. Horses screamed from the vicious work the English housecarls did with their two-handed axes, but they were trained warhorses, and many kicked and even bit their attackers. Others fled, trampling their fallen riders, or fell to expire in a pool of blood. The English were again getting the best of their opponents. Before the horns sounded for the second wave of cavalry, Richard shouted to his men, "Look at the Norman knights! They can't even use their shields! Keep one spear! Remember your . . ." A pair of blasts from the gjallarhorns drowned him out. Richard led his conroi in the charge.

As the second wave moved toward the battle lines, they had to evade the retreat of the battered first wave. Richard saw that the number of missiles thrown by the English were less than the earlier attacks. *Perhaps the English are running short. At least our waves of attacks are spaced close enough to prevent the enemy from retrieving their spears and axes.* Thirty paces from the English, Richard ordered his knights to hurl their spears. He noticed eager housecarls had stepped free of the shield wall, holding bloodied axes, having gained confidence routing the infantry and cavalry in their first assault. Richard's knights had each retained one spear and with the weapon's long reach they lanced the isolated and overconfident housecarls. After reining their horses to the right, they rode with their shield side toward the enemy line. Richard extended his spear to its furthest reach and stabbed over and over at the joints of the shield wall and over the top of the English shields, inflicting casualties along the enemy battle line.

Lambert's spear was hacked to pieces. He pulled back from the attack and drew his sword to return and fight. Suddenly two elite housecarls, skilled in use of the two-handed axes, stepped in front of Richard's hurtling steed. Time seemed to slow down as he realized the pair were working together. One ducked and chopped at the horse's front legs as the other swung his axe at Richard's head. Their round shields were slung across their backs, the long, heavy axes requiring both hands. When Richard's horse reared to avoid the low attack, the axe blade meant for Richard cleaved the animal's neck. As he hit the ground, Richard thrust his stabbing spear into the groin of one of the housecarls. He had pulled his leg from being crushed by his mount, but his knee was twisted, and he could not stand. The second housecarl placed a foot on the steed's fallen body and raised his axe. During the shock of the fall Richard had lost his grip on his shield, but the enarmes had kept it securely fastened to his left arm. He raised his shield, blocked the axe, and felt the ground tremble as blood spattered over the top of his shield. When he lowered it, the housecarl lay dead, his throat cut. Lambert had dismounted and finished off the other housecarl who was trying to extract the spear from his groin. The yelling horns sounded their double call, signaling the next wave of cavalry was coming. Lambert helped Richard into the saddle and sat behind him as they rode to the Norman army at the bottom of the meadow. "Can you walk?" said Lambert. "I barely got you on the horse."

"I'll be all right when I get another horse," answered Richard.

"That won't work—if you become unhorsed, you're done!"

Osborne and Gauthier arrived with the conroi to join their retreat as the third wave of cavalry advanced uphill. Lambert's horse was struggling with the weight of two armored knights, but they were far enough from the battle lines and the men dismounted to walk the rest of the way. Richard stayed mounted as Lambert jumped to the ground. "Don't tell them about my leg."

"Ozzie! Gauthier! But where is Drogo?" asked Richard.

"I'm here with your new horse," shouted Drogo. "God rest his soul who no longer can ride it."

The squires took care of their horses as the FitzPons conroi gulped watered down wine, rested, and counted their losses. Richard couldn't hide the knee injury, but he forced himself to tread with a painful limp. The third wave of knights was still at the battle, and the archers, replenished with ammunition, were forming ranks. "I believe our leaders will order us to go through another round of the same. Archers, infantry, then knights," said Gauthier.

Richard looked to his brothers and Lambert. "Report your losses."

As Lambert dropped his head, Gauthier looked at him and said, "We have lost Leufred and Pippin."

Osborne added, "Bertulf is dead. Grimald somehow made it out alive. He lost most of his right arm, a tourniquet was helping stem the blood, as his comrades rushed him to the camp to cauterize it. No further word on him yet. "

Drogo reported, "We carried Fulk out and he is being cared for in camp, but he cannot fight."

There was a pause. Lambert was in tears. "Lothar is also gone. My brothers from Le Mans, both dead!"

"Lambert, we are going to win this," said Gauthier, "and give your brothers, *our* brothers, a proper burial!"

"You must continue to fight for your brothers—us, your brothers," Osborne said. "You are now the fifth FitzPons. You can't let us down!"

Drogo pounded Lambert on the back, who acknowledged, "Yes, those are good words."

"Our conroi is reduced to fifteen, but we are strong," said Richard.

"YES WE ARE!" said Osborne as he stood up. "*DIEUX AIDE!*"

They all stood and shouted, "YES, WITH GOD's HELP!"

The FitzPons conroi gathered in a circle after bandaging their wounds and replacing lost or damaged weapons. Richard bowed his head. "Lord, give us the strength to finish this battle and spare as many lives as possible. We are all Christians and we accept the duty to amend Harold's broken pledge that he made on the saints' relics. Amen."

The Norman army continued to batter the English shield wall through the morning. A second round of assaults, including another arrow onslaught, an infantry assault, and cavalry charges were carried out. Hundreds more casualties occurred on both sides and the FitzPons conroi lost another man. The English continued to target the Norman horses, and Osborne's steed was axed from under him. As his mount collapsed and fell, he untangled himself from the stirrups, landed on his feet, ran his spear through one soldier of the English fyrd, and drew his sword and put another adversary out of action. As he strained to retreat on foot, he discovered his ankle had been injured, but Gauthier had seen Osborne's green plume tumble and arrived with a stray horse. This second run of attacks on the English finished at the end of the fourth hour.

The knights of the Fitzpons conroi rested between assaults and ate the biscuits the squires provided. Osborne was rotating his ankle and wincing, testing it out by taking steps. "Gauthier, thanks again for getting me off the battlefield."

"Anytime, Ozzie," Gauthier laughed. "I am just keeping my promise to Mother to watch your back. By the way, do you have the money you owe me? And don't worry, it could happen to any knight. I heard Duke William has had three horses cut out from under him today."

"I hope William and his commanders are devising a new strategy," said Richard. "I do give William credit for his eagerness to start the battle. The lack of English archers tells me they rushed here before collecting enough men. It has become a battle of attrition, which we can't win. There are thousands of the fyrd that could arrive at any moment. It's hard to figure how many English soldiers are up there or how many we have killed. When we are at the top of the ridge in the fight, every instant is filled with surviving against spears, axes, missiles—there is no time to look around. But I could tell the English are standing five or six men deep, at least in the center."

"The English are in high spirits. And they should be. We can't break their shield wall and they look down on us and can easily see our losses. William is stubborn. He will continue to attack, just as he has been," added Gauthier.

"The archers and infantry are supposed to create openings in the shield wall, so the cavalry will break through," said Drogo. "It is not working. What about all the hours we trained in the feigned retreat? As I said before, the tactic worked in Sicily. Why doesn't William try it?"

It was after the end of the fifth hour and for a third time the infantry was approaching the top of the ridge to engage the English. The archers were returning to the camp to obtain more arrows. One of them yelled, "Duke William is dead! They said he was crushed under a horse on the last charge!" Repetitions of the man's anxious cry rippled left and right through the army. There was jostling and shouting among the knights. William's half-brother Robert galloped across the front of the army. A minute later, the commander of the left-wing, Count Eustace, spurred his mount the other direction toward the Norman knights assembled in the center. A guttural roll from angry men floated among the soldiers. There was a commotion behind the troops. The camp followers had taken down their tents and were leaving. Monks were packing their carts. A group of archers was trying to steal the reserve horses from the squires.

"There is something amiss. I sense panic rising among the ranks," said Richard. He looked around at his knights. "Our best chance is to stay together."

The groans from the mass of Norman knights to their left changed to cheers. Shouts of "IT'S WILLIAM! THE DUKE IS ALIVE!" flowed through the knights like waves and reached the FitzPons brothers. Duke William, sans helmet, and revealing his monk tonsure and signature moustache, galloped along the troops. The cheers followed William as he rode with his Papal banner. Cheers erupted again as he passed going the other direction, and soon the whole army was shouting *"Saint Denis Montjoie! Dieux aide!"*

Just when the morale of the Norman army appeared to be

restored, there were new cries of anguish. Drogo pointed to the top of the ridge where the infantry was trying again to break the English formation. Instead, the Bretons on the left wing of the infantry were fleeing downhill as a mass of the English fyrd, the peasant militia, chased them. The Norman center was being outflanked and was in danger of having enemy soldiers at their back. Within seconds William could be seen charging up the hill, still without a helmet. Hundreds of Norman knights armed with lances followed him. The English fyrd in pursuit was half way down the hill, far outside their shield wall, and the Norman cavalry smashed into them from the side. Few of the English survived to return to the shield wall, which was still anchored by the disciplined housecarls at the top of the ridge. The shield wall for the first time was noticeably diminished. William returned from his successful charge in high spirits and paused the assaults.

The sun was not overhead, but it was the highest it would attain on the day of October 14. The knights of the FitzPons conroi sat on an old fallen tree eating hard biscuits and drinking weak diluted wine. "The assaults might have worked if we would have staged them in a faster order," said Drogo.

"But the ground is uneven and there is not enough room to maneuver," said Gauthier.

"I agree," said Drogo. "But look what happened when the Breton infantry on the left wing fled and the English broke from their shield wall. The knights slaughtered them! We should start a feigned retreat!"

"That is up to the commanders," said Richard.

Count de Eu rode by slowly on his mount, surveying his troops. Drogo said, "There, Richard, he is your commanding officer, talk to him—convince him to change the tactics!"

"The last time I made recommendations to the count was in Brittany, and we were punished—twice!" answered Richard.

As Count de Eu rode nearby Drogo stood and raised his lance and shouted, "*Saint Denis Montjoie! Dieux aide!*"

The count slowed and responded, "*Dieux aide!* Yes, yes, um, good knight, keep up your faith, we will win!"

Despite Richard's earlier dissuasion, Drogo intercepted the

commander and said, "Count de Eu, the feigned retreat by the Bretons and Duke William's counterattack was inspiring! Will it be our turn next?"

"Your *turn*?" asked the count.

"Yes, we are ready to follow you. God has blessed us with the best leaders. It will be as at Messina!"

With brightened eyes the count said, "You were there with Roger? The feigned retreat that defeated the Arab Saracens?"

Drogo nodded.

Count de Eu smiled. "Roger is my son-in-law, married to my sweet Eremburga!"

The count examined the enemy's left flank on the top of the ridge. Drogo imagined he was envisioning his knights dislodging the English fyrd. He looked over Drogo's shoulder and saw Richard sitting on a log. "Which brother are you? I know the FitzPons brothers furthered the shipbuilding."

Drogo bowed his head. "I am Dreux—Drogo FitzPons, sir."

The count broke into another smile. "My shipyard built sixty ships for the invasion." He slapped Drogo on the shoulder. "You saved me a great deal of money with your ideas."

Count de Eu tightened his grip on his reins and kicked his steed into a gallop, heading toward William's field headquarters.

The Norman assaults resumed by the seventh hour with the commanders initiating two changes in the attacks. They instructed the archers to change the trajectory of their missiles and shoot farther over the shield wall into the massed English. The archer fusillade was followed by the infantry attack. The foot soldiers had received directions to engage, then run and fake a panicky retreat. Unlike before, the English right flank, mostly from the fyrd, did not break formation and chase the Normans. The English center, made up of professional housecarls, also did not fall for the ruse. The fyrd on the English left flank, however, wavered and about a hundred militia broke from their lines in pursuit, much less than the thousand odd when the Bretons had been chased earlier. Count Eu led the first wave of Franco-Flemish cavalry and cut off the wayward English before they could retreat to their lines. The knights dispatched the peasant soldiers, piercing them with couched lances or running them down with their warhorses.

Drogo pointed at the English line. "The English are jostling each other. They have been under attack constantly from either our archery, infantry, or cavalry, whereas we have been able to rest between attacks. I would lose my patience too and would also want to fight and get this battle over!"

Count Eu passed them going downhill as the FitzPons conroi prepared to charge with the second wave. He nodded at Drogo, "Every little crack we put in their defense moves us closer to triumph."

When they drew close to the English, they realized the shield wall had withered as a result. On the far right of the English line a few knights were now able to gain access to a level area and charge with their lances. The English tried to spread back out to fill the gap, but it created openings, which the knights exploited with more lance assaults. When the FitzPons conroi completed their assault and then returned to their assembly area, the commanders of each wing were dispensing new orders.

Reorganized into joint assault forces, each cavalry conroi was now accompanied by a score of archers and a troop of foot soldiers. The three Norman divisions moved up the slope toward the English. For the next several hours each of these groups alternated among attacking, resting, and returning for arrows. They continued to degrade the English defenses until the members of the fyrd were either dead or had fled north through the forest. The Normans paused in their assaults. At the highest point on the ridge there remained a few hundred housecarls gathered around King Harold's banner. Harold was not to be seen, but they showed no indication of surrender.

It was late in the afternoon and the sun would set in an hour. Count Eu returned from William's headquarters and gathered the leaders of his conroi to announce their next plans. Count Eu, FitzOzbern, and Count Eustace held a conference with four chosen conroi leaders of the Franco-Flemish wing. Similar meetings were taking place at the same time with the Norman and the Breton divisions. With equal respect, Count Eustace regarded each officer: his infantry commander, the cavalry commander, and four chosen conroi captains, including Richard FitzPons.

"Good knights, this struggle has taken a huge toll on our army, not just in the thousands of casualties, but in morale and the men's ability to continue the fight. But William cannot let Harold escape today to rally more troops. The housecarls will fight to the death and this last round will be vicious. After all your efforts today, it is difficult to realize this battle is just the start of our conquest of England. We will need our men to be faithful to the cause for years, so your example of leadership will inspire them. William and Bishop Odo will lead a conroi of nobles including Count Eu, Alan Rufus, and me. Sir FitzOzbern will stay here. Your conrois will aid us in the final assault. Gather your archers and foot soldiers and be ready for instruction.

After the assault troops were organized, William rode to the top of the ridge, leading a royal conroi of his commanders. Accompanying them were nine more conrois, each supported by a contingent of foot soldiers and archers. The supply of arrows and bolts had been depleted, because during a battle, archers, in part, depended upon salvaging the enemy's arrows. This had not been possible due to the scarcity of English archers. At the top of the ridge, however, the Norman archers recovered thousands of their own arrows.

The English housecarls awaiting the Normans appeared like their ancient Germanic ancestors, the Angles and Saxons, who had engaged in battle on foot using the shield wall, but also like their Viking ancestors, wielding the terrifying long axes. Their wild hair, bristling moustaches, and fierce black look seemed like the manifestation of a pack of Viking berserkers.

Their adversaries were no less capable or warlike. The Norman leaders were descended from Danish Vikings and had retained their bellicose spirit. Their French allies, the descendants of Franks, Gallo-Romans, and Celtic Bretons, also represented a long history of accomplishments on the battlefield.

Waiting for the duke were some two hundred housecarls packed together into a circle, their shields facing outward. Littering the surrounding ground were a thousand corpses, the men's skin ghostly pale, their life blood soaking the earth. The carcasses of horses created a hundred obstacles for the next fight. The putrid odors in the sluggish wind varied from metallic to feculent. The English surrounded the personal banner of Harold with its image of the *Fighting Man,* which was a rendition of Harold armed with the feared long axe. As William issued his last details for the next charge, he ordered the reserve knights to block the English if they fled. But the housecarls stood resolute and showed no inclination to leave their high ground, their comrades, or their king. Other Norman knights were riding through the woods flushing out members of the fyrd, although many peasant farmers who lived nearby had already fled back to their villages. Meanwhile on the battleground below, camp followers and Norman foot soldiers stripped the bodies of the fallen English.

The assault conrois spread out one hundred paces from the English. William adjusted his lance, draped with a red pennant with the two lions of Normandy. Bishop Odo wielded his battle club and played the whited sepulcher, declaring it was a weapon that would not shed blood. The duke addressed his fellow nobles. "Do any of you see Harold among them? He is not tall, and they all are armed alike, but I would recognize him."

Eustace answered, "I am looking around their banner, but I cannot see him."

"No matter," said William as he leveled his lance. "I am going directly at the *Fighting Man.* Sound the gjallarhorn!"

When the Normans drew within fifty paces, the horn blew once, and a hail of arrows and bolts riddled the English formation. The yelling horn blew twice, the foot soldiers and archers ran ahead, spaced to permit the infantry and mounted knights to clash with the English at the same time. It was a melee of weapons, horses, and men. Horses fell and crushed their own riders, two-handed axes cleaved comrade and foe in one swing. More conrois charged, the housecarls' formation was broken, and the battle turned into several pockets of resistance. William's horse was cut from under him a fourth time, but he was determined to reach Harold's banner and fought ahead on foot, as his men formed their own wall of shields to help the duke fight his way to the center. The housecarls fought to the last man, and next to Harold's banner they found the king dead, killed by an arrow that had pierced his eye.

The battle had taken a heavy toll on the victorious side as well. One in four soldiers in the Norman army were dead. Angered they had lost so many comrades, the cavalry, intent to exact revenge, pursued the fugitives into the surrounding forest. It was near sunset. Richard was disgusted with the hunt for the English fugitives, but told his men that he would not prevent anyone who wanted to participate. Instead, Lambert and the Fitzpons brothers searched the battlefield, not to *rifle et rafle*, to strip the dead bodies and to carry off loot, but to find Leufred and Lothar. Although there were some soldiers rifling dead bodies, he also saw others honoring their friends and digging graves.

As they moved along the ridge, Richard discovered tangled among the bodies a blue pennant covered with diagonal red and white stripes. *The banner of County Evreux!* He dismounted and inspected the nearby bodies, hoping his suspicion was wrong. *For Amicia's sake, I hope her fiancé is not dead.* He turned over a face-down knight who still grasped the lance with the banner. *It is Guillaume, the son of Count Evreux! Amicia will be devastated!*

Gauthier shouted, "I have found Leufred's body!"

Then Osborne yelled from nearby, "Lothar is here, too!"

Richard detached the banner from the lance, mounted, and was about to join his brothers, but went back and using his dagger point, twisted, turned and snapped off a ring, one of the hundreds which made up Guillaume de Evreux's chain mail. He mounted and started to weave his path through the tangled bodies of men and horses. His brothers were hard at work, absorbed in digging the graves for their two friends. Richard saw figures edging along the ground. *Are those wounded English?* The slinking forms unexpectedly reared and charged. Richard spurred his horse into a gallop and shouted to his brothers. *They can't hear me!*

A pair of strangers appeared in the enemies' path, one swinging a heavy staff, the other wielding a long bow as a bludgeon. By the time Richard arrived, the ground was strewn with unconscious English soldiers. The two men who had intervened did not appear to be Norman or French. One of the strangers wore the garb of an archer and on his back hung an empty quiver. He had short hair, a huge blonde mustache, and blue eyes that conveyed a mischievous air. The other was bearded and mustached with russet hair. He was fitted with a vest of chain mail like some of the mercenary infantry. This man hailed Richard, *"Bonjour monsieur."*

"Who are you?" demanded Richard. "Lambert, do you know these men?"

"Blue eyes looks like an English archer," said Osborne. "But I never have seen a bow that long! And the other one is wearing Saxon chain mail! They look English to me!"

"No English. *Fi yw Cymraeg!*" answered the archer.

"The truth is, as my comrade just said, is that he is Welsh," the second stranger added in French. "He doesn't know your language. We are mercenaries, ready to fight for Duke William."

"What! But you fought for the English in the battle!" said Gauthier. "How did you survive? The Normans are not taking prisoners."

"But see, we defended you. We will be your bodyguards. No? Did you see how good I am with the *bata*? Half of a spear makes a good cudgel. Who needs a spear! As for the battle, we got lucky. The last thing I remember is that we were fighting back to back, and my spear was broken." He held up the wooden spear shaft void of its point. "Chopper had run out of arrows and . . ."

"Your mate's name is Chopper?" said Drogo. "That sounds like an English axe man's name, not the name of an archer. You *are* English!"

"No, no! He is Welsh. As for his name—just look at his jowls. Does that convince you? And as for me, well, my father was Scotti and my mother was from faraway Paris. She loved Paris. That's how I learned French. I am just me, Louis, a mercenary."

His partner, speaking Welsh, added a few comments, incomprehensible to everyone except Louis.

"What did he say?" asked Drogo.

"Chopper said I should let him do the talking. He said I am doing a terrible job, you are angry, and I will get both of us killed!

We offer our services, you will not regret it."

"You will help us finish these graves before dark," said Richard. "We must also bury Count Evreux's son. Then I will turn you over to my commander."

By the time they were done burying Guillaume, their two comrades from Le Mans, and prayed over their graves, it was almost dark. They rode toward the cookfires of the encampment. Richard and his brothers tied the two strangers' hands behind their backs and took them to Count de Eu. After they told him of the prisoners' heroics, being overwhelmed with many duties, the count told Richard to decide their fate himself.

Ale was distributed that evening before they retired. Around the fire the FitzPons conroi shared drink with their prisoners. "Thank you, Sir Richard, for retying our hands in the front," said Louis. "Now we can drink our ale."

Chopper held up his cup with joined hands and toasted, *"Iechyd da!"*

"Sante!" said Louis. "He says 'good health' in his Gaelic tongue."

The men replied, *"Iechyd da!"*

"I think I am going to lose a tooth," said Drogo as he wiggled one. "I was hit in the mouth several times during the battle."

Chopper said something, and his comrade interpreted. "My friend has a joke for you."

The men looked at each other with amusement as he continued, translating for Chopper. "I knew an old Bishop who had lost some teeth and complained of others being loose and he was afraid they would soon fall out. 'Never fear,' said one of his friends, 'they won't fall.' 'And why not?' inquired the Bishop. His friend replied, 'Because my testicles have been hanging loose for the last forty years, and yet, there they are still.'"

The Welshman told more jokes as Richard thought, *A way to forget the battle. How can I get the banner to Count Evreux? Will I even survive this war? We have lost so many and there is hardly any food. There could be thousands of the English fyrd coming this way right now.*

MICHAEL A. PONZIO

CHAPTER SIX

.

Duke William's March to London

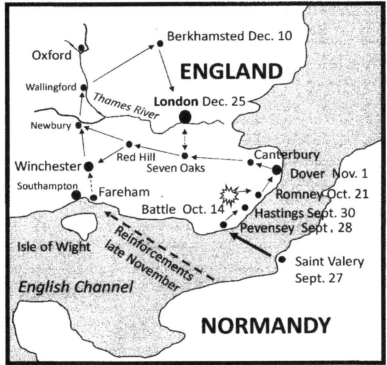

ENGLAND

NORMANDY

Berkhamsted Dec. 10

Oxford

ENGLAND

Wallingford

Thames River

London Dec. 25

Newbury

Red Hill

Winchester

Seven Oaks

Canterbury

Southampton

Dover Nov. 1

Fareham

Romney Oct. 21

Battle Oct. 14

Hastings Sept. 30

Pevensey Sept. 28

Isle of Wight

Reinforcements late November

Saint Valery Sept. 27

English Channel

NORMANDY

CHAPTER SIX

The morning of October 15, 1066, Duke William inspected the battlefield. The grisly scene portrayed the huge losses his army had sustained and the significant reduction in the strength of the army. The FitzPons brothers along with most of the Norman army were hard at work burying their fallen comrades. William had ordered them to leave the English where they fell, without burial. He also made known that anyone stealing armor from the Norman dead would be punished. The armor was to be gathered and stored for the army, although the duke allowed the pilferage of weapons or other articles.

Richard and Lambert removed the armor of another knight, placed his body in a grave, and covered it with soil. After Lambert said a short prayer, he commented, "Thank you, comrades, for helping me find my brothers and bury them last evening. It looks like most of these bodies were looted last night. The only honor we can give these men is to bury them and say a prayer."

"I am certain it was not only the camp followers that rifled the bodies," said Richard, "but also our own soldiers. That is surprising, considering the punishment for rifling armor from a Norman soldier is a severe lashing. The officers are also going to inspect the camp and make sure armor isn't peddled to camp followers. The sentinels posted around the battlefield during the night kept the English riff-raff from stealing in, but I am sure our own soldiers rewarded the guards with some of the loot. Comrades and foe alike have been stripped of arms and valuables."

"It's good we already buried Lothar and Leufred. We beat the riff-raff to their belongings," added Lambert. "As remembrance, I will wear Lothar's helmet and I have Leufred's dagger. If I ever go back to Le Mans, I will take the rings we saved from their chain mail as a memento for their families."

They continued burying more of the dead, when Gauthier said, "Look!" He pointed to a litter carried by four men, the *Fighting Man* banner draped over the body. Riding down the hill behind the procession were Duke William and his brothers Odo and Robert. "That must be King Harold. What will they do with his body?"

The second day after the battle, William led the Norman army, reduced to about 5,000 fighting men, to Hastings. There the army recuperated and sent out small raiding parties to scavenge food. Unbeknownst to William, even his ally, the nearby Fecamp Monastery, was looted to the point the monks themselves were in want. The duke kept the army in Hastings for almost a fortnight, expecting the English to send envoys announcing their surrender. One evening, the knights of the FitzPons conroi were having meager servings of porridge. They had not been sent out with a foraging party, and the food supply was almost depleted. As they sat around their campfire, Osborne said, "The gossip in the ranks says William arranged for Harold's body to be brought to Hastings where they buried the king on a hill overlooking the English Channel."

"We saw them carry his body off the battlefield," added Gauthier. "I am pleased the duke gave Harold that respect. There was also talk that William expected the English to send a delegation to surrender, but that hasn't happened. Are we just going to wait for another English army? When are we going to leave this place?"

"There must be thousands more of the fyrd still available to fight," said Drogo.

"I would say tens of thousands if all the English fighting men were mustered. It is a large kingdom," answered Osborne.

"I don't think that detail really matters. Just say there could be too many!" added Drogo.

"And thank you, Ozzie, that makes us feel even better!" said Gauthier.

Richard arrived from an officers' meeting. "I heard you. William knows we need to move on to obtain enough food, and we must force the English to surrender. William's scouts have found no organized troops between here and London. You will get your wish. Tomorrow we head to Dover."

"Dover is not on the way to London," said Osborne.

"No, the duke plans to take control of the southern towns first and station them with garrisons before our move on London," answered Richard. "On the way to Dover we'll secure the village of Romney. A monk from Fecamp Abbey reported to William about two longships that got separated from our fleet during the crossing. They landed at Romney and the townspeople there killed all the soldiers on board. Our conroi is part of a contingent that will search the town."

"Good, we may be the first to the village and find something to eat this time," said Drogo.

Richard nodded. "Let's sleep. We'll be riding at the first hour tomorrow."

The Norman army crossed the battlefield where they had fought and died two weeks prior. Many of the bodies of the English soldiers had been removed or buried. The old Roman road continued for sixty miles north to London, but they turned off to the east on a dirt track toward Dover. The second night from Hastings they camped several miles north of Romney. The next morning the army continued to Dover, and the FitzPons conroi, part of a force of several hundred knights commanded by a Norman baron, proceeded south until they came to Romney Harbor. A few miles across the harbor was an island.

The men dismounted, let their horses graze, and ate some hard, dry biscuits. They waited for the ships that would take them to the island. After several hours, Gauthier said, "I can't believe I now long for the wine I used to complain about. This water doesn't taste right."

Drogo pointed across the harbor. "Maybe they have brought us some!" A handful of longships were approaching, flying red banners with the two gold lions of Normandy. One conroi of knights stayed on shore to watch the horses as the FitzPons brothers and the rest of the troops boarded the longships. The boats were the escorts for the *Mora* and had a full complement of oars as well as a few archers. The knights manned the oars and rowed five miles across the harbor to the island. There were several ships tied up at the docks. Drogo called out, "Some of our men did land here. Two of those ships are from our fleet, the same kind in which we installed only one set of oars to make space for cargo and horses."

Their ships beached near the docks. The village appeared empty. The archers removed their crossbows from their waterproof sacks and disembarked first, setting up positions to support the knights' landing. Richard joined the other conroi leaders as the Norman commander gave orders. "This village appears to have less than a hundred cottages, but there could be fyrd stationed here," said the baron. "The two ships that arrived had only four knights each, so the townspeople themselves could have overwhelmed them. Be aware." He regarded the captains, "Each conroi will have two archers with them and will search the village. I will stay here with the reserves. If you hear the horn, follow the sound. This island is a few miles long and half as wide. Outside the town we'll regroup and sweep the woods and fields."

The conroi leaders turned to join their men and paused. With a grim face, the baron added, "We will not garrison the village after our search and William does not want to leave any English fighting men here or take any prisoners. And no looting until we have secured the town and I give the order." The conrois assembled and then spread out, moving away from the waterfront and along the streets.

The FitzPons knights searched shops and houses as another conroi moved down the other side of the street. As they entered each building, Richard placed the archers and two knights outside.

No one was discovered in the first two houses. As Drogo entered the third dwelling, a muffled voice made him freeze and listen. He looked back at Richard and held a finger to his lips. Two men went upstairs and returned without finding anyone. Then a baby's cry seemed to come out of the wall.

After checking the layout of the house, Richard was certain the sound came from a hidden room. He ordered the men to exit the house and continue to the next building.

Shouts erupted from across the street followed by the screams of women, and then stopped. The search team on the other side left the house with bloodied swords.

"I am not going to kill any women or children," said Gauthier.

Richard halted. He was livid. "No soldier under my command will kill unarmed townspeople. You can leave now if you do not agree." All his men were stone-faced and quiet.

The men continued to move along the street. Shrieks and wailing came from the adjoining alleys. In the next house Lambert discovered a trap door in the floor. He lifted the door. The tiny cellar was crowded with women, children, and several elderly men. He was closing the hatch as a woman said, "*Eglise!*"

He kept it halfway open and answered. "Shh! We know you are English. Stay here, we are not English!"

She shouted, "*Eglise! Alle Eglise!*"

"No, I think she is trying to say the word *church* in French," said Gauthier. "She said, 'Go church.' Perhaps she means, 'Go to the church.'"

"Close the trapdoor," said Richard. "Drogo, take the men and finish searching the rest of the houses, then meet us at the church." Osborne and Gauthier left with Richard and hurried towards the steeple of the church, which was visible above the housetops two streets away. As they neared, cries of anguish and pain echoed down the streets. In the paved area in front of the church were the bloody forms of women and children scattered on the ground. A crowd of knights stood by and watched as their comrades dragged screaming women from the church, although several knights, outnumbered by the executioners, fought to stop more slaughter.

As Richard hurried with his brothers to help the rescuers, he shouted to soldiers standing by. "These women did not kill our comrades! If you are a Christian, help them!"

More knights then joined the brothers to intervene, and the carnage was stopped. Fires had been started in the town. Drogo and the rest of the conroi arrived, escorting more women and children to protect them. They led them into the church. Shoving and jeering among the opposing knights escalated but subsided when the yelling horn sounded at the edge of the square. The baron arrived and shouted for the knights' attention. He called the conroi leaders together. "Fools! What the hell is going on? Forget these people. And no fires until we get the food! Then we destroy the town for killing our comrades." The officers dispersed to organize their men and sack the town.

Within a few hours, as plunder and food were loaded on the ships, the baron led several conrois across the island. A hundred English men were flushed out of the woods, overwhelmed, and killed in a brief skirmish. The Normans learned from the surviving townspeople where their missing knights had been buried. The baron said a brief prayer over their graves and the troops left, much of the town burning except for the church they had left untouched.

The troops were transported back across the harbor to their horses and rode to Dover, joining the rest of the Norman army which now occupied the town. Dover had surrendered without a fight. There was no widespread revenge as in Romney, and although food was taken from the townspeople, its men were not executed. Duke William and his brothers took up provisional residence in the fort at the highest point in town. The original Roman fort, maintained for centuries, was perched above massive white cliffs of chalk, and commanded a view of the sea. The town was in a fertile valley and located at the mouth of the River Dour. Dover also had a fishing fleet which could provide sustenance for the troops. In addition, Dover was at the narrowest part of the English Channel and was the shortest and fastest crossing to Normandy.

The FitzPons conroi and other knights were camped outside

the city walls where their horses could graze. The brothers and a few comrades went into the city to search for food. Although much of the foodstuffs had been acquired by the soldiers upon the initial occupation of the town, it was hoarded and not shared except among their own units.

They heard, however, that William was distributing food to his troops at an old Roman villa near the south gate of the city. Osborne had been told the villa was a large house with red roof tiles and would be easy to find. Approaching the city, they traveled along a road that provided a remarkable view of the town and castle above white cliffs overlooking the channel. They topped a rise and the house they sought came into view. It was the remains of a Roman manor, a large U-shaped building hundreds of paces long and two stories high. There were outbuildings that appeared to be barns and stables. Soldiers were forcing townspeople to deliver food on carts. Hundreds more soldiers were milling about and congregating on the steps outside the manor house.

"That was a Roman villa? All the people in the village of Pons could live there at once," said Osborne.

Gauthier pointed. "I wonder how far you can see from that watchtower outside the castle? It's four or five stories high."

"I think . . . that tower is a lighthouse," said Richard.

"Light—house. What is a lighthouse?" said Osborne.

"A fire is made at the top of the tower to guide the ships' helmsmen to avoid crashing on the shore, or to just find the port."

"That is a good idea, but it would take a lot of work. Extra wood, carrying it up the tower, keeping it lighted."

"Yes, Amicia told me that in her homeland of Galicia there is a Roman lighthouse which is hundreds of pieds high, twice as tall as this tower."

"You have mentioned Amicia often, brother," said Drogo.

"I became fond of her, but then I learned she was betrothed. Now she has lost her fiancé at the battle. I feel somewhat guilty thinking about her."

They arrived at the manor house and Richard noted an occasional shriek of terror from inside the building, above the noise of the crowd. *This was never part of my life as a knight in*

Aquitaine. Soldiers' brothels and now worse, the raping.

They procured biscuits and salted fish and loaded their saddlebags. Richard commented, "Still no wine, and the Normans drank all the ale in town before we arrived. I don't like drinking the water here." Two men of Richard's conroi went upstairs, saying they would meet them back at camp.

About to leave, a commotion attracted their attention at the bottom of a staircase. A woman struggled to break free and screamed as she was dragged back up the stairs. The FitzPons brothers looked at each other with disgust. "Let's go," said Gauthier. "I don't want to see this."

A wagon, drawn by two ponies and guided by a townsman arrived. It was crowded with women and girls, some who were merely juveniles. There was terror on the girls' faces and some were whimpering. The women were pleading in English. A few soldiers were cheering. Richard dismounted, and his comrades followed without comment.

Richard moved toward the driver. "Those women don't look as if they want to work for favors."

The wagoner, an Englishman, didn't respond. but a Norman knight came down the steps from the villa and called out, "What is the problem, soldier?"

Richard turned to the knight. "I don't speak English," said Richard, "but I believe these women are screaming *no*."

"That's war, comrade. Spoils go to the winner," said the knight.

Richard heard a commotion behind him and saw his brothers holding the driver. "Quit struggling, you cur," said Drogo. "You are lucky we stopped you. If you had struck him, I'd be pounding you into the ground."

Several other men joined the Norman confronting Richard.

Richard spoke louder, so the crowd of men could hear. "Some of these are only girls, not women. Is this the Christian way?"

A shout came from the crowd: "The English are all sinners! Just as Harold disobeyed his vow to William, the Pope has given us approval!"

"Would you stand by in France if the Pope gave the English permission to violate your own wife, your sister, your niece, or your daughter?"

The men grew silent. Many of them yelled, "Let the girls go!" The soldiers were divided in opinion, and they began shouting and pushing each other.

Richard knew daggers would be pulled shortly. *I hate what I am going to say, but it may be the only way to save the girls and avoid bloodshed now.* He shouted, "At least free the girls and let them have a Christian life!" Richard watched and did not interfere as several of the women were removed from the wagon and taken into the manor house. The girls were set free and ran back toward town. Richard guessed, *The women led into the villa appeared calmer, as if they had won a victory by sacrificing themselves for their young womenfolk.*

The atrocities against the population did not end when the army departed. Much of Dover was put to the torch as the soldiers left, although William had not ordered the action. He understood the benefit of the news spreading to London and did not punish the arsonists. The duke left a garrison in the castle and the army moved north toward Canterbury. They camped halfway to the town where many of the soldiers became sick with fever and diarrhea. Those who were fit enough moved onto Canterbury, which surrendered and opened their gates, hoping the town would be spared. William made plans to move on and left a third of his men, sick from dysentery, to recover and join him later.

The day before the army headed west, Count Eustace, commander of the Franco-Flemish cavalry, summoned the FitzPons brothers. On the way to the count's tent, a handful of other knights fell in step with them. One of them said, "Do you think we are in trouble about the women at the manor?"

"I would do the same again," said Richard. "But had we done more, I think there would have been bloodshed."

"Do you remember what Father told us years ago, when he was trying to teach us about women?" said Drogo.

"No, all I recall he appeared uncomfortable, but whatever he told us, he would have told us to do the right thing."

"All I remember is that he said, 'Never force a woman,'" said Osborne.

They arrived at the count's tent and joined other knights, a few who had been with them on the mission to Romney. "Knights, the army has been reduced to half strength since we landed," said Eustace. "We lost thousands at the battle with Harold, and the army was further reduced when we left men to garrison Pevensey, Dover, and Canterbury. Now the sickness has, temporarily I hope, claimed hundreds more, probably from the water. You have been chosen to return with your conrois to Normandy, assemble reinforcements, and rejoin us in England. You will soon board horse transports on Dover beach to cross the channel."

The men filed out of the tent and Eustace said, "Richard, please, you and your brothers stay a bit." He produced a skin and passed it to Richard. "The last of my wine. Please enjoy."

The count was quiet as the brothers passed around the drink, then said, "Odo and Robert wanted you and the other knights to be punished for instigating dissension in the ranks."

"Do you mean at Romney?" said Gauthier. Richard glared at his brother as if he spoke out of turn.

"That's fine. Speak freely, men," nodded Eustace. "Yes, the baron told William and his commanders about Romney and the incident at the Dover villa. William cannot tolerate anything that divides our men or lowers morale. Instead of the punishment, as his advisors recommended, he chose to remove you, at least for the time being, by sending you to acquire reinforcements."

They each took another sip of the wine. "Sir, I am curious, said Drogo. "Did all of William's advisors call for us to be disciplined?"

"Um . . . well, yes, I did say speak freely. William recognized that the FitzPons brothers have shown their courage and worth to the army before," answered Eustace.

"There is something else?" added Gauthier.

The count put one hand on Gauthier's shoulder and looked at each brother. "Your father and I served together in Spain during the Reconquista. He was a fierce warrior, a true knight, and a highly moral man. And I see that his sons have the courage to follow his example! *Sante!*" The count raised the skin and imbibed the last of the wine.

The FitzPons brothers waited on the beach below the cliffs at Dover, expecting soon to board the horse transports. "It's no wonder you chose the ship to Pont de la Arche, to see pretty Amicia!" said Osborne.

"I will be returning Guillaume de Evreux's banner to his father. And the ring from his chain mail. I will give Amicia my condolences."

His brothers laughed when they said, almost in unison, "Of course!"

A convoy of fifty transports arrived and anchored offshore, and pairs of knights were ferried by punts to the ships. Richard and Drogo sailed together to Pont de la Arche accompanied by a small fleet of ten ships. Gauthier and Osborne were sailing to Dives with another flotilla. Other groups of transports crossed to the ports of Dieppe, Treport, and Barfleur to gather more knights recruited by nobles in Normandy.

After a calm night at sea, Richard and Drogo arrived at the port of Honfleur at the mouth of the Seine River. The ships were anchored there to wait for the reinforcements, which were gathering in Rouen. The brothers procured horses and within two days arrived at the city's castle. Only about half the recruits had gathered, so Richard and Drogo rode to report to Count Evreux the sorrowful fate of his son. The roads were good, and they reached Pont de la Arche for the night. They arrived at the town of Evreux the second day, late in the afternoon, and went directly to Chateau Evreux. As they entered the chateau's hall, the count sprang from his seat, beamed with joy, but just as quickly lost his cheer when he saw their grim faces. He then noticed the folded banner under Richard's arm and fell back into his chair. "Don't say it! I know why you're here. I only want to hear it once." The count motioned to a servant. "Tell my wife and Amicia to come right away."

As the ladies joined them, their expressions turned somber as they considered the men's seriousness. "My lord, Guillaume was killed in the battle with the English," said Richard. "I am very sorry. God rest his soul. He fought valiantly for the Pope's crusade and I am sure he is now in Heaven." Richard held the banner out to the count. The women sobbed, and the count squeezed the arms of the chair, his face turning red. Suddenly the left side of his face sagged; when he tried to speak, he slurred his words. His wife cried out, calling for the chateau's steward and servants. As they removed the count to his bedroom, his wife spoke through her sobs. "Sir Richard, what dreadful news you have brought! Oh, no, I am sorry. It's not your fault. Stay, I will be down as soon as I can. Please, stay and comfort Amicia."

The young woman sat with them. "Sir Richard, with all this unhappy news, I hope that your brothers did not meet tragedy as well."

"No, Lady, they are all safe. Amicia, my brother Dreux. Dreux—Lady Amicia." They briefly nodded, both considering why the men were there, plus the blow to the count's health. Richard produced the steel ring. "Amicia, here is a memento of Guillaume. I retrieved it from his chain mail."

She hesitated and did not take the ring. "I hardly knew him, but he was a gentleman, and did not deserve his fate." She sobbed. "Perhaps you should give it to his parents. Uh . . . I feel I do not deserve it."

"Not deserve it?" said Richard.

Amicia added, "Yes, because my feelings are not those of true mourning, as I should have for a husband, or even for one to whom I was betrothed. I am sorry for him, but sadder for his parents. They treated me like a daughter." She looked blankly across the room in silence. "Guillaume was their only child. I will stay here as long as they need me."

"You are very kind, Amicia. Is there anything I can do to help?" asked Richard.

Amicia gave a shy smile. "Do you remember our secret?"

Drogo looked uncomfortable and stood to leave. "No, Sir

Dreux, please stay. It is fine," said Amicia.

"Yes, I remember," answered Richard. "I will support you in any way, as an older brother would. Yes, that's right, I am your older brother away from home, away from Galicia."

Drogo smiled. "Does that make me your brother too?" His grin made them both laugh.

"Drogo! This is a time of mourning," said Richard.

"No, he is helping," added Amicia. "His jesting is a good relief."

The count's steward appeared. "The Countess will be staying with her husband this evening. His strength has increased. Your dinner is ready in the next room. You will stay the night?"

Richard nodded.

In the morning the steward notified Richard and Drogo that the Countess wished for them to see the count before they departed. As they climbed the stairs, Amicia and the countess were laughing with the count. The brothers looked at each other in surprise. When they entered the room, the puzzle continued as the women quieted and looked somewhat secretive. The count was sitting erect, propped up by pillows in the bed. He seemed dazed, but his speech was no longer slurred. He addressed Richard. "Son, I am so pleased you were able to visit. I know you must return to England and continue the conquest with Duke William."

"Yes, sir, and again we are so sor . . ." Richard was interrupted by the count.

"You brought your best man! Wonderful!" said the count. "I know this is unplanned, but let's not wait for the end of the campaign? And give me this wish now. I don't have much more time in the world. You must get married before I pass away, son." He waved a hand toward the steward. "The priest is here, your mother is here, your best man. Guillaume—you are marrying a lovely young woman. We are all fortunate."

The steward held a Bible, and the expressions of the countess and Amicia compelled Richard to cooperate with the count's delusion. The steward had Richard and Amicia recite a semblance of the Christian wedding vows. Richard could not believe what they were doing. He spontaneously presented the ring from Guillaume's chain mail and slipped it on Amicia's finger. The steward ended the ceremony with, "I pronounce that they be man and wife together, in the name of God, our bishop, and our duke who is the protector of the Holy Spirit and our people. Amen."

Still acting their parts, the brothers were relieved it was time to depart and said their farewells to the count and countess,. While Drogo went to the stables to arrange for a servant to ready their horses, Richard and Amicia waited in front of the chateau. "Amicia, will you go back to Spain after the count and countess finish grieving?"

With a weak smile, Amicia answered, "Shh, the count might hear you. I am still living in the count's fantasy. Returning to my home is not part of his illusion. So I must act the part, waiting for my husband to return to Evreux. I wish . . . I mean . . . um . . . I must be here to help the countess take care of her husband."

"Of course. Your presence will comfort the countess and she will comfort you as you both must mourn the loss of Guillaume," added Richard. "There may be years of war in England yet, but if I ever return to Normandy, I will visit." She did not comment, but looked down. Richard tried to sound cheerful. "After all, as your big brother, isn't that what I should do?"

Amicia exhibited a genuine smile. "Yes."

Richard looked to make sure no one saw and kissed her on the cheek. "*Au revoir*, Amicia."

Drogo arrived with their mounts, and as Richard turned to leave heard, "*Au revoir*, Richard."

I will not look back. I should have kissed her lips! But no, it's good I didn't. I may never return. That would have been cruel for both of us.

After making the channel crossing without incident, the fleet of horse transports sailed along the east coast of the Isle of Wight, a few miles from their journey's end. Richard marveled at William's good luck. Two months earlier the island had been the headquarters of the English fleet, but those ships had been sailed up the Thames River to London and pulled from the water for winter storage. Richard and Drogo quietly watched the shoreline. Drogo slapped Richard lightly on the back. "Brother, are you thinking about Amicia?"

"Yes, I thought I would find the right woman in a few years, after the conquest was finished, but I didn't realize it would be this soon."

"You are a lucky man, but don't let your mind be faraway on the battlefield. We may have a long way to go yet."

Within an hour they were beached at the village of Fareham and offloaded the men and horses. They did not sail to the fortified port of Southampton, closer to Winchester, because the town had not yet been taken by the Normans and could have offered stiff resistance to their landing.

The FitzPons brothers were eventually reunited and assembled their conroi for the ride north. "I already miss the ale in Normandy," said Gauthier. "Hah! We were ordered to fetch barrels and barrels of wine instead of good ale."

"I'll take either over the water in England. I'd guess that is why so many were sick in Canterbury," added Osborne.

"Richard, do you think we were assigned this mission—to bring the reinforcements—as another punishment?" said Osborne.

"No, I think we have a guardian angel, Ozzie."

"Count Eustace?" said Gauthier.

Drogo added, "I am thinking the same, but the count is rather shrewd. He seems to have assigned us to this duty before William could get wind of our rebellious acts. Got us out of the way."

"We did the right thing, according to the way we were raised and according to what Jesus would have done. Although I wonder if our actions have threatened our reward. William did say every knight who joined his quest would receive land," said Osborne.

"Are you jesting? When he learns we brought him barrels of wine, he will reward us even more!" laughed Drogo.

"I wager the duke sought the wine more than the reinforcements!" added Richard.

The FitzPons conroi finished their wine, mounted, and joined the column of four hundred knights riding north to Winchester. They would meet a contingent from William's army, which had already occupied the city, a special prize, being the location of the mint and treasury of England.

After traveling a few miles on a wide dirt track, they came to a road and headed west. Paving stones were missing in some areas, but the road offered good transit as it turned northwest. Within several miles it was intersected by another paved road from the south where the force stopped to rest. They drank some diluted wine while Lambert read the engraving on an old Roman milestone at the intersection. "It points south to 'CLAUSETUM $\overline{IV}$ PASUUM' and to the north, '$\overline{X}$ PASUUM VENTA BELGARUM.' Ozzie, I remember you said the line on top of the number means thousands, so it is four thousand paces, four miles, to some place called Clausetum and ten miles north to the other place."

Nearby, another troop of knights mounted up. As they began to ride south, Osborne called out to the departing chevaliers, "Where are you going?"

"To Clausetum, like the sign said," Lambert said with a grin.

The knight reined in his horse and said, "To Southampton and make sure there are no threats. The town is still in English hands."

"I guess those engravings on the milestone were the ancient Roman names for the towns," said Lambert. "If Clausetum is Southampton, then Venta Belgarum is Winchester and we only have ten miles to go."

Osborne said, "At least in Aquitaine and Normandy, the Roman names and the French names are more alike, so the milestones are helpful. Another thing is different here—have you noticed, there are no castles?"

"You are right, there were the Roman forts at Pevensey and Dover, but no castles like those in France," added Richard. "When we erected the motte and bailey castle inside the Roman fort at Pevensey, we may have built the first castle in England. We'll see if Winchester is any different."

The road north remained level and in good order, and the knights rode their horses at a trot for a little over an hour to reach the city. The column of knights turned off the main road and halted outside the walls at the village of Westgate, a settlement that had grown beyond the city fortifications. As the force prepared their camp, a messenger arrived from the leader of the Norman garrison in the city. The baron and conroi captains were ordered to report to the Royal Palace.

Richard and a few other officers followed the messenger through the city gate on foot, past Norman guards. The city walls encompassed a rectangular area one mile on each side. The wooden houses were crowded together, making any horse traffic difficult. They passed two stone buildings and went toward the middle of town where a large timber edifice loomed ahead. Other than the city walls and the two stone buildings which appeared to be minsters, churches with attached monasteries, the town structures were all built of wood. When they neared the center of the town, the streets widened into a gardenlike area surrounding the Royal Palace, previously occupied by the late King Edward.

They were escorted into the great hall and took seats with some Norman officers. Richard saw Alan Rufus among them, commander of the Breton division of the army. He was pleased that Count Eustace was also present. A woman of regal bearing attired in sumptuous clothes entered the room, escorted by Bishop Odo. "Brave knights of the Papal banner, I present to you Queen Edith, wife of Edward, the late king of the Anglo-Saxons. The queen confirms her husband's wish for William to inherit the crown. To show her support she has generously awarded the treasury and the city of Winchester, capital of England, to Duke William."

The nobles present, including Rufus and Eustace, greeted Edith. After a few brief introductions, she departed with Odo. Eustace sought out Richard as he was leaving and embraced him. "Sir Richard, you have done well! With your help," the baron said, "we have four hundred fresh knights! After our losses they were sorely needed to help us push onto London."

"Yes, the deaths of so many comrades was very painful," answered Richard.

"Besides the thousands we lost at Hastings, and those that died from sickness, there was a battle at Southwark," said Eustace.

"Southwark?" asked Richard.

Eustace continued, "While you were in Normandy, the army camped at Seven Oaks, about thirty miles south of London. William sent five hundred knights to test the English defenses. The English crossed London bridge, fought our knights in Southwark, and stopped our attempts to enter the city. The English retreated to the north side of the Thames and our men burned the buildings south of the river, then returned to Seven Oaks. William decided to continue to harry the areas around London. The army is now in Red Hill, waiting for the reinforcements.

"Where are your brothers?"

"Camped at Westgate . . . guarding barrels of wine," laughed Richard. "Care to join us?"

"I miss the atmosphere of a tavern. The city is intact and undisturbed, so I assume we can find some good monks' ale. Winchester surrendered to us through Edith's influence. There was no fighting and William told us not to sack or burn the city. He wanted it undamaged, particularly because it is where the English mint is located. Let's get your brothers and find some brew! I have to return tomorrow to Red Hill and join William."

They collected Richard's brothers, walked down High Street and passed the minsters on both sides of the avenue: Saint Mary's Priory where sisters of the Church lived and Saint Swithun's Priory for the monks. Gauthier said, "Listen . . . down that side alley, from the voices, I believe men are imbibing some ale!"

Hanging above the door was a shingle, *Hogshead Royal Oak Tavern*. Inside there was a standing crowd, mostly Normans and Bretons, noisy and merry with drink. As the group worked their way into the tavern, Richard overheard stories of battles and fights with the English. There were few tables, and they were all occupied. "Count Eustace!" A Norman knight sitting at a table with several other men had addressed the count. "Sit here, Count! Please, take this table."

The count thanked them, and he sat with the FitzPons brothers. After being served, Osborne gulped some ale. "Best ale I've had in England."

"The only ale we've had, brother," answered Gauthier. "And

I am enjoying it."

"This is very good, even compared to the monks' brew in Normandy," added Richard.

"This ale was made at the nunnaminster we passed on our way here," said Eustace. The count guzzled his drink, stood, and chuckled, "Save my seat, comrades. I need to make more room!" He headed out the back door to the ditch behind the tavern.

"It is good ale," said Drogo. "The count said the abbey was a nunnaminster. Is he implying the nuns and monks brewed it together? They must have a merry time tasting the ale to see if it ready."

"They aren't living *together*," said Richard. "They are celibate."

"I know that—I spent the night at the double abbey near Honfleur," answered Drogo. "The nunnery and monastery were isolated from each other."

"How do the clergy do that for years, stay celibate?" said Osborne. "And Drogo, at Honfleur, I'm guessing you stayed with the nuns, right!"

"What? No . . . but I have heard stories of monks and nuns breaking their vows of celibacy."

"I don't blame them. It's not natural to be celibate," said Osborne.

"And that's why there are also tales of insanity among some clergy!" added Gauthier. "Even whoredom!"

"Forget this talk and get back to the ale!" said Richard. "'Whoever keeps his mouth and his tongue keeps himself out of trouble.' That's from somewhere in the Bible, I think."

"Yes, we're gossiping," added Gauthier. "However, the monks brew the best ale, just as in France. *Sante!*"

The men quieted and swigged their ale in silence, then Gauthier said, "I wonder what Father would think. I believe he would be pleased that we served *and* shared ale with Eustace, his old comrade-in-arms."

"How long do you think the conquest will take?" said Richard. "It may be years before we can even dispatch a letter and that would be very expensive. It's not impossible, but it would have to go by hired courier."

"It might be possible to send a letter with some pilgrims," said Drogo. "They frequently pass through Pons."

They suddenly were interrupted when a Norman knight pounded his fist on the table, spilling ale. He stared at Drogo then Gauthier. "Your long hair tells me you are English or Saxon or whatever you call yourselves. We spared your town, but it is ours now. What right do you have to be here, sitting at a table as if you are nobles?"

In the clatter of the tavern, only a few men standing near the table noticed his outburst. The FitzPons brothers sat without comment. Richard said, "Comrade, let me purchase you a brew."

The knight ignored the offer, and he reached out and stroked Gauthier's blonde mane. Gauthier rose up, seized the knight's hand, twisted him sideways, and drove a roundhouse punch downward into his temple. The man lay unmoving on the floor as several Normans stepped toward the brothers' table. Gauthier plopped into his chair and guzzled a large draught of ale.

"I am surprised, Gauthier—you usually stay calm and back us up when *we* get into trouble. What happened?" said Osborne.

"Good move, *hand man*," said Drogo.

"I just wanted to drink my ale!" answered Gauthier. He raised his cup to the Normans who raised their cups in salute, appeared to agree, and then backed off.

Eustace returned and stepped over the man. "Someone had too much ale." He addressed the closest soldiers, "Take him back to camp."

Eustace sat and studied the FitzPons brothers. "The reason I wanted to talk was to describe your next mission. With your success in bringing the reinforcements you are each promoted to the title of marshal, with Richard in charge. You will jointly oversee Winchester, acting as its military governors. William wants to guarantee protection of his rear bases and supply lines to Normandy. When I suggested the FitzPons brothers, I reminded him of your ability to achieve success by cooperating with one another. He approved. Once Winchester is under your strict control, Alan Rufus will command the forces to take

Southampton. Our reconnaissance shows there should not be much resistance. After the city is secured, Alan Rufus will then rejoin William's army. To garrison Winchester, I am leaving a squad of archers to support the French and Flemish knights under your command. Money from the treasury will be distributed by Queen Edith to pay for the garrison.

"Tomorrow I will return to William's army. He plans to circle London and continue harrying the surrounding towns, then enter when the timing is right."

"What time do you expect that to be?" asked Richard.

"Following the battle with Harold, William thought the English leaders would abdicate, but they have not. He will now drive fear into them. And he believes the English clergy will side with him soon, after they have learned that the Pope declared the invasion a holy crusade. Well men, good luck with your command here."

Over the next few months the FitzPons brothers governed Winchester with little resistance. News of the duke's brutal harrying of the English countryside had reached Southampton and the fearful citizens did not contest Norman occupation of the city. Richard assigned some of his French knights to garrison the city, and word was sent to Pevensey to transfer part of the fleet to Southampton. The Archbishop of Canterbury defected to join Duke William, and then Edgar Atheling, the English king appointed after Harold's death, abdicated the crown. Duke William was crowned King of England in London on Christmas Day, 1066. The fighting subsided, but rebellions flared up for the next five years before England was fully subdued under the new king's control.

CHAPTER SEVEN

Domesday Book records "Walter fitz Ponce" and "Drogo fitz Ponce" as holding manors in Oxfordshire, Berkshire, Wiltshire, Gloucestershire, Worcestershire and Herefordshire and also shows "Drogo FitzPons" holding Seagry in Wiltshire; Frampton on Severn and Eastleach Martin in Gloucestershire; Hollin, Stildon, Glasshampton and Martley in Worcestershire; also several properties in Herefordshire. (ref 54)

Osbert (Osborne) after the Conquest Lord in 1086:Saunderton, Desborough, Buckinghamshire, Milton [Keynes], Moulsoe, Buckinghamshire, Leckhampstead, Stotfold, Buckinghamshire (ref 52)

Richard FitzPons probably built the first castle at Bronllys, a typical Norman motte and bailey stronghold. Situated on a well-appointed site overlooking the junction of two rivers, the Llynfi and Dulais, the castle guarded the main route into Wales. (ref 24)

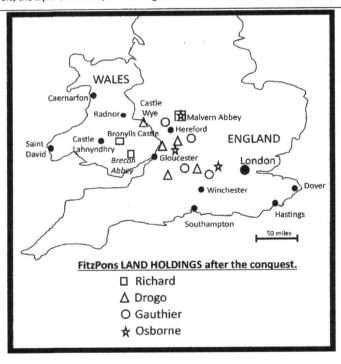

CHAPTER SEVEN
1086 A.D.

With a crack of wood on wood, a ball skipped across the green lawn of the bailey and flew between the vertical poles for a goal. Seona yelled, "*Shin t'ye*! Another hail for the girls! Ha ha!" The members of the girls' team held their camans, the curved sticks, in the air and shouted: "*Shin t'ye!*"

Simon, ten years old, the second oldest of the children after Alejandro, looked indignant. "If we played by the rules, the boys would be winning!"

"Young man, we agreed we would not shoulder each other and there'd be absolutely no hacking, so your little cousins may play," said his mother, Mailisa. "Besides, don't you want Zizi and Papa to play? You wouldn't want your grandparents to be knocked down."

"Come on, son, let's play on and score a hail," said Osborne, as he threw the ball above Simon and his sister Minuet to resume play. The boy swatted the ball out of the air to Drogo who dribbled the ball with his caman across the grass. Seona moved to tackle the ball from him, but he remembered she had stolen it earlier and instead passed it to little Walter, who was challenged by his cousin Willow. He avoided her tackle and deflected the wooden ball to five-year-old Sully, who faced his grandmother Zizi playing goalkeeper. He swung the hooked stick and hit the ball through the goal for a hail.

Mini hugged her young grandson and said, "That was an

excellent strike, little Sullivan, I couldn't block it!" She looked over the boy's shoulder and winked at his siblings and cousins.

"That ties the score. That's enough shinty for me!" said Pons. "Let's eat."

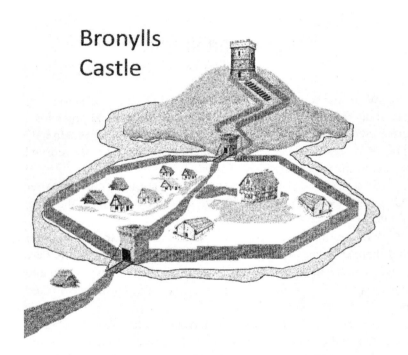

The Pons family gathered around a long table set up outside the manorhouse. The farmers had arrived from the land surrounding the motte and bailey castle. Their thatched roof houses spread out over the manor owned by Richard FitzPons, granted to him by King William twenty years prior. The craftsman and professional soldiers lived in the wooden houses located inside the timber palisades that surrounded the bailey, the grassy area where the Pons family had played shinty and now were preparing to have a feast with their vassals.

The palisades were surrounded by a ditch filled with water. A stone gate tower and drawbridge guarded the entrance. When the original ditch had been dug two decades earlier, the soil from the excavation had been heaped and compacted to form the motte, a mound on which the wooden keep and tower had been built. A wooden chateau, Castle Bronylls, had been built by Richard, then replaced by a stone structure ten years later. Now in 1086, it towered over the bailey and hamlet in Breconshire Wales, where they celebrated the arrival of Richard's parents from Aquitaine.

Long tables made from barrels and planks were set upon the green. More planks were placed across small kegs to provide benches for the nobles and the soldiers, craftsmen, freemen, serfs, and their families, all vassals of the manor.

The aroma of pork and lamb roasting on the outdoor grills, as well as those of fried cheese laverbread and mint sauces filled the air. The diet of the Welsh farmers of Bronylls Manor consisted mostly of the grains and vegetables they raised, so the meat supplied by Richard for the feast was unusual and especially appreciated by them. Mini sat between two of her grandchildren, Minuet and Laynie, Willow's sisters. She smiled and caught Catriona's attention from across the table, where she had just mediated an argument among her three sons, Dickins, Pons, and Sullivan. "Cat, you were certainly having fun in the game today! You have experience playing shinty?"

"Yes, Lady Pons, I played growing up in Radnorshire, a village of Irish descendants. My grandparents were from Ireland where the sport is called hurling. The two games are similar, but the sticks used in hurling are heavier and not curved at the end."

"I know we have finally met just today, but as Drogo's wife, would you please call me Mini! If it weren't for the kindness of pilgrims who carried letters to us, we wouldn't know anything about our sons' lives in England. Drogo did mention you were of Irish descent living in Wales, and the daughter of a lord."

"Drogo was granted manors in Herefordshire which bordered my home shire. He then developed his business and bought more land."

"Business?" Mini had an inquisitive look.

"Yes. Like when the pilgrims would drop off letters? Drogo pays these travelers to obtain saffron, cinnamon, and other spices when they visit Spain, and then to bring them back. The sales from small amounts bring high profits."

"How did you and Drogo meet?"

"When he built a castle at the Wye River, the border between England and Wales, the people of Radnorshire became alarmed. We expected the Normans to invade any day. My father was lord mayor of Radnor town and *attorneyz generale* of the shire, and he traveled to Castle Wye to meet Drogo. He discovered, instead of a planned invasion, Drogo was erecting the fort to protect his land in Herefordshire from the Welsh. My father is an expert negotiator and formed an alliance with Drogo. Father agreed that Radnorshire would be a buffer against other Welsh that might raid Drogo's holding. In turn, Drogo pledged alliance and protection of our shire."

"Then your marriage was arranged for political reasons?" asked Mini.

Catriona laughed. "No, not at all! After they made the alliance, my father invited Drogo to Radnor where we had a feast to celebrate the agreement. We met for the first time there. Then Drogo in turn bade my father to visit Castle Wye, and bring his family, and, uh . . . me. At first, I kept my heart guarded, as I was smitten by Drogo, but after he told me of his experiences, I thought he was too wild for me. But, we fell in love during frequent visits; then ten years ago, we were married. Your son is very considerate and encourages me and bolsters my confidence!"

"You must be the perfect woman for him," said Mini, "Dreux

is very particular. He said you are so kind and thoughtful! Do you enjoy living at Castle Wye?"

"My mother taught me to be kind. And at Castle Wye, I can gaze across the river and see my beautiful homeland of Wales. I enjoy traveling with Drogo as he inspects his manors in England. I had always loved growing flowers. After hearing the farmers discuss the sowing of the seeds, the growth of their crops, and the harvest, I developed a passion for cultivation. Now I desire to spread the knowledge of the land to Drogo's other manors to increase their productivity."

Pons was enjoying sausage and telling stories of France and Spain to his grandchildren. Richard and Amicia's son Alejandro asked, "Papa, are the Moors black people? I heard stories they were scary! Are they hard to fight?"

"They are fierce warriors, and they are to be respected. Some are honorable, some are untrustworthy, not much different from the English and the French. As you grow up, you will see that there are good and bad people everywhere. And, no they are not black, they are different shades, just like us! Look at your Uncle Drogo and then at Uncle Gauthier. They are brothers and yet one is darker, one fairer. In fact, when Drogo returned from being in the Sicilian sun years ago, he was as dark as a Moor!"

The boys laughed, and Alejandro elbowed Simon and Walter, the sons of Osborne and Mailisa, and said, "These cousins are the white ones!"

Pons glanced at Richard. "Yes, sometime enemies can become friends. Son, tell them the story how the two strangers, Chopper and Louis, who had just been in battle against you at Hastings, fought off an attack against your brothers."

After Richard described the event, Pons asked, "What happened to them?"

"Chopper sold the land awarded to him for his service and opened a tavern, which of course, he named Chopper's, just outside Saint David's Monastery on the west coast."

"That seems risky. What about the Viking threat along the coast?" asked Gauthier.

"Ha!" laughed Osborne. "Chopper is such an entertainer; if the Vikings showed up, he would just serve them ale and make them laugh!"

"And what of the other one, called Louis?"

"He settled up north and returned to his Scotti clan, the Murdochs," said Gauthier. "And remember how good he was with the bata? Well, I am sure he spends a lot of time playing and watching shinty with his cousins . . . and with his ale."

Three of Mini's granddaughters brought her colorful flowers and she called out, "Oh, how beautiful! I see you have a pretty lilac. That flower is the symbol of Joanna, one of Jesus's disciples. Do you follow Jesus . . . Joanna?"

"Yes, Zizi! And yes, and that's my name!" said her granddaughter.

Next to Joanna was a little girl holding bright orange marigolds. "Your name must be Marie. You have gathered the flowers of the Virgin Mary. She was Jesus's mother."

Marie smiled and looked down.

"And you are Lily," said Mini. "That's why you have those brilliant white flowers!"

"How did you know our names, Zizi?" said the girl.

"Why, because of the flowers you picked!"

The girls glanced at each other with expressions of wonder. Simon joined them carrying a warped ball and was accompanied by Walter. "Girls, the cook fixed us a pig's bladder for us to play football. Are you coming?"

Mini looked doubtful, but Seona added, "Mother Pons, I talked to the children, including those from the village. There will not be any *mob football.* No pushing the little ones, so they can play too. Don't worry."

A farmer's wife placed a wooden slab on the table filled with cakes, still warm, and said, *Pice ar y maen!*"

"My, those smell good!" said Mini. "What did she say?"

"She said cakes on the stone because they are baked on hot stones. And they are best eaten still warm," added Catriona. She spread butter on one and handed it to Mini.

"Mmmm."

The boys and girls looked at her with envy.

"May the little ones have a cake too?"

The children hesitated and looked at their fathers, who nodded. The youths grabbed buttered cakes and stuffed them in their mouths as they ran off across the green, leaving the adults to themselves.

Mini and Catriona were joined by the FitzPons women. They placed a trencher, a large slice of bread used as a plate for food, in front of each one seated at the table. Mailisa poured wine as Amicia and Catriona sat opposite the grandmother. Slabs of wood full of food were passed around. Seona said, "Mini, you must try at least one of each."

She took a small bite of a sausage. "The aroma of the meat is delicious, but I prefer vegetables."

"Try the other sausage, I think you will like it. It is a sausage, but a vegetable sausage, made of laverbread," said Mailisa.

Mini nibbled. "Yes, I do like this! What is laver . . . bread?"

The daughters-in-law smiled and Amicia answered, "Laver is a puree made from seaweed. It is collected south of here, washed, and boiled for hours and added to oatmeal to make bread."

"Well, that is strange, but it is tasty." Mini sampled more food. "This is quite different. I see it is baked bread covered with cheese, but shaped like a sausage."

"That is a cheese sausage. The curds are made from sheep's milk and the bread is stuffed with leeks," added Seona.

"Your sons said you favor sweets, so we are baking more cakes on the stone and will top them with honey," said Amicia.

Mini peered down at her trencher, soaked with the juices from the pork sausage. "I will save my bread for Pons, who will enjoy it more than I."

Mini glanced at the children kicking the ball and asked Mailisa. "I heard Seona say 'mob football.' I recall Osborne telling me he met you at a folk football game? Are they the same? Is it wild?"

"Yes, they are the same game although folk football is a

rather tender name for the mob football game. But the game is dear to me. That's where I met Ozzie, although it's not a game for ladies. A lord who owned manors north of Gloucester once invited our family to join my father on business, to enjoy the countryside. I soon tired of reading and staying indoors, so without the knowledge of my parents, I joined a football game. There were two hamlets on either end of the farmland and before the planting, a wild, free-for-all game started. The goal was to kick the ball to the opponent's village. It was fun and dirty. Scores of people including men, women, and children played. I was doing well and had moved the ball across the field when a well-built man tackled it away. But he did not shove me and was smiling while he took away the ball. A few more times he appeared when I neared the ball, then to my surprise I stole the ball from him! He had not lost his smile, which made me think he was enjoying the game, and he was a gentleman, unlike many other men playing who had knocked me down and were aggressive and rough. The humorous ending to this story is that the next day, the lord of the manor invited our family to attend a supper with local dignitaries, as my father had been doing business with him. I put on a favorite dress and when we arrived for dinner, the handsome man I had played against in football was the Shire Reeve of Gloucester, your Osborne! At first, neither of us recognized the other, because the day before we had been covered with dirt and grass."

"How amusing!" said Mini. "And your family is in Gloucester?"

"Yes, I was born there. My father's parents moved from Rouen in Normandy twenty years ago at the invitation of King William. My late grandfather was part of the Jewish mercantile community in the city, well-known for their ability in trade. William recognized that the merchants would help the kingdom prosper and encouraged many Jewish businessmen to immigrate to England after the conquest. So my grandparents moved to Gloucester, where my father was born. He eventually took over their business and in his travels to the north, my father met Mother in Scotland, and they settled in Gloucester. He became a Christian when he married my mother."

"Quite a story, young lady!" said Mini. "Osborne told me he was a county official who enforced Norman laws and mediated in legal disputes, but you said he was a *shire reeve*. I am not familiar with that title."

"Pardon me, shire reeve is the old term for his position. Osborne is the sheriff."

"Your children are precious. It must take all of your time tutoring them."

"They go with me to the abbey where the monks educate them, while I help at the abbey hospital."

Mailisa glanced across the table. "Seona and Gauthier also had an amusing first meeting."

Seona sipped her wine and seemed embarrassed, but then smiled. "Yes, it was after a shinty game. Also, not a game for ladies. I had convinced my parents as well as the escort who walked me home after my classes at the Saint Guthlac's Abbey that my lessons extended an hour past the time we were dismissed. Often I changed in the nunnery and donned the clothes of a serf, then stole out the back of the abbey and played shinty with men. The monks even played. It was so much fun!"

"That explains your skills today!" laughed Mini.

"One day as I joined a game, far across the field it seemed there was another woman playing," continued Seona. "I first noticed the long blonde hair tied behind in a tail, but then I thought, my she is a robust lady. But it was Gauthier! I was on his team and noticed he played defense and I always wanted to shoot for hails. He favored me and often passed me the ball, so I could strike at the goal. The game ended, and I was ready to leave and change clothes in the women's abbey, so I could return home. The men drank ale and wine after the game, though I always left before they started. That day I stayed, attracted to the man with the blonde hair. I thought he was a Norman due to his accent but was puzzled why he played games with the common folk. Even in my disheveled state, hair tangled, and coarse woolen tunic, I had the courage to talk to him. I was bold and said, 'Wouldn't a noble such as you rather be out hunting than rummaging through the muck playing shinty?' He laughed, gulped his ale, one too many, and looked starry eyed as he said, 'I want to be wherever *you* are, my beauty.' His servants arrived with a cart and rolled him into the bed of the wagon. As they led him away, he called out, 'Lady, join me in my cart!' I did not, but after he left, I learned he was Lord Gauthier FitzPons of Hereford. That was over ten years ago. Now I make time to help the convent in their artwork, illuminating Bibles."

"How wonderful. I would like to see some of your art," said Mini.

"Someday I may show you, however, women aren't recognized for their work on the manuscripts. The nuns tell me it is because they have taken a vow of humility, but the monks are publicly acknowledged for their great toil and labor on the manuscripts . . ."

"I understand, and I sympathize with you, Seona. Uh . . . has your family always lived in Hereford?"

"No, I was born in Ayrshire, Scotland. My father was a merchant and relocated his business to Hereford when I was a child."

"How is it we have all been brought together! It must be God's plan," said Mini. "Our sons are from Aquitaine. You are from Scotland. Mailisa is from Gloucester, Catriona from Wales, and Amicia's native land is Galicia in Spain." Mini glanced at Amicia. "Your son's name, Alejandro. He was named after your father?"

"It is the Spanish version of the French name Alexander," said Amicia.

"A very noble name, indeed!" said Mini. "Richard told me how your father taught you the skills of shipbuilding. Amazing! He also mentioned that you used your talent to design the expansions to the nearby monasteries at Brecon and Malvern."

"Yes, we visited an abbey where Richard had donated funds. There I noticed a weakness in the original chapel walls as well as the newer structures that were being built," answered Amicia. "The framework that reinforces a ship's hull is wood, but the strengthening principles are the same, so I suggested some modification to the buttresses that support the walls. It helped make the buildings more stable."

"And the builders listened to you, a woman?" asked Mini.

"I have learned to be tactful in this man's world," said Amicia. "Richard informed them of the designs."

"Well, I am impressed by your abilities, and by all the competencies of my daughters-in-law. What capable young women!"

Lord Pons relaxed and savored the large family gathering as a man sang and plucked the strings of his crwth. He ambled to the opposite end of the table where his wife chatted with her daughters-in-law. He sat with them, his smile almost sad as he appeared on the verge of tearing. "Daughters! We always treasured Sara, until now our only daughter. Now Mini and I are very blessed that you are part of the family. Years ago, in one of the few letters that made it to Aquitaine, when our sons told us of their marriages, we loved you immediately . . . of course, because our sons loved you. Then when a second rare message was delivered by pilgrims, you each wrote of your love for our sons, and our love for you increased a second time. Now after we have met you and see for ourselves how kind, beautiful, and strong each of you are, our love is tripled! Those are our three loves we have for you."

The women were quiet, absorbing the homily. Several of the residents called to Pons and waved hello; then a group of villagers motioned for him to join them to share wine. Pons moved to the next table and toasted, "Your land is beautiful, *Sante!*"

They raised their cups and replied in unison, "*Iechyd da!*" One man returned the French, "*Sante.*"

"Oh, my apologies! I don't speak English. I speak only French," said Pons.

A fellow in the group stood and bowed, speaking in French, "Lord Pons, it is my pleasure to meet you. I am Lambert, a friend of your sons from before the conquest."

"Yes, yes. Osborne told me about you. Yes! As he said, you are the fifth FitzPons!" He laughed as he said, "But you know, they have an older brother, so you are the sixth FitzPons!"

"And Lord Pons, these gentlemen also are not fluent in

English. We are in Wales. Most of them speak Gaelic. '*Iechyd da'* means *good health*."

"I have a decent grasp of Gaelic," said Richard as he gestured, "but Pont de Dinan, my comrade here and perhaps one of your distant cousins speaks Briton, close enough to Welsh Gaelic."

A dark-haired short man stood and nodded. "Sir, I speak French and English as well. I would be glad to accompany you and translate when you choose to mingle with the people of Bronylls. I also arrived in England in the wake of King William's conquest twenty years ago. Now I live west of Bronylls in Lahnyndhry Castle in Carmarthenshire.

"You are the minstrel! Sweet music, sir! And another close friend that my sons have mentioned," commented Pons. He put his arm around Pont's shoulder and steered him toward a nearby table to socialize with the villagers. "I will take your offer to translate. Maybe we are distant cousins? —We see eye to eye!"

Pons enjoyed the conversation and toasts with his new acquaintances. His sons joined him, and their father commented, "Your vassals respect you very much. But I have a few . . . private questions." He led them out of earshot of the villagers and they sat alone at a table.

Pons's voice was barely above a whisper. "Stories reached us in France that King William ravaged England with fire and sword for years after the invasion, killing thousands, including many women and children. There were reports he devastated parts of England north of York, making the region almost uninhabitable!"

Richard was grim, as were his brothers. "Yes, it was our duty to kill the English soldiers during the battle with King Harold. We were fortunate we were not ordered to perform those despicable tasks and face such a moral dilemma. After the battle, Eustace sent us to Normandy to recruit reinforcements, then we were assigned to the garrison in Winchester while William led his army to attack London. There were rebellions over the next five years and rumors the Welsh and the Scots were preparing to invade England. So luckily, we were sent here to build castles and create the Welsh

March as a buffer against Welsh incursions."

"Recall, brother," said Drogo, "we thought Eustace influenced William to send us to Normandy and obtain reinforcements to keep us out of the duke's judgments."

"What?" said Pons.

"Our standing with William often wavered," said Gauthier.

Their father looked puzzled.

Gauthier described their rebellious deeds when they rode to Dinan without orders, and their discord with the troops at Romney, and at Dover.

"Well, uh . . . you have had the adventure of a lifetime. You have come out in good shape, despite . . . no . . . I am proud of you, sons. Your mother would say God was watching over you.

"But you mentioned Eustace?" said Pons. "He was your superior officer?" They nodded. "My comrade at the Reconquista!"

Richard described how Eustace had supported them, which markedly pleased his father.

"I hope to see him again someday, but tell me about your manor, Richard."

Richard seemed relieved to change the subject and pointed up the long flight of steps climbing the motte to the tower and keep. "Twenty years ago the keep was made of wood, but we rebuilt it of stone. The next project is to replace the wooden palisades around us with stone fortifications. We have started the work. You can see now a stone tower protects the drawbridge. There are still threats from the Welsh."

Richard nodded at Pont de Dinan. "Our, um . . . distant cousin from Brittany," he laughed, "is visiting from the Lahnyndhry Castle, which along with this castle and Drogo's castle at the River Wye, protects the frontier between England and Wales."

"But I thought the Normans invaded Wales," said Pons.

"That's true," replied Drogo, "and William's army marched right through this region to Saint David on the west coast of Wales."

"Then why do your vassals appear so loyal and content?" asked their father. "They are not Normans, they can't speak French. Didn't William harry and destroy parts of Wales as in

England? Am I still to be proud of my sons? Have you been true Christian rulers and treated them accordingly?"

The brothers looked at each other. Gauthier said, "We hope you are proud of us, Father, and we treat our vassals fairly, but there are other reasons they are loyal. Ten years ago, William replaced Stigand, the Archbishop of Canterbury, with his lifelong tutor and comrade Bishop Lanfranc, who urged William to abolish the slave trade in England. The Normans had already eliminated the practice in their lands. But the English and Welsh had a practice of enslaving their own people and selling them to Irish pirates and slave traders. When William marched to Saint David years ago, he freed hundreds of Welsh slaves. The people who work on our manors were among those freed, so they benefited from the Norman invasion. But there are thousands of other Welsh who want us out of their country."

"Slavery has not entirely ended," added Drogo, "but the number of slaves has decreased from before the conquest. William's law prohibits the sale of any man by another."

"Many of the Welsh also respect William for his protection of the priory dedicated to Saint David, the patron saint of Wales," said Osborne. "King William visited the monastery as a Christian pilgrim. The priory is often raided by Vikings, so he improved the fortifications. He occupied only a few coastal towns of Wales where he constructed castles. He did not allot every acre of land as he did in England."

"True, brother, and there is another reason most of Wales is independent," added Drogo. "The Welsh are masters when fighting among their mountain strongholds. The Normans are not committed enough to tangle with them there."

"And they are experts with the longbow," added Osborne, "which I believe they invented."

The arrival of galloping horses drowned out the shouts of the children playing football. The riders dismounted and one of the knights of Bronylls hurried to the FitzPons brothers. Between breaths that forced his words out, the knight said, "Lord Richard, I need to notify Lord de Dinan that the Welsh have Castle Lahnyndhry under siege. And a Welsh army is headed this way!"

CHAPTER EIGHT

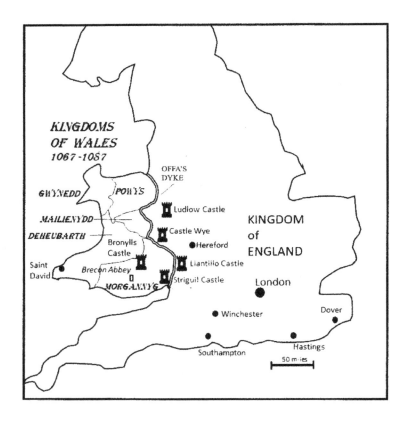

CHAPTER EIGHT

Lord Pons observed from the top of the stone tower. In the fortified village below his sons led the defense against the Welsh attackers. A pair of soldiers with crossbows patrolled nearby along the top of the keep. The enemy had not approached the Bronylls palisade, and they continued to shower the hamlet with arrows from their longbows. The onslaught was without much effect, however, because Richard's force of about a hundred vassals, a score of professional soldiers, and a handful of knights, were pressed against the wooden palisade, safely under the arcs of the missiles.

Raising his voice above the clatter of arrows impacting the wall, Richard crouched next to the palisade as he addressed his brothers. "Lambert is riding to Striguil Castle for help, but until reinforcements arrive, if they do, we must discourage the Welsh from rushing the walls. We may not be able to withstand an assault." He clutched a yelling horn. "We don't have enough arrow slits along the palisade and we can't string the crossbows fast enough to match the firing rate of the longbows. Gauthier, redeploy more crossbowmen to the gate tower. When I sound the horn, loose their bolts en masse. "Go!"

Richard carefully peered through an arrow slit. *Yes, they are becoming more confident. The Welsh archers are leaving the edge of the forest and crossing the meadow.*

Eight stories above the palisades, Simon asked, "Papa! Lift

me up, so I can see!"

"No!" yelled Pons. "Simon, you could be hit by an arrow, stay inside!"

Mailisa had chased the boy, caught him, and now pulled him back down the stairs and into the keep. Lord Pons followed them down the steps into the safety of the keep where the grandmother and mothers played with the children, trying to distract them from the sounds of battle. There was anxiety in the children's voices. "Where is my father? Where is Uncle Drogo? Will those men hurt us?"

"I have a story for you!" said Pons. During the last few days his grandchildren had relished the stories he had told them about their parents. He sat on the floor and gathered the boys' wooden soldiers, diverting the children's attention from the mayhem below.

"Toy soldiers? Is that a good idea?" said Mini, her arms crossed on her chest. "Be careful what you tell them. They are just children!"

"Years ago in Aquitaine," said Pons, "the village priest asked Uncle Richard—he was a boy near your age, Simon—to be in the procession for the Epiphany Celebration." The grandfather lined up the wooden soldiers and marched them forward as if they were in a parade. "These two figures walking in front are the monks carrying gifts from the magi, followed by the priest with his incense—and these soldiers with spears, imagine they are each holding a shepherd's staff—are Uncle Richard and his older brother Simon. They acted the part of the shepherds and walked behind the priest."

The children had formed a circle around their grandfather and were watching intently. On the other side of the hall, the mothers, now temporarily relieved, were inspecting crossbows and taking inventory of the bolts, while Mini went upstairs to review the situation in the hamlet.

Pons continued his story. "Behind the priest, Uncle Richard and Simon began to fight with the staffs." Pons made the two soldiers act as if they were fighting, and the children broke into laughter. "Zizi was very upset with the boys fighting," continued their grandfather, "but the people lining the street and watching were smiling and laughing. The priest had no idea that was happening."

"You said Uncle Richard was a shepherd in the parade," said Willow, "but where was my father and where were Uncle Drogo and Uncle Ozzie?"

"They were with us alongside the street with the villagers, who were lighting candles, getting ready to follow the parade after it passed. Wouldn't you know, but young Gauthier, Ozzie, and Drogo were sword fighting with their flaming candles!" The children screamed with laughter and their eyes were bright.

"Tell us another story, Papa," said Laynie.

"Before the next story, who can tell me what Epiphany is about?" asked her mother, Seona.

"It is when the three wise men visited baby Jesus," answered the grandson Pons.

"Very good!" said Seona.

"Now tell us a story about my father," added Sully.

"Well, the boys, your uncles and your father, Drogo, were all very young, but Drogo was only three. Uncle Simon, Richard, and Sara were the oldest and were able to ride their own ponies."

"I want to ride a pony!" said one of the children.

"Before you know it, the battle will be over and you will! As I was saying, Uncle Gauthier rode with Zizi on her horse and Uncle Ozzie rode with Simon, and I had Drogo with me. It was a family outing as we rode through the Baconnais forest near our village. I remember it was a sunny day, and as we crossed a river, the hooves went *clomp, clomp, clomp* on the wooden bridge. Drogo glanced to the left and said, 'One river!' Then he looked to the right and said, 'Two rivers!'"

There was silence, then the oldest children started laughing. Alejandro shouted, "There weren't two rivers!" and continued laughing.

Half of the children appeared bewildered and Willow said, "You don't understand? You are as silly as that baby Drogo!"

"We want to hear another story!" said Dickins.

One floor above them Mini watched the battle escalate. The Welsh archers were shooting a steady barrage of arrows and firing as they advanced toward the palisades. Hundreds of armed men followed them. A green flag with a red dragon was carried among the foot soldiers. Her anxiety increased as she observed the battle. *It's frightening that their archers can loose five or six arrows in the time it would take a crossbowman to shoot one or two! Where are my sons? There—the gold plume of Richard who is crouching behind the wall speaking to a group of archers. And I see Gauthier's blue crest— next to Richard. I can follow Ozzie's green as he runs to the left and the bright red tail on Drogo's helmet moving to the right side of the tower, each leading a group of men. Knowing they were far from home and fighting in the conquest was stressful enough but watching them here is terrifying.* When the enemy was less than 100 paces from the palisade walls, Richard blew the gjallarhorn and a storm of arrows zipped from the gate tower. An instant later a score of the enemy archers fell to the ground. The attackers continued forward, most unaware of the devastating crossbolt attack, when another score of their archers collapsed with crossbolts protruding from their bodies. The infantry fled back to the forest two hundred paces away and the remaining archers followed.

Mini returned and her daughters-in-law met her with anticipation. She smiled and nodded.

Pons set a helmet on the floor and draped a green scarf over it. He turned a cup upside down and placed it at the top. "Little ones. This cup is our donjon, our castle keep, where we are safe. He placed five toy soldiers on top. Look at the steep mound. Do you think it is easy for anyone to climb up this hill?"

A chorus of denials came from the children.

"When your uncles and fathers grew up, they lived at a castle like this, with a steep grassy hill. One late spring after it had rained for days, Gauthier and Ozzie went outside, against Zizi's wishes and slid down the hill into the muddy ditch." Pons made a pair of the toy figures slide down the scarf. "When they climbed back up to do it again, they were covered with mud and it was dripping from their arms and legs. Only their white eyes showed through on their faces and their hair stuck up in the air like goat horns! Their brothers were amused and hollered that monsters were invading the castle. Your Zizi heard the commotion. She said, 'I'll lock you out all night if you don't wash!'" The grandchildren laughed. "Their brothers joined, and they all looked like mud monsters, even holding the castle's cats in their laps as they slid down the hill. They had to spend all night outside! The next day their punishment was to join the maidens at the creek and wash their own clothes."

Mini detected smoke and climbed the stairs to take measure of the events below in the hamlet. From the meadow, the enemy archers shot fire arrows into the village. The thatched roof of a house was on fire. A family fled the blaze, seeking shelter in another house. A second house was aflame. More villagers bolted to escape the fire, and a few children were hit by arrows. Richard brandished a white cloth above the palisade and the enemy stopped firing. Mini's sentiment was in tumult. *He is surrendering? But of course! The poor children.*

The Welsh king also raised a white cloth. Richard left the walled area unarmed and advanced across the meadow. He was accompanied by Pont de Dinan and the manor reeve, the foreman of the Bronylls manor. They met a pair of Welshmen halfway across the meadow between the hamlet and the edge of the forest. Both parties were taking the same risk. At one hundred paces, an arrow shot from the Welsh longbows could penetrate armor and the crossbows along the bailey walls could kill the Welsh envoys. The two groups met, and Richard spoke first. "We are honored that you respect the white flag of truce. As my Welsh is not good enough to carry on negotiations, I leave this to my foreman, a Welshman as yourself, Reeve of Bronylls."

One of the Welshmen said, "I am Jestyn ap Gwrgant, King of Morgannyg."

"First, I ask as a fellow countryman," said Richard's foreman, "Our wives and children were in the houses that caught fire. I plead that you let them leave in safety and we continue the fight after that."

"You say I am your countryman, and you are Welsh,"

answered Jestyn, "but you are a slave to these Normans who fight us."

"We were freed by the Normans and are no longer slaves. We fight for the safety of our families."

"I respect that, but this land belongs to the House of Morgannyg. Depart now with your families and you will not be harmed. The fight with your masters will continue. If you do not take leave, we will not be responsible for the deaths of your women and children."

Pont de Dinan confirmed the translation of the king's demand. The reeve appeared uneasy but calmed when Richard nodded in agreement to the king's proposal. They returned to the palisade as Richard deliberated. *I will have less than thirty men after my vassals go.* He looked up at the tower and was filled with distress for his family. *I would also want my family to leave if I was in the reeve's place. Now where is Lambert?*

Lambert had pressed his mount onward all day and into the night and had just crossed Offa's Dyke. The earthen wall and ditch was named for the King of Mercia who had built the barrier hundreds of years earlier. It stretched along the border of Wales and England and had been created to keep the Welsh from raiding his kingdom. Lambert finally arrived at Striguil Castle, which overlooked the Bristol Channel. Tower banners fluttered in the night breeze as the reflection of the full moon rippled on the waves. The steward at the castle refused to wake his lord, Richard FitzGilbert, the Earl of Hereford, and Lambert was forced to wait until the morning to appeal for help.

The earl was a powerful noble who oversaw the shires of Hereford and Gwent, as well as the marches, the frontier between Wales and England. While FitzGilbert ate breakfast, Lambert described the assault on Bronylls Castle. The earl looked annoyed. "Sir Lambert, years ago after King William's incursion to Saint David to pacify the area, he bestowed the role of Marcher Lords to the FitzPons brothers and yourself. There was an understanding you were to continue to lead sorties into the Welsh kingdoms. Either you didn't follow these orders, or your skirmishes have failed to weaken and discourage them. At most, I would expect the Welsh to carry on scattered raids, but not threaten an invasion of England." The earl finished eating, dipped his hands in a bowl of water, dried them, and stood. "I will lead my knights to Bronylls and repulse the Welsh, but I will not continue farther west to your castle, Sir Lambert, because then I would be absent from Striguil Castle for too long. You will need to find help from the Marcher Lords to recover Lahnyndhry. And because you and Richard permitted this rebellion to organize, and I must quell this uprising, you will both pay me a handsome levy for this rescue."

Within two hours, the earl had mustered twenty knights. Two score mounted infantry accompanied them armed with crossbows. They covered half the distance to Bronylls before dark and made camp outside of Castle Carleon. Its environs consisted of the village and manor of Lord Iacobus, a Norman knight who had fought at Hastings. The earl declined an invitation to spend the night in Iacobus's castle and requested him to join him in his tent along with his second in command to discuss the mission. He also had the intention of recruiting knights from Carleon to reinforce his expedition.

"Lord Iacobus, you, like myself and the other March Lords, pledged to buffer England from the Welsh," said the earl as they shared ale in his tent. "I would assume you will join our expedition to help expel the invaders from Castle Bronylls."

"Yes, your lordship, I have already notified my knights. I will lead them in the morning to accompany you to Bronylls." He raised his cup. "To success!" The other two answered in kind as Iacobus soon excused himself to organize his men for the next day's march.

Iacobus parted the tent flaps and was only several steps away when he stopped to listen. He overheard the earl say to his second, "Your men will receive their regular wage and a bonus for this service."

"When?" asked his officer.

"As soon as we defeat the Welsh. I will collect the penalty from Richard in silver coins and you can distribute the money at once to your men. That will satisfy them."

The earl's subordinate asked, "What about me?"

"You will receive the largest amount, as usual."

"I have been loyal for many years, Lord. Give me Richard's keep as his penalty. And being your vassal, your share of the profits from the land would greatly increase your revenue."

He coughed out a sharp laugh. "That could be done . . . but, no, his three brothers all have influence and power," said the earl. "They would consider that too harsh and would not allow that. I do not want to fight the FitzPons brothers. I fought alongside them at Hastings. To battle them when they are in concert is like battling a four-headed dragon. Besides, King William himself granted them the rights to the land."

"Lord, there is a way. What if we arrived at Bronylls too late and found the Welsh had overrun the castle and slain everyone?"

"It would have to be everyone," answered the earl.

Iacobus headed toward his castle gate, worried how he could alert his comrades at Bronylls. He passed a campfire, and recognized a man preparing to bed down for the night. "Lambert, is that you!"

They enjoyed a short reunion, reminiscing of their comradeship at the Battle of Hastings, although it had been almost twenty years. Iacobus whispered what he had heard from the earl and finished with, "I cannot stop him but I will be most effective in ensuring justice if I accompany him to Bronylls. You must warn your FitzPons brothers. I will provide you with a spare mount."

Lambert quietly saddled his horse and rode in haste and darkness toward Bronylls, a second horse trailing. He was confident his mount would lead him safely to Richard's castle. They were retracing the route he had ridden just the day before and with a crescent moon, his steed could easily follow the road. Bright starlight alone was enough for a horse to see the way.

Earlier at Bronylls, Richard and the Welsh king Jestyn finished their parley. The vassals left the bailey palisades with their families and dispersed to their farmsteads nearby. Ozzie and Gauthier were moving their war horses out of the bailey and to the slopes under the keep, inside the inner palisades. As Richard shouted orders to his knights, Drogo approached accompanied by two knights from Castle Wye, followed by smiths and craftsmen of the Bronylls manor. Richard surveyed his skilled vassals. "You must leave now! That was the agreement, to protect your families."

"Our families are safe with our friends," said an old blacksmith. His barrel chest and thick forearms made him look younger than his five decades. He nodded toward his comrades. "Jestyn will see a hundred farmers leaving. He won't notice four or five of us. We choose to fight for our homes . . ." he bowed to Richard, "and our Lord. We might still be slaves were it not for King William's decree and your generosity."

"I am your servant as well," said Richard as he nodded. "Together we can win this fight! There are not enough of us to defend the bailey's walls, so collect weapons, food, and water and regroup at the keep's lower palisades."

From the top of the keep, Mini and Pons watched the activity below. The warhorses had been led inside the gate tower guarding the bottom of the motte. Crossbowmen were positioned on top of the inner gate tower and a score of others spread out along the palisades flanking the gate. The villagers had departed to their farms as the Welsh forces of Morgannyg Shire filed across the meadow, through the main gate, and into the bailey. The shadows began casting toward the east as the sun lowered to the knolls. Pons slumped against a crenellation atop the keep. "It's all my fault! We should not have come! I have endangered all our children and grandchildren!"

Mini put her arm around his shoulders as her husband lamented, "This was to be a wonderful and peaceful gathering! We had never seen our grandchildren. And I promised my sister I would find them."

"Find whom, my love?"

He was silent for several moments, then said. "At home, in Pons Barony, before Mother died, she confided to me that prior to her marriage to Father, she had been espoused once before. Her first husband was a Welsh nobleman from Shire Deheubarth, just north of here. I recall my mother crying as she told me she had borne two beautiful daughters to him. He left her without notice or funds, but fortunately his own mother loved them and cared for the two girls and my mother. For several years they had a happy life, but Mother's husband returned, demanded the girls live with him, and took them away. Mother was devastated and tried to forget. She went on a pilgrimage to Compostela. At the resting place in village Pons, she met my father."

"My God! You never told me any of this! Why not and what happened to your half-sisters?"

"If they were anything like Mother, they would have survived. I imagine them using intelligence and toughness to carve out Christian lives. I never mentioned them because Mother asked me to tell only my sister."

"And you thought you could find them in Wales, after all these years?" asked Mini.

"I have sent only two letters to my sister in Paris in my lifetime, both carried by pilgrims. The first letter years ago told her of our half-sisters. The second letter was just last year, informing her that we were journeying to Wales on an extended visit. I did not remember to mention our half-sisters. She responded right away with a letter sent by private courier, at great expense, and reminded me of our half-sisters and to find them." He shook his head, as if to clear his thoughts. "But now, we must concentrate on this crisis and survive."

Mini gently squeezed his shoulder. "We are not beaten, and I know you will not let anyone harm our family. You will keep the promise to your sister. I recall your mother would say, *It's always darkest before the dawn.*"

The sun dipped below the mountains. The Welsh intruders occupied the village and lighted cook fires, beginning the siege of Bronylls Castle.

The children woke the next morning complaining of hunger and confinement, but settled as they were provided bread, jam, and water. At their own homes, they would have been cared for by servants, but the tower did not have room enough for the few domestics that the FitzPons families had brought with them from their manors. The children brightened when Lord Pons donned his armor. "Your fathers . . ." Pons hesitated and glanced at their mothers who were inspecting crossbows. Their faces were set in fierce determination. Several more crossbows had been collected from the tower's armory and lay on benches. "Your mothers and fathers will never let you be harmed, but they might need my help!" said Pons. He was short, but his erect and confident bearing projected a strong presence. His grandchildren showed a mixture of emotions. The younger ones, not understanding the real danger, appeared thrilled, but a few of the older children now seemed concerned.

With her foot inserted in the stirrup, one of the women held a crossbow securely to the floor and struggled to pull a bow string to the trigger. "Only a very strong man can string a crossbow that way while standing," said Pons. "Here, I will show you how to use your legs."

The grandfather sat on the floor with one foot in the stirrup. He pulled the string back into position, his leg doing most of the work, as if he were rowing a boat.

"Lord Pons," said Catriona, "will this help?" She had retrieved a thick leather belt from the armory and strapped it around her waist. A brass hook was attached to the front of the belt.

"Yes, yes! I thought all of those were taken by the archers. Bend your legs, that's it, hook the string onto the brass piece, and stand up to string the bow."

She tried but could not bring the string far enough. "Let Amicia try," said Pons. "She has strong sea legs from her time on the ships."

Amicia was able to string the crossbow and said, "Being shorter . . . I have better leverage. You can do it, try again." With her encouragement, the women each strung a bow.

"Daughters," said Pons, "start shooting."

Pons negotiated the long path from the keep to the bottom of the mound. The Welsh began shooting arrows from behind the houses and barns in the hamlet. Pons used his long teardrop shield to protect himself until he reached the palisade.   Richard's crossbowmen manned the palisade and shot through arrow loops into the bailey. Several more of their archers atop the inner gate tower fired from the crenellations. Pons finally joined Richard at the top of the gate tower. The high pitched roars of injured horses added to the din of battle and forced Richard to shout, "Father! Why did you come?" He looked up the motte slope, as a warhorse fell, pierced with arrows.

"I wanted to mount a warhorse and charge with you into the bailey, but now I see we have only a few horses left!"

The Welsh archers, trailed by foot soldiers, charged the inner gate, sensing the defenders had run short of bolts or were reloading. The FitzPons brothers ordered spears thrown as the enemy closed on the wall, then suddenly bolts from the keep impaled several attackers. Another hail of bolts discouraged the Welsh and they retreated behind the buildings at the far end of the bailey.

Ozzie and Drogo waved lances as they looked up at the tower, their green and red pennants flapping the air. The women let out whoops in response. "I can't help but feel the thrill of battle," said Richard, "but I never thought it would be mixed with the terror for my family. I am afraid with another charge they will breach the walls."

During the pause in battle, from atop the gate tower, Pons observed the castle's soldiers treating their own wounds. Among the enemy wounded, he noticed several women dressed in white. They had apparently accompanied the Welsh king's army, and were bandaging and helping fallen soldiers back to the safety of the bailey houses.

Pons saw movement to the east at the edge of the woods. A rider emerged from the trees on a warhorse, heading toward a section of the moat distant from the battle, and leading a second mount. "Richard. A knight, by the looks of his armor. A group of the enemy have noticed him, but he has a chance, none of them are archers. "

The horseman spurred his mount into a gallop towards the moat as enemy foot soldiers hurried to cut him off. He drove his warhorse into the water. The spare horse followed. As the powerful chargers swam across the moat, the rider swung his shield across his back. The enemy shelled him with spears and stone-headed throwing sticks. Osborne ran to the moat, leading a handful of soldiers. Some of his men hurled spears at the enemy.

"The Welsh are backing off," shouted Pons. "Isn't that your comrade Lambert?"

"He'll make it, somehow," said Richard. "Lambert will never give up."

Halfway across the moat, the warhorse, encumbered by the armored knight and exhausted by several days of long rides, struggled to keep above the water. When both animal and rider floundered, the enemy foot soldiers again hurried toward the moat.

As the enemy pelted him with missiles, Lambert rolled off the saddle but held onto the cantle. His steed recovered, swam on, and dragged him through the water. Osborne and his men threw the rest of their spears and drove the Welsh back again. Lambert's grip weakened, but he still hung on with one hand. Abruptly, Lambert lost his grip, sank out of sight, and his steed reached the shore without him.

Richard gasped from atop the gate tower, "He's gone. God's bones, no!"

Osborne unstrapped his helmet and tossed it, then pulled off his tunic. A soldier helped him remove his long hauberk and he removed his padded shirt. Watching from the gate tower, Richard said, "Ozzie is going in after Lambert!"

Osborne was about to dive in when the second horse made it to the bank. Clinging to its mane was Lambert. He lost grip and fell into the shallow water at the muddy bank.

"He's not moving and looks drowned," groaned Richard, "after all that. They are taking him back towards the palisade."

Osborne's men helped him carry Lambert's body to the palisade that led to the tower keep. As they passed him up a ladder, Lambert's body doubled over the top of the wall. Water gushed out of his mouth and then he coughed violently.

"He is alive!" shouted Richard still watching from the top of the gate tower.

"Wonderful *and* astonishing, son! Your mother would say, it's the work of the Lord," added Pons. "And I pray he has news that the Normans from Striguil are right behind him."

The Welsh charged the walls again, barely slowed by a meager response of crossbolts. Richard looked up to the tower. "They are out of bolts as well!" Then he saw that several enemy soldiers had penetrated to the backside of the mound and were attempting to climb the tower. The attackers in the bailey had reached the walls and were scaling the palisade. Richard and Lord Pons rushed down to ground level from the gate tower and joined in the hand to hand combat. Outnumbered, the remaining score of knights and soldiers along with Drogo and Gauthier fought the enemy at the bottom of the stairs leading to the keep. Osborne had left Lambert in the care of a squire and joined them. He shouted, "Lambert told me that FitzGilbert could be here soon, but he plans to kill ALL of us!"

Richard pointed to the top of the hill. "Father, go to the tower! The children!" Pons rallied two soldiers who followed him up the slope. The FitzPons brothers and several knights fought as they backed up the hill, exhaustion setting in until they could no longer slash with their swords but resorted to blocking and shoving with their shields.

At the top of the stronghold Catriona and Amicia had been loading bolts and setting the triggers, then handing the crossbows to Mailisa and Seona. Working together, they had hailed a steady volley of bolts upon the attackers. They discovered that a novice could quickly learn to aim a crossbow, and they were improving their accuracy, but were soon short of bolts. Amicia shouted down to the next level. "Mini, are there more bolts down there?"

Her mother-in-law, trying to comfort the grandchildren, searched the room then answered, "No!" She didn't notice that the three oldest children, Alejandro, Willow, and Simon had gone downstairs.

Mini heard a door thud below her on the front side of the tower. Seona, who could see them from above, shouted, "Willow! Get back inside!" She yelled down the staircase, "Mother— Alejandro, Simon, and Willow are outside the keep!"

Amicia, Seona, and Mailisa rushed to the first level of the keep. Catriona had remained at the upper level of the tower and saw that a score of attackers had crossed the moat at the backside of the tower. Their archers drew their bows. She ducked behind the wall and heard whistling, then loud grunts. Crawling along the floor she came to the bodies of the tower guards. Both had been mortally wounded by arrows. She glanced through a crenellation as missiles continued to pelt the tower. Enemy soldiers heaved iron hooks attached to long knotted ropes up toward the top of the keep. The clanging of metal on stone repeated as the attackers adjusted their throws to reach the top. The scraping metal jumbled with the clatter of wooden arrows ricocheting off the walls. Catriona stooped down and crawled to the village side of the tower. She saw the three grandchildren collecting arrows and piling them up near the lower door. Their mothers appeared and quickly drove them all into the keep. The door opened again, and they retrieved the arrows.

The mothers seemed in a panic running up the staircase with armloads of arrows. Catriona motioned them to stay low as enemy arrows bounced off the walls. Without even trying to string one arrow, Amicia moaned, "These are from the long bows! They are twice as long as the crossbow bolts. Will they work in the crossbows?" A grappling hook suddenly caught hold on the wall just above their heads. They faced each other and for an instant froze. Amicia and Catriona inserted the long arrows in the crossbows and handed them to Mailisa and Seona. As enemy arrows continued to rattle off the stone parapet, they quickly glanced over the edge of the wall, and shot the recovered arrows. Their targets below were a man holding the bottom of the rope and another starting his climb on the rope.

Mailisa and Seona dropped back down to the floor. "The arrows did not fly true!" said Seona. "The flights curved and missed." Another hook caught at a crenellation. The women could not disengage the hooks because of the weight of the men as they climbed.

Mailisa broke two arrows in half and gave the fletched ends to Amicia and Catriona. "Load these." They shot over the parapet again. Both sunk back to crouch and seemed defeated. "Closer, but we missed again! yelled Mailisa.

Amicia broke several more arrows and handed one to Catriona. They strung all six of the crossbows. "Keep shooting. We'll get more arrows." Seona and Mailisa continued to fire arrows and a few hit the intended targets.

"Two men are halfway up the ropes to the top," yelled Seona. "We may have one more shot before they get here! But you must wait for them to get to the top. When they climb on the edge, shoot. We can't miss at that distance!"

Within seconds the face of a soldier appeared. The women hid the bows behind them and he continued to pull himself up over the edge. Mailisa whispered, "Wait for a bigger target. They don't have armor." The soldier pulled himself up to his waist and Seona shot him in the chest. He fell to the ground four stories below. A second man appeared and was dispatched by Mailisa with her bow.

A hail of arrows prevented the women from looking over the edge of the parapet. An enemy soldier had climbed up the back side of the keep and suddenly appeared, rushing around the corner of the tower. He ran toward the women, with drawn sword. When he saw they had no arrows, he seized their bows and tossed them behind him. "I will not hurt you, ladies. You will be valuable hostages." He sheathed his sword and leaned through a crenellation to pull up a second Welshman.

One floor below, Catriona, retrieving more arrows, heard the enemy soldier and pointed up the stairs. The children were terrified and were crying. Amicia and Mini were trying to reassure the children. "Children, let's pray that the fighting will stop, and your fathers will return unharmed," said Mini.

Amicia quoted Psalms 23, "The Lord is my shepherd; I shall not want. He maketh me to lie down in green pastures: he leadeth me beside the still waters . . ." As she continued, the children were calmed.

Mini looked up the stairs and offered a sword to Catriona, "Help them!"

"I don't think I can kill anyone!" said Catriona. The

commotion upstairs grew louder, and startled into action, she picked up a broom instead and ran to the top floor. Seona and Mailisa had each grabbed a leg of the enemy soldier as he was helping a comrade to reach the top. Just as they lifted and pushed one soldier over the wall, the second pulled himself into view. Catriona arrived at a run and thrust the broom in his face. He lost his grip on the rope and fell backwards, knocking loose another soldier climbing below him. The women leaned over the parapet wall and saw the men had landed in a heap upon the ground. While the women were distracted, two more climbers slipped in undetected behind them and rushed down the stairs towards Mini and the children.

Pons reached the tower and pounded on the heavy wooden door with the pommel of his sword. He cursed himself for thinking a simple knock would gain entry. When he was about to identify himself, Mini swung the door open. Her terrified look beyond him compelled Pons to turn around and see his men fighting several attackers. His escorts held off the enemy with their shields. He joined the melee, tipped the balance in their favor, and they put the enemy soldiers out of action. Pons's right hand was slashed during the fight. As one of his men cut a piece of cloth from his tunic and tightened it to stop the bleeding, Pons surveyed his sons fighting as they retreated toward the tower. "Guard the door for Richard and his men," he ordered his guards. "but close it if you cannot defend it." Pons approached the door once more and saw Mini waiting up the stairs on the first landing with Alejandro and Willow at her sides.

"Quickly, husband," said Mini.

Something's amiss. She opened the door before she knew it was me. I have a feeling. Then she nodded encouragement for him to enter. He armed himself with a brace of daggers, dropped to one knee as he crossed the threshold, and stabbed back with both blades. A sword cut meant for his neck missed, trailed by a clang on the wall. The metallic ringing competed with the thud of a crossbow hitting the stone floor, the zip of a crossbow bolt, all followed by the skittering of the errant arrow. A pair of enemy soldiers sunk to their knees, with their hands pressed against blood-soaked tunics. A sword and a longbow lay on the floor. *That was lucky. Hardly any of them have armor.* Pons hollered to Mini to go inside and lock the door at the next floor.

He started to return outside and Mini cried, "They threatened to shoot the children if I didn't open the door!"

"You did the right thing, you kept them safe," answered her husband with a smile. Pons retrieved the weapons and rushed out of the tower. The FitzPons brothers were halfway up the hill, fighting as they backed up the slope. Lord Pons saw more Welsh entering the bailey. *Another hundred! How can we endure? No, I see, it's the villagers, they have returned! Does the Welsh king see them? Thank God.* He shouted to Richard. "Blow the yelling horn!" He pointed across the village to the newcomers.

Richard blew the horn, but the enemy had already slowed and were retreating down the hill. Richard held up a white cloth and yelled, "King Jestyn! King of Morgannyg! We must talk!"

Richard's vassals now blocked the front gate at the entrance to the bailey and the Welsh king saw that his men were trapped between the keep's motte and the outer palisade. It did not matter that most of the villagers carried farm tools, enough spears also bristled from their ranks to be menacing. The fighting stopped everywhere, and it grew quiet. Jestyn, atop the gate tower leading to the mound, raised his arms to show himself. Richard moved down the steep hill to the same level as the king, fifty paces between them. He raised his voice. "The villagers want to live, raise their families, and worship Christ. We all want the same. Let us stop fighting and join our forces against a common threat. You saw a messenger arrive earlier on horseback. His message is from the Normans. From Lord FitzGilbert. FitzGilbert is coming to kill ALL of us. Yes, you can flee, and then the villagers, your countrymen, may continue to till their fields, but they will live under Norman rule. And you will be next. Would you rather have the FitzPons families or the Normans rule this land?"

There was a flash of color several hundred paces to the east, where Lambert had ridden out of the forest. Richard shouted, "We may be too late. With God's favor they may only be FitzGilbert's scouts. But he will be here soon. Make a decision!"

The earl's vanguard led by Lord Iacobus halted their mounts and studied the tableau. He held up a white cloth and with his ten mounted knights he slowly made his way through the Welsh farmers at the entrance of the bailey. Iacobus then rode to the base of the inner gate tower occupied by King Jestyn. Other than low mumbles and jostling from the fighters, the manor was silent.

Iacobus was tall and as he sat on his steed, he towered over everyone. "The earl's army is an hour behind me. I will deny I said this, but he is intent on killing everyone here so he can seize the manor."

Among the murmurs from scores of Welsh soldiers could be heard, "Kill us all. That's what Lord Richard said!"

King Jestyn bellowed, "Everyone sheath your swords and pass this message across the bailey to all! We must convince the Normans we are one people, that we have won the battle, and that the rebels have fled. Begin digging graves in plain view of the Normans. By the time FitzGilbert arrives, he will see that we didn't need his help at all!" The faces of the gathering were blank with disbelief. The people were silent. Jestyn understood. "We all desire to take our dead back to our homes and bury them there, but our survival, the success of this plan, depends on burying our fallen here. And it is still in our home shire." He looked at Iacobus. "Will your knights be faithful to this plan?" Iacobus nodded.

Iacobus sent a messenger to FitzGilbert, who was advancing toward Bronylls with his main force. Upon hearing the conflict had ended, he slowed his progress, no longer in a hurry. By the time he arrived hours later, most of the dead had been interred and more graves were being dug. As far as he knew, all the Welsh were Richard's vassals. Richard immediately paid his penalty in silver coins to the lord hoping FitzGilbert would soon return to Castle Striguil.

The Bronylls Welsh and the Welsh of Morgannyg Shire were exhausted and grief-stricken. When these former adversaries began identifying their dead, their hatred for one another took up again, yet burned away as they focused on the hard labor of digging their comrades' graves. The tension lessened as Christian prayers in their common language resounded across the manor for all who had fallen. Water, herbs, and bandages were shared for the treatment of the wounded. Lord Pons stood atop the gate tower and observed two women tending to the wounded. Word of their exceptional healing skills had spread, and they were frequently besought for help. They had worked through the night with little sleep. He called to the women, "Are you angels who came down from heaven to save us?" *I swear by the saints they both look like my mother!*

They noticed him. One said, "You are bleeding."

He raised the hand and said, "Can you stop it?" *That's it — I must be delirious—I have lost too much blood. Mini did an excellent job dressing my wound, but I took it out of the sling she made and was helping bury the dead shoveling. Now I am bleeding again! But . . . they can't be my sisters!*

When he met them at the base of the tower, one said, "Sit down and raise your hand. After we fix your bandage, you must keep your hand elevated for several days to prevent it from bleeding again."

"I am Pons. Please, my ladies, what are your names?"

"I am Ceingwen and this is my sister Brangwen." As she applied herbs and a clean bandage, Pons grunted in pain, "What is that green paste? Smells like something I would eat with fish."

"The scent is from mint which will heal the wound," said Ceingwen. "Another herb in the plaster is bloodwort, which will help staunch the bleeding."

"Where are you from and how did you learn French?" asked Pons.

Ceingwen used strips of cloth to make a sling for his arm and tied it around his neck. "You have lost three fingers and if this bandage and elevation does not stop the bleeding, your hand will need to be cauterized."

"We live at Brecon village near the monastery and work in the abbey hospital there. We have had Welsh, Norman, and English patients from time to time and the monks have taught us much."

Their hair is like my mother's. They have high cheek bones and are short in stature like Mother. I must ask. "Was your mother's name Maeve?"

The women flashed looks at each other, eyebrows raised, and appeared shocked. They broke into sobs. One said, "Yes, how did you know? Our mother left us when we were young. She went on a pilgrimage and never returned."

Several weeks later, the castle bailey was finally peaceful again. The spring and early summer rains were encouraging grass in the field after the scouring and trampling in the battle. Tables were now laid out with food and drink for the gathering held in honor of the fallen. The Welsh of Bronylls Manor and Morgannyg Shire together celebrated their alliance. The children of the hamlet and the visiting FitzPons children played their games of shinty and football. Ceingwen and Brangwen sat at a table with Pons, Mini, and their family. Pont de Dinan joined them. Pons and his sisters reminisced about their mother Maeve.

"I remember Mother was small, but very sturdy," said Brangwen. "She was a strong walker and even swam in the cold river, as if she enjoyed it! I can envision her thriving, even on the long pilgrims' walk to Compostela."

"Yes!" Pons explained. "Even when she was elderly, she still had strong legs. And she loved her garden, especially growing flowers.

"Sisters," he continued, "I am half Welsh through our mother. I assume you are solely of Welsh descent?"

"Yes," Brangwen smiled, "but in our native tongue our land is called *Cymru*, not Wales, and we are *Cymry*, instead of Welsh."

"Welsh is an English word," added Ceingwen. "It means *foreigner*."

"Does Cymry have a special meaning?" asked Mini.

"Yes," said Ceingwen. "It means the opposite of the English word. It means *countryman*."

Mini playfully bumped her husband with her shoulder. "You always admire your Gallo-Roman ancestors, easily traced by your name. You should laud your *Cymry* folk more often!" Mini raised her cup. "*Iechyd da*! Good health! To our Cymry ancestors!"

The family returned her toast. "*Iechyd da*!" Mini surveyed her sons. "And of course, our children are as much Welsh as Aquitanian."

"That's right, Mother," said Richard. "Your father was originally from Wales and married your mother in Anjou!"

"What was your father's name?" asked Ceingwen.

"Davies," Mini answered.

Brangwen and Ceingwen laughed. The others looked puzzled. "That is a very common name in Wales," said Ceingwen. "The name means *son of David*."

The FitzPons brothers and their wives cast knowing glances. "Yes, yes . . . the Welsh want to honor their patron saint, so many name their boys David," said Gauthier. "Then to avoid confusion the next generation is named Davies, son of David."

"That is like my name," Drogo said. He saw his brothers' knitted eyebrows. "Um, *our* name. FitzPons, in Norman French, son of Pons, written in Latin as *Filii de Pontius*."

"It is the same as the name on my locket," said Pont de Dinan. "*Marcus Pontius Laelianus,* who was my ancestor and a Roman senator."

Drogo laughed. "You are another of our brothers—Pons . . . or FitzPons." He then said, "Father, I am Drogo FitzPons, so I have two names. But the Roman named on Pont's locket had three. Why three names?"

"They had a given name, a family name, and a name for the tribe or clan. So for Pont's ancestor, Marcus Pontius Laelianus— Marcus would be this Roman's familiar name, of the family Pontius, and the clan of Laelianus."

"Your own father was also Pons," said Drogo. "That would make you Pons FitzPons?"

His father laughed. "Yes, you are right, when he was alive, that is what I was called."

"Do you think our ancestor was named Pons after Saint Pons of Cimiez, for the same reason the Welsh name boys after their patron saint?"

"Hm, I never thought of that." Pons curled his bottom lip as he hesitated in thought. "There are many Pons cousins throughout Aquitaine, Toulouse, and Provence. I believe colonists from Italy with the surname Pontius arrived in France when the ancient Romans built their cities in Gaul. There may be many named Pons who are descendants of Pontii and there may also be those who adopted the name because they revered Saint Pons. Does it matter? Everyone who is here, I see as my family. We are from widely scattered heritages. Yes, sometimes I put too much emphasis on blood relations, but for a family it's more important how we think of one another . . . how we love one another—how we treat each other—our hearts."

There was a pause as they absorbed his last statement. Lambert joined them, perspiring from his comic attempts to referee the children's football game. "Here is a man with our heart—the sixth or seventh . . . FitzPons," said Osborne. "I have lost track." He laughed and said, "We adopted him at the Battle of Hastings!"

Mini glanced at Catriona. "Does your family also consider Saint David your patron saint?

"Of course we respect Saint David, but we consider Saint Patrick as our benefactor."

"Yes, now I remember you told me," answered Mini. "Your ancestors were from Ireland. Saint Patrick was Irish?"

"That is the popular belief," answered Catriona, "but no, he was a Briton or Roman. Many people think he was a Roman because he was educated, could read and write, and in his own confessions he wrote his name as Patricius. He was born hundreds of years ago, in Roman times, in Glennoventa." Catriona paused and smiled as she glanced at Seona. "Near the place where Seona was born."

"Yes, I was born near the Roman Wall," said Seona.

Mini looked puzzled, "Near a wall . . . the *Roman wall*?"

"Yes, there is a wall that divides England from Scotland to the north, built by the Romans long ago."

"Vallum Hadriani," inserted Osborne.

"What? Who?" said Catriona.

"I saw it on an old map at Brecon Abbey. *Vallum Hadriani* means Hadrian's Wall, built by the Roman Emperor *Hadrianus*. It is eighty miles long and spans the width of England—from sea to sea."

"Ozzie, now I remember how you always studied any maps you could find," said Mini, "rare as they are."

"Did the monks at Brecon tell you the other name for the wall, Ozzie?" said Seona. He shook his head. "Many people call it the Pict Wall," she said, "after the tribe of wild northerners the Romans could not subdue."

"Ha!" blurted Osborne. "The fierce way you play shinty, you must have Pictish blood!"

Catriona continued after their laughter quieted. "Oh, yes, to finish my story of Saint Patrick. Irish pirates captured Patrick when he was a youth and sold him into slavery in Ireland, where he became a shepherd. Years later he escaped to France, where he joined an abbey, and then returned to Ireland to spread Christianity."

Brangwen said, "How interesting! And Seona, I heard you were born near the Roman Wall, um . . . Hadrian's Wall. Was your birthplace the same as Saint Patrick, at Glennoventa?"

"No, but I was born nearby, beyond the wall just across the border in Scotland. My father was lord of the manor of Ravenglass. He sold the manor, being certain the Normans would invade Scotland, and we now live in Herefordshire,"

"It is a blessing that your family now lives in England," said Brangwen. "Is Saint Patrick the patron saint of Scotland, as in Ireland?"

"No, Saint Andrew, a disciple of Christ, is the most revered saint," answered Seona. "Legend says a Greek monk brought a few of the apostle's relics to Scotland and that is how he became our patron saint. He—"

She was startled when suddenly interrupted by one of the children. "Papa! The Normans are coming! The Normans are coming again!" shouted Alejandro as he bumped into the table out of breath. "Look! Coming over that hill, knights carrying the banner of King William, with the two lions! Is there going to be another battle?"

Richard signaled for his brothers to follow as he turned to his father. "They are not approaching in a menacing way. I don't think this is a reprimand called for by FitzGilbert. But organize the women and children and lead them to the tower if I signal, in case I am wrong." He began to follow his brothers to the front gate, then turned. "I am sorry, Father, if it sounded like I ordered you."

"No, son, you . . . and your brothers together . . . you are an alliance, you are *brothers* . . . and, with your wives, you are the leaders of the family now. Your mother and I are just, er . . . advisors."

Richard nodded and went on. With his brothers he met a group of twenty mounted Normans outside the front gate of the palisades. As they dismounted, the FitzPons squires took hold of their mounts. There were introductions and courtesies. The Norman leader did not mention nor ask about the recent battle. He spoke in Norman Anglo French, a patois which just twenty years after the conquest had already incorporated English words. "At the last Christmas court in Gloucester, King William decided to send scribes throughout his domains to record the ownership of land, stock, and all possessions. We are but one group of many censors who have been sent over England into every shire to find out how many hides there are, what land, cattle, sheep, other livestock, plows, and every tool. This wealth will determine the amount of taxes each man owes the king. In addition, we will count every person, whether freeman, slave, knight, or soldier."

The Norman began to talk of details, and Richard discovered the census officials had already stopped at his brothers' domains. Since the landowners had to be present during the census, the brothers arranged to return east and meet with the officials at their respective manors. "Please come and sit at our table and have refreshment after your travels," said Richard. "We will start tomorrow after I inform our people, yes?"

The Norman knight tipped his head.

The brothers returned to their families in good spirits, to the relief of Mini and Pons. Richard said, "The Normans are here to take a census of everything and everyone in the country. Ozzie, Drogo, Gauthier, and their families will need to return to their manors tomorrow to assist the census takers."

"Sounds as if we're also being judged," said Osborne. "Like we are being entered into God's Book of Life."

"Yes, we're all going to be entered into a book of doom, the Doomsday Book," laughed Gauthier.

The Normans appeared happy to enjoy the ale and food by themselves and the brothers returned to their families.

Up to now the adults' conversations had been uninterrupted; however, Pons noticed the youngsters' games were ending and the horde was converging on their tables. He quickly proclaimed to his family, "It is a blessing we are together. Our diverse origins make our lives that much richer!" He laid his arm around Mini's shoulders and said, "We plan on staying and becoming *Cymry,* Welsh countrymen."

The daughters-in-law beamed with surprise. "Our sons have asked us to stay permanently," continued Lord Pons. "We will not return to Barony Pons, where sadly, your older brother Simon continues to destroy himself. One day he is excessively happy and gregarious and the next moody and sullen. He pilfers the barony's wealth to lead a wild life of excess. He did well at first managing the barony, but in the last several years he has deteriorated. We are thankful for our many good memories with Simon and Sara in Aquitaine. Sara is happily married in Saintes, so we are not worried for her welfare. Now we are also thankful to reunite with our four *conquering* sons. We will visit each of their homes and likely choose a place near their manors . . . and close enough to visit Ceingwen and Brangwen as well."

"Father," said Richard, "your experience with the manor's watermill in Aquitaine can help us. Gauthier has built a mill at his manor in Herefordshire and we plan on building one here."

"Very good!" said Pons. "I do not see a fish pond here. The excavations from the diversion ditch for the mill can be used for the pond dam."

The grandchildren arrived, crowding around the seated adults and demanding water after their play. Servants caught up to them, but the mothers politely waved them off and talked over each other, reminding their children they could go to the well themselves and help each other get a drink. Catriona caught the eye of Pont de Dinan, and announced to the children, "Come back soon. Uncle Pont will sing about King Arthur!"

Pont didn't need any more encouragement and left to get his crwth. Smiles extended around the table. Richard looked about the villagers and surrounding land. "You will be happy you decided to stay, this land is beautiful, as are the people." He nodded toward the children playing and laughing. "My hope is they will live here, marry within the local people, and become *Cymru*."

The children returned in a rush and Pont readied to perform before the gathering of adults and youth. "I discovered when talking with the villagers that the legend of King Arthur is alive here in Wales as well as in England. I will soon be journeying to the town of Bath to investigate the claim that the legend began there! I feel drawn to the place, as if I was once there." As he plucked a familiar tune on the strings, Pont sang:

Long ago Gildas the Wise, wrote of our ancestors' plight.
Then Arthur, against them he led the British kings to fight.
Saxons increased their numbers and raised a mighty horde
Four hundred and ninety years after the passion of our Lord.
Arthur with the power of Christ, twelve battles he did wage
The final struggle was at Baden Hill, penned by Gildas our sage.
Our hero slew 960 pagans, Saxon warriors of faithless nations
Freed were the Bretons after Baden, for many generations.

He continued with the couplets, each more spellbinding than the previous. The family didn't notice that the villagers gathered with them as well.

MICHAEL A. PONZIO

AFTERWARD

The earliest recorded use of the appellation *William the Conqueror* was in 1120, sixty years after William's conquest of England, which is why I did not refer to him as *the Conqueror* in this novel.

Early in his lifetime, his loyal followers called him the Duke of Normandy or William FitzRobert (he was the son of Robert I, Duke of Normandy). He was dubbed William the Bastard by his disparagers, as he was the illegitimate son of Robert and his mistress Arlette (Hervela).

Source:https://www.historyextra.com/period/norman/10-surprising-facts-about-william-the-conqueror-and-the-norman-conquest/

ANCESTRY NOVELS

A new subgenre of historical fiction

Have you ever wanted to live in another time in history? And if so, did you imagine what it would be like to take the place of an ancestor? My lifelong experience reading books on history combined with love for family has inspired me to bring these visions alive, by writing a series of "Ancestry Novels."

It began over fifteen years ago. My father, Joseph Ponzio, also read books on history as a hobby. We traded books and discussed the possibility of being related to ancient Romans. I then wrote novellas for my father of our "ancient ancestors." The first story was about an Etruscan, Pontias Larth, whose only historical record was his name engraved on a tomb in 474 BC. I wrote another story about Pontius Cominius, a scout in the Roman army. He was mentioned by the Roman historian Livy in his narrative on the sack of Rome by the Gauls in 390 BC. The source of the third novella was *generous*, being a few pages of historical record that described the defeat of the Roman legions by General Pontius Gaius at Caudine Forks.

I suggest two criteria when writing Ancestry Novels. The main character must be documented in history, and there should be a possibility that the historical person could be related to your family based on surname. The source for the main character can be as little as a name inscribed on a tomb or a page in a historical record. Sparse historical records are preferred, because when the character is well documented, the author's experience is lessened and there are fewer chances to develop characters and stories.

Write the novels you want to read but that no one has written. Experience the story and live the dream as one of your ancestors. Use the personality of a relative for the main character and include memories of family experiences. Memorialize a favorite departed pet by adding it to the novel. Use the results of family DNA tests to add previously unidentified ethnicities and localities to the stories.

233

I have published three ancestry novels that take place during ancient Rome. The first novel is about Pontius Aquila. He infuriated Julius Caesar when he refused to stand with other officials as the dictator's chariot passed them during a parade in Rome. The second novel takes place 100 years after Aquila. Emperor Tiberius Caesar ordered Pontius Pilate to return to Rome from his post in Judea, because of a complaint that the governor had used excessive force to put down a rebellion. In the third novel, Saint Pontianus, as the Bishop of Rome, must deal with the persecution by Roman authorities and fight street battles with the followers of the anti-pope, Hippolytus. When the novels are read chronologically, connections are revealed as to the relation of the characters across generations; however, the stories stand on their own and each book may be read alone.

The fourth novel occurs during the Middle Ages. *Ramon Pons: Count of Toulouse,* which chronicles the ruler of a region in the south of France in 924 AD. Ramon Pons longs to fulfill his dying father's request to build a monastery in honor of their ancestor, Saint Pons of Cimiez. Fulfillment of his promise is delayed, because he is obligated to marry and produce an heir, put down rebellions by vassals, and protect his domains against Saracens and Hungarians.

Novels by Michael A. Ponzio

Lover of the Sea series about Ancient Rome

Pontius Aquila: Eagle of the Republic

Pontius Pilatus: Dark Passage to Heaven

Saint Pontianus: Bishop of Rome

Warriors and Monks series about Medieval Europe

Ramon Pons: Count of Toulouse
1066 Sons of Pons: In the Wake of the Conqueror

ABOUT THE AUTHOR

Since childhood, Mike Ponzio has read books about ancient history. He traded books and stories with his father, Joseph E. Ponzio, and they discussed the origins of the family surname. Mike traveled around the Mediterranean to Europe, Asia, and Africa, visiting many of the locations he would later write about. He continues to travel and writes stories which he imagines may have taken place during the lives of ancient ancestors.

Mike met his wife, Anne Davis, in 1975 at a University of Florida karate class. Since then both have taught Cuong Nhu Martial Arts. In collaboration with John Burns, they wrote and published six instructional books on martial arts weapons. Mike retired in 2015, after working as an environmental engineer for thirty-seven years. Anne and Mike have raised four sons. They are engineer graduates, following in the footsteps of their Davis and Ponzio grandfathers.

For more information use the link to

Amazon's Michael A. Ponzio Author Page

https://www. **amazon.com/author/michael_a_ponzio**

Or the author's website:

Ancestry Novels: Pontius, Ponzio, Pons, and Ponce

https://**mikemarianoponzio.wixsite.com/pontius-ponzio-pons**

MICHAEL A. PONZIO

AUTHOR'S REQUEST

Please write a brief review of *1066 Sons of Pons: In the Wake of the Conqueror* on amazonbooks.com.

Comments are welcome: mikemarianoponzio@gmail.com

SOURCES

1. Anglo-Norman Studies VII: Proceedings of the Battle Conference 1984, edited by Reginald Allen Brown.
2. Anglo-Norman Studies XXX: Proceedings of the Battle Conference 2007, edited by C. P. Lewis.
3. Aulus Cornelius Celsus, De Medicina, Book V, Loeb Classical Library Edition, 1935.
4. Balfour-Paul, Jenny (2006). Indigo. London: Archetype Publications. ISBN 978-1-904982-15-9.
5. Barton, Simon F. (1997). The Aristocracy in Twelfth-century León and Castile. Cambridge, Cambridge University Press.
6. Bradbury, Jim, The Medieval Archer, Barnes and Noble Books, New York, 1985.
7. Burke, John, A Genealogical and Heraldic History of the Landed Gentry; Or Volume 3, 13 Great Marlborough Street, Henry Colburn Publisher, London, MDCCCXXVIII.
8. Douglas, David, Charles, William the Conqueror: The Norman Impact Upon England, The Yale Press, 1999.
9. Elisabeth M.C, van Houts, 'The Ship List of William the Conqueror,' Anglo-Norman Studies X: Proceedings of the Battle Conference 1987, Ed. R. Allen Brown (Woodbridge: The Boydell Press, 1988), p. 161.
10. Francese, Christopher, Ancient Rome in So Many Words, 2007, K & P Publishing, New York. Hippocrene Books, Inc.
11. Harkins, Susan Sales, Harkins, William H., The Life and Times of William the Conqueror, 2009, Mitchell Lane Publishers, USA.
12. Howarth, David, 1066 The year of the Conquest, Barnes and Noble, New York, 1977.
13. Light in the East, Chapter 3-The Norman Conquests, Constable, George Ed., Time-Life Books Inc., 1988.
14. Lloyd, Alan, The Making of the King: 1066, Holt, Rinehart, and Winston, New York, 1966.
15. Morris, Marc, The Norman Conquest, The Battle of Hastings and the Fall of Anglo-Saxon England. Pegasus Books, New York, 2013.
16. Neveu, Jean Louis, Charentes Forests, Le Croît Vif, 2001.
17. Powlett, Catherine, Lucy, Wilhelmina, Duchess of Cleveland, The Battle Abbey Roll: With Some Account of the Norman Lineages, Volume 3, John Murray, Albemarle Street, London, 1889.
18. Reno, Frank D., The Historic King Arthur: Authenticating the Celtic Hero of Post-Roman Britain, McFarland and Company Publishers, Jefferson, NC, and London 1996.

INTERNET SOURCES-Search Google or Bing

19. Battle of Hastings.
20. Castle Wales, Bronylls.
21. Charge, (warfare).
22. Clinker Boats.
23. Dyes and Colors.
24. Duke William Raises Papal Standard.
25. Early Music Muse.
26. Elite Warrior of the Dark Ages Norman Knights.
27. Essentially England.
28. Famous Irish Sayings with Gaelic Translations.
29. FitzPons.
30. Genealogy Eustace.
31. Henbane.
32. How Did William the Conqueror Raise the Army for the Invasion of England.
33. In Defense of Fitz.
34. How could the Viking Sun compass be used with sunstones before and after sunset? -Royal Society Publishing, Proceedings A, Proc Math Phys Eng Sci.
35. How the Oldest Medical Document after the Hippocratic Writings Survived the Middle Ages.
36. How to organize a Norman invasion fleet.
37. Inventions_Inventors/Longbow.
38. Jongleur.
39. Longbow.
40. Maniacal Medievalist.
41. Matilda-William the Conqueror Queen facts.
42. Medieval Medicine and First Aid.
43. Medieval Watercraft.
44. MED William.
45. Middle Ages – The Bayeux Tapestry.
46. Military history on-line Hastings.
47. No, Medieval People didn't drink Booze to Avoid. Contaminated Water.
48. Normans and Slavery.
49. Norman Descendants – The Norman Conquest of Sicily.
50. The Normans-Their history, arms, and tactics. An article by Patrick Kelly.

51. On the Origins of William the Conqueror's Horse Transports, JSTOR JOURNAL ARTICLE.
52. Open Domesday.
53. Pons.
54. Pinxton Community Profile.
55. Saint Andrews, Patron Saint of Scotland.
56. Seasoning Wood for Ship Construction.
57. December 1942, United States Department of Agriculture Forest Service Forest Products Laboratory, Madison, Wisconsin.
58. Swords, Norman.
59. Swords, swallow.
60. The Anglo-Saxon Harp, 'Spectrum, *Vol. 71.*
61. The Meaning of "Mora", the Flagship Matilda of Flanders Gave William the Conqueror ~ a guest post by Elisabeth Waugaman, The Freelance History Writer.
62. The Medieval Bow and Arrow.
63. The Town of Pons.
64. Thoughts on the Role of Cavalry in Medieval Warfare Jack Gassmann, Artes Certaminis.
65. Topographia Hibernica, III.XI; tr. O'Meary, p. 94.
66. Troubadours and Trouvères, Matthew Steel.
67. Trouvere.
68. Waterfalls Cascade de Mortain.
69. What is the capital of England?
70. William the Conqueror, 1027-1087.
71. William Conqueror.
72. William the Conqueror – Hero or Villain.
73. World Changing Weapons of the Middle Ages.
74. William the Conqueror and the Channel Crossing.
75. When Did the White Flag Become Associated with Surrender?

Made in the USA
Middletown, DE
23 June 2020

10680421R00139